# The Children's Block

Otto B Kraus

First published by Ebury Press in 2019

First published as *Smoke is my Brother* in Czechoslovakia and elsewhere as *The Painted Wall* in 1993

3 5 7 9 10 8 6 4 2

Ebury Press, an imprint of Ebury Publishing
20 Vauxhall Bridge Road,
London SW1V 2SA

Ebury Press is part of the Penguin Random House group of companies whose addresses can be found at global.penguinrandomhouse.com

This novel is inspired by the author's experiences.

www.penguin.co.uk

A CIP catalogue record for this book is available from the British Library

ISBN 9781529105568

Typeset in 11/15.4 pt Bodoni MT Std
by Integra Software Services Pvt. Ltd, Pondicherry

Printed and bound in Great Britain by Clays Ltd, Elcograf S.p.A.

To my wife, Dita,
without whom this book wouldn't have been written.

*How goodly are thy tents, O Jacob:*
*And thy tabernacles, O Israel* (Numbers 24:5)

# AUTHOR'S NOTE

The events described here really happened. The book is based on research, my personal experience and on interviews with surviving instructors of the Children's Block in the Czech Family Camp in Auschwitz-Birkenau.

The characters – except for Fredy Hirsch, Jakob and Miriam Edelstein and their son Aryeh, Slavek Lederer, Dr Mengele, Eichmann and the SS guards – are composites of several people and shouldn't be identified with any particular person.

Otto B Kraus

# INTRODUCTION

WHEN WWII WAS OVER, SURVIVORS BEGAN RETURNING FROM the Nazi concentration camps. But people who had stayed in their homes during the war were unable or unwilling to listen when the prisoners described what they had been through. They said that to listen to these horrors was too painful and would give them nightmares, or else they dismissed our descriptions as wildly exaggerated.

We therefore ceased to speak about our experiences, except when we were among fellow survivors.

On one such occasion Harry T who, like my husband Otto, had been a counsellor on the Children's Block, turned to Otto, and said:

'Don't you think, Otto, that the time has come to write about the Children's Block in Auschwitz-Birkenau? There was nothing like it in the entire Nazi machinery of the extermination of the Jews. A few of us are still alive, but after we are gone, there won't be anyone left to tell the story. You're a writer, you should do it.'

Otto started making notes of the events he remembered and I too supplied my own. Later he began visiting former co-workers from the Children's Block, who were scattered in the kibbutzim and towns all over Israel. It took him years to collect the material because Otto worked as a school teacher and was free only at weekends. We had no car and he was obliged to travel by public transport which, as is known, keeps the Shabbat. People didn't have phones yet and visits had to be arranged by letter.

In the course of these encounters with his former fellow counsellors and teachers, Otto discovered a surprising fact. Comparing the mortality rate among the prisoners, he found that a much larger percentage of those who had worked with the children remained alive, than of the other prisoners.

The reason couldn't be that they had received more food. They hadn't. Even on the Children's Block the adults had eaten the same soup as the rest of the prisoners. Children had been given a more nourishing soup, but the Block Senior, Fredy Hirsch, had forbidden the staff to take even a spoonful of the children's soup.

Otto came to the conclusion that it was their mission that had given strength and stamina to the counsellors. They'd had a goal which helped them overcome the dread of their looming death and their pity for losing their young lives. They dedicated themselves to alleviating the suffering of the children. This is in accord with the philosophy of Victor Frankl.

Planning the structure of the novel was a slow process. Otto didn't want it to be just another document about the tragedy of the holocaust. Many such books already existed. I often saw him sitting at his desk staring into space. He explained: 'Don't think I am idle, I am thinking.' He created the characters in the book from people he knew. But he changed their identity in such a way that they couldn't recognise themselves. For example Lisa Pomnenka is a composite of two young women who decorated the wall in the Children's Block. Scenes I myself witnessed or events which actually happened to me, Otto attached to other characters. Also the hero of the novel, Alex Ehren, is fictional, although Otto mixed into his personality some of his own biographical elements. And of course, no such secret diary existed in reality.

Finally Otto was ready to start writing. After school he would sit at his desk, or under the tree on our porch and write. There were moments when he had to stop, overcome by emotion. On one occasion I found him with his head resting against his crossed arms on the desk, sobbing. He had just written the poem, 'Green'.

One line of the poem became the title of the Czech edition of the book: *Smoke is my brother.*

When Otto's lifelong friend Pavel Stránský came from Prague to visit us in Israel, he offered to translate Otto's novel to Czech. The first Czech edition of the book was published in Prague in 1993. In 1995 it came out in English but was distributed only in Israel, where there is only a limited English readership. In later years the book was also translated into French (2013) and Hebrew (2014).

Now the book is available worldwide thanks to Penguin Random House. Otto would be glad to hear about it, but he is no longer with us. I'm going to whisper the happy news to his grave. Perhaps it will be delivered to him.

Dita Kraus

# PROLOGUE

THIS BOOK IS A STORY BASED ON ALEX EHREN'S DIARIES. I had to edit the script, which would have been obscure to readers unfamiliar with the Czech Family Camp in Auschwitz-Birkenau. I filled in the gaps where pages were missing, either lost or simply not copied in the hasty specimen I received from Antonin Dominicus. I kept the narrative close to the original, though I have changed the names of people; many of them are dead but those who are still alive might feel embarrassed by events mentioned in the diary.

As I leaf through the pages I see in my mind the cache we dug under our bunk. We took turns scooping out the dirt with our mess bowls and then we strewed it on the camp road where it melted with the mud. We worked with our spoons but were careful not to break their handles because, had I lost my spoon, I would have had to lap my soup like a dog. We covered the hole with a plank, which Shashek pried loose from behind his cot, where it was dark even at noon. Had somebody reported the missing board, the Block Senior would have sentenced us to twenty lashes of the cane. We saved some of the dirt and spread it over the plank to make it look like the pressed earth of the floor and we opened our cache only at night to conceal in it the pages Alex Ehren had written during the day. By the end of June, which was the time scheduled for our execution, we had one hundred and twenty-three diary sheets written in Alex's small handwriting, in which the end strokes curled upwards like piglets' tails and the letter 'g' looked like the figure eight.

We lived on a bunk built for four, but in times of over-crowding – namely before the departure of the September transport and after the arrival of the May contingent – it slept seven and, at times, even eight. There was so little space on the berth that when one of us wanted to ease his hip, we all had to turn in a tangle of legs and chests and hollow bellies as if we were one many-limbed creature, a Hindu god or a centipede. We grew intimate, not only in body but also in mind, because we knew that although we were not born from one womb, we would certainly die together.

We decided to write a diary to establish a link with the world. We were like a stone cast into the void of the universe, out of time, damned, forsaken and utterly alone. We believed that by leaving a written record we wouldn't vanish from human memory, like a word torn away by the wind or a letter written on running water. We knew that there was little chance that anybody would ever read the diary. The pages might fall into the hands of the Block Senior, who would burn them to ashes. Yet even if the folder survived it might never be found after we were marched to the gas chambers. Still, our enter-prise brightened our nights and bolstered our spirits dur-ing our smoke-filled days. We chose Alex Ehren to write the records because he had access to a pencil and paper. He also had a table and the privacy of the stall when the children met their parents before the evening roll call. Besides, Alex Ehren was a poet and had a way with words. I still remember crumbs of his verses, although after so many years I have probably changed some lines or lost the fall of his rhythm or confused his phrases with some other poems I read later. His verses may sound trivial today but we were silently impressed when he whispered the words into the murkiness of our bunk.

Alex Ehren was a poet but the records were not entirely his. We shared not only the narrow space of our berth but also our thoughts and fears, which Alex moulded into round sentences and paragraphs. We were all actors in a play and, though we were not on stage, our voices did play a part. I do not know if there were lines Alex kept for himself, thoughts and events he was too shy to share.

We wrapped the diary in tar paper torn from the roof and in an oilskin sleeve, which we had bartered for a bread ration with a Russian prisoner of war. The oilskin must have belonged to a Baltic fisherman because it smelled of mermaids and fish and decaying algae. When we touched it we closed our eyes and dreamt about the freedom of the ocean, the ships that sailed to exotic places, islands fragrant with spices and coastlines sweet with lemon blossom. Each time we buried the parcel, its scent lingered on my fingers and reminded me that, although I would dissolve into a wisp of smoke, the records would prevail and bear witness that we had lived.

After the war I was too busy to travel to Auschwitz-Birkenau and excavate memories I had tried to forget. I was recuperating from a bout of typhoid fever contracted in a Soviet quarantine camp and when I finally returned to Prague I was eager to build a world for myself to replace the one I had lost. I had no family, no home, no friends and Alex Ehren's diaries seemed of little importance.

I basked in my new freedom and walked the streets, watched the flow of the river under the Charles Bridge and climbed the steps of Petřín Hill. It was exhilarating to be alive and able to roam wherever I chose. Lilacs were blooming in the parks and I sat in their scented dusk, watching the gait of young women and aching at the sway of their breasts. For the first time in five years I wasn't considered subhuman, a monster or vermin that was to be exterminated. After months of abysmal starvation I had enough bread to fill my stomach and, as people didn't shrink from me as if I were a leper, I was learning to feel human again. Indeed I'd refused to return to Auschwitz to look for the diary. I didn't want to descend into the abyss of sorrow and to reopen my wounds, which had barely begun to heal. I didn't want to burrow into the silt of Birkenau, which contained the ashes of my father, my friends and the bones of the girls whose elbows I had touched in the intimacy of a movie theatre in my green pre-war years. Yet, above all, I wanted to forget the narrow faces of the children with whom I had worked during my last months in Birkenau.

All that kept me from trying to recover Alex Ehren's diaries. There is a myth that man cannot survive a face-to-face encounter with God. Yet if a man exposed to pure light will die, will he not lose his soul after he has experienced ultimate evil? There were times when I witnessed events so unnatural that, had I not grown a shield of unfeeling around my heart, I would have perished in terror or lapsed into insanity or, if I did survive, remain crippled for life. It wasn't a flood that only came and went; it wasn't a sudden stroke of disaster, a death of a beloved person, but a continuous exposure to death, where one horrific morning was followed by worse fears at night. I had nightmares but when I awoke on my straw mattress, my dreams paled against the horrors of reality. The longer I was exposed to fear and helplessness the thicker the shield of ice grew until there was barely any heart left under the glacier of unfeeling.

Over the course of the years the shield of ice has grown thinner, though it has never melted entirely. I know when it is time to laugh and when to weep, but my tears and my laughter are only a mask. For I am a man set apart from the rest of humanity, only partly able to love, to hate and to feel.

There are no accidents in our lives, because events are an outcome of all that has ever occurred, and whatever befalls us had to happen and couldn't have been avoided. I'd refused to recover Alex Ehren's diaries because I was reluctant to deal with my past. The human mind stores pain in its cellars and I didn't want even to have the keys to rooms I had locked and forgotten. And yet the records caught up with me in a way and in a place where I least expected them.

It was at the end of summer, twenty-three years after I had left Auschwitz, when I met the Czech publicist Antonin Dominicus. He was, like so many of his compatriots, an incurable romantic with a penchant for good food, comfort and financial security, which made him a pleasant companion but a poor martyr. He had fled Czechoslovakia after the Soviet invasion in 1968 and had come to settle in Jerusalem with the intention to write about freedom, truth and goodwill among the people of the earth. I met him for the second time before he left for Canada to become the editor of a Czech periodical in Toronto.

We were sitting in a Greek restaurant near the Jaffa Gate and spoke about the Jewish persecution complex. He killed his cigarette with his delicate fingers and ran his hand through his hair.

'Yes, yes,' he said, 'I do understand. I've visited Auschwitz.' He felt guilty because he had spent the war in the safety of his home while I had been shipped off to the camps. He leant over the table and contemplated his cup of coffee.

'Most of the Birkenau barracks are gone,' he recalled, 'burned by the Russians or dismantled. I left my tourist group and roamed. The wind made the grass ripple like water and the chimneys stood out like fingers of a buried hand. A surrealistic experience, as if I were in a Salvador Dali landscape. Or a Hieronymus Bosch,' he added and looked away.

'There is a memorial, of course, but no Jews are named. The Bolsheviks are terribly conservative, stick to Marx and Lenin and all that. Jews have no nation, you know. They read their Lenin like the Gospel, or the Ten Commandments, if you wish. Take your pick.' He paused in his monologue.

'Of course there are documents. Thousands of them. There is a museum in Auschwitz with an exhibition and even pictures that some inmates had scribbled on the walls. Most of the papers are locked up in Warsaw and not available to the public. But they told me that I could use them for research. Mind you, I was on an official mission then. An artist. A member of the Writers Union, a cadre communist, "one of us",' he added with a self-deprecating movement of his hand.

'There was a Czech diary or something.' He touched his short beard. He paused and contemplated me queasily. 'Could have been from your time.'

'It should be here in Jerusalem,' I said.

'Possibly. But the Poles won't let it out. Certainly not after the Dubček spring in Prague. A Zionist plot and all that rot.'

'Did you read the diary? Whose was it?'

'No, I haven't read it. How could I? Just opened a page here and there. There was no time between the addresses and toasting the brotherhood of the Czechs and the Poles. No more fascism, no more war. With the Soviet Union for ever and ever. Brotherhood, my foot. One could be choked by too much love. Friendship grown out of the barrels of guns.' He laughed bitterly and his voice was full of resentment. He lit yet another cigarette though his saucer was already brim-full with stubs.

'The diary,' I said, 'was it written in pen, in pencil? How many pages?'

'It was a long time ago and I had only a glimpse at it. It was pencil, I think.'

His answers were tentative but after a while I had no doubt that what he had seen was Alex Ehren's diary. I was greatly excited but, at the same time, in a strange, perverse manner, also glad that the pages would remain unread until they fell apart, destroyed by mould. I had a safe job, a family to support and no wish to struggle with the ghosts of yesteryear.

For several days afterwards I was uncomfortable, as if I had left a task unfinished. But then my conscience would fall asleep and I kept to my routine, got up to work, ate my meals and twice weekly made love to my wife. I was sure that I would never again meet Antonin Dominicus and soon forgot the whole matter.

But one day he was back.

'Like a bad penny,' he said on the phone. 'I won't stay long, two, three weeks perhaps. I was commissioned to write a story about a Czech medieval knight. I came to see the Crusader Halls in Acre. Imagine a Czech crusader in Acre. A compatriot in the Holy Land. Just like you.'

Dominicus sounded enthusiastic, friendly, Czech and familiar with the accents of my childhood.

'Still interested in the Auschwitz manuscript?' he said.

'You said there was no way to get access to it?'

'Why don't you come and have a beer with a countryman?'

He was staying in one of the elegant Haifa hotels and his shirt and shoes were new and expensive. We sat on the terrace and he looked out at the hazy shores of Acre.

'What clever people you Jews are. Make the desert bloom, build kibbutzim and blow up Russian tanks. But you've never learned how to brew decent beer. No kick.' He grimaced but poured himself another glass. 'There is a man who could produce a photocopy. Still,' he cautioned, 'you might pay and get nothing. Nobody to complain to, understand? The Pole may be a cheat, or chicken out at the last moment. It's like shooting in the dark, but it's better than not shooting at all,' and he sighed again over the poor quality of the Israeli beer.

After a year I wrote off the two hundred black-market dollars I'd given him, which I hadn't told my wife about. There were other things I'd lost and I felt relieved that I wouldn't have to go back to my past. It was a surprise when I received a manila envelope with a note from Dominicus and inside a photocopy of Alex Ehren's manuscript.

Even looking at the copy I could tell that the original seemed to have been well preserved although a few pages were missing and it seemed as if others had been slightly damaged, as if an insect or an animal, possibly a mouse, had nibbled at their edges. I never learned how the diary parcel was found. The manuscript was still legible in spite of the long time it had lain in the damp hole under our bunks. The night after Dr Mengele's selection we had wrapped the sheets for the last time in the tar paper and the oilskin sleeve, which smelled of mermaids and fish and freedom.

Alex Ehren is dead. He was shot on a death march near a place called Bischofswerda in Lower Lusatia or Lausitz, as the Germans used to call that part of Silesia, barely a week before we were set free by the Red Army. That morning we'd walked through blossoming cherry orchards, and though I'd been weary and starving, I'd felt elated by the approaching spring. We had shuffled in our wooden clogs, more dead than alive, but had tried to keep our rows tightly closed because by touching one another's arm we'd supported the weakest from falling. Those who had stayed behind had been shot in the neck by the SS sentries at the tail of our miserable procession. Some of us had dragged a cart with our dead whom we had buried in the fields at night.

By noon we had reached a crossroads and because of the ever-growing stream of German refugees, we'd turned onto a track that had led through pinewoods, soft with bracken and blueberry flowers.

Alex Ehren had taken my arm and his eyes had come alive. 'Let's run,' he had said. 'There won't be a better time.'

Yet I had been weak and resigned to death. In fact I had been certain that the SS would shoot us and then disappear among the local population, rather than be caught by the advancing Russians.

Alex Ehren had moved to the edge of our column and when the track had bent to the left he'd run into the darkness of the pines. One of the sentries, the man whom we used to call the Priest, had noticed and followed him into the wood. We'd heard the staccato of his automatic and I'd known that he had shot Alex. Nobody had been sent to fetch the body and he was left where he had fallen among the bracken and the gently blooming blueberry flowers.

When I finished re-reading the diary I drove to Jerusalem to see other documents in the Yad Vashem archives. I listened to the oral evidence collected by the late Gershon Ben-David of the Hebrew University, spoke to survivors and read as much material as I could find. There is no such thing as the Holocaust of six million but rather six million separate Holocausts, each different from the other, each one with its own suffering, fears and scars. For a whole lifetime I tried to forget, to suppress and erase the memory of my Holocaust. However, when it caught up with me, I was eager to know and to understand, because only by bringing my nightmares into the open could

I rid myself of my guilt. I was like a solitary tree in a felled forest and I felt guilty that I had lived while so many others had died.

And then, out of the mist of too much information, I stumbled upon two amazing facts. I realised that the Czech Family Camp in Birkenau hadn't been just a whim of an official at the Reich Main Security Office, but a part of hideous scheme, a game the Nazis tried to play with the allies.

In 1943, after the loss of Africa and the retreat from Stalingrad, SS Reichsfuehrer Himmler became aware that the war had been lost. In an attempt to save Germany from total destruction and himself from the gallows, he tried to negotiate a separate peace with the British and the Americans. Like other Nazi leaders he was a prisoner of his own words, and he feared that the Jews, who supposedly ruled allied politics, would jeopardise his plans. To disprove reports of the annihilation of Jews in Europe, in June 1944 the RSHA – the Reich Main Security Office, or *Reichssicherheitshauptamt* – permitted (after prolonged and tedious negotiations) an International Red Cross Commission to visit Ghetto Theresienstadt. The ghetto was well groomed for the visit: several thousand of its inmates were shipped to extermination camps; the outer walls of the houses were repainted; and shops, a café and a park were opened only to be closed immediately after the departure of the Swiss investigators. The ghetto inmates were cautioned not to reveal the horrible truth that existed behind the whitewashed walls. Yet, there had been still some danger that the Commission might learn about the transports to the east and inquire about their fate.

It was the Czech Family Camp in Birkenau, or at least some of its inmates, that had provided an alibi against rumours about the organised murder of Jews in Auschwitz-Birkenau. There were three shipments of Theresienstadt prisoners to Birkenau: two transports in September 1943; two in December 1943; and then more trainloads of 7,500 people in May 1944. Each contingent was to stay in Birkenau for six months, then die in the gas chambers and be replaced by the next transport. In case they were needed as evidence, a few suitable families, men, women and children would be selected, fed well for several weeks, and paraded, decently dressed, clean and alive, before the Swiss Red Cross Commission to disprove once and for all any allegation of a Holocaust.

The second fact was even more puzzling. Out of the total of 17,517 prisoners who had been brought from Ghetto Theresienstadt to the Family Camp BIIb in Birkenau, some died of disease and starvation, but most of them were murdered in the gas chambers. The first batch of 3,800 died in the night between the 7th and 8th March 1944 and the second contingent of more than 10,000 on the 11th and 12th July 1944. A further 2,750 inmates were sent to Germany and of these only 1,167 were still alive in various slave labour camps at the end of the war.

According to these numbers the overall survival rate of the Czech Family Camp inmates was as low as 6.6%.

However, there was a group of fifty men and women, of whom a full 83% were still alive at the end of the war in May 1945. My discovery became even more perplexing when I found out that most of them were intellectual types who were neither used to manual labour nor possessed the animal vitality essential for survival in the jungle of the concentration camps. True, they were relatively young and healthy because otherwise they wouldn't have passed Dr Mengele's selection. There were no skilled artisans among them or people in privileged positions who might have had access to additional food. They were rank and file prisoners who shared the fate and suffering of other ordinary prisoners.

Yet they had one thing in common. They all had worked at the Children's Block during the last three months of the Family Camp in Birkenau. And though Alex Ehren's diaries are not explicit about the reason for their survival, the clue to the riddle is hidden among the lines of the manuscript. At least, so I believe.

# 1.

## Auschwitz-Birkenau

THE IDEA OF AN UPRISING CAME TO ALEX EHREN AS IF BY itself. It was like a bubble of air rising from the bottom of a pond or like a winged insect emerging from its chrysalis.

True, every night he had dreamt about an escape because in the darkness everything seemed possible, even crossing the electrically charged fence, scaling the ditch, avoiding the chain of dogs and the sentries. It was never utterly dark at night because the projectors swept the camp with a bright beam and the fence was dotted with lights on pillars that bent forward like snakes. He would close his eyes and think of freedom. Yet never before had he dared to dream about a mutiny, an armed struggle against the Germans.

Alex Ehren had arrived at the Family Camp in Birkenau in December 1943. The 5,007 prisoners – men, women and children – had travelled in two trainloads, one that left Ghetto Theresienstadt on the 15th and the other on the 18th of the month. After many days in a stinking boxcar the prisoners reached Birkenau on Christmas Eve. There they were stripped of their meagre possessions, had a serial number tattooed on their left forearm and were marched in pitiful rags to BIIb, the Czech Family Camp. BIIb was one of the seven Birkenau enclosures. Next to it was the Quarantine Camp and on the other side the compound where the SS corralled young Hungarian women before dispatching them to forced labour in Germany. In another Camp, seven thousand Gypsy families were housed in wooden barracks and further on were the Men's Camp and the Women's Camp. Finally, at the far end of the encampment, stood the Hospital Camp where the SS doctors performed their horrifying experiments. When the December transports arrived at the Czech Family Camp, they met the previous Theresienstadt contingents that had been shipped to Birkenau three months before, in September 1943.

The September people had an advantage over the newcomers because they had been allowed to keep some of their own clothes – dirty and bedraggled by three months of camp life – but still their own. More than a thousand of them had already died of starvation, disease and hard labour, but those still alive had grown wise to the unspeakable conditions of a concentration camp.

The two groups lived together in the overcrowded blocks for another three months. On the first of March both transports – those that arrived in September as well as the December newcomers – were allowed to write a postcard with twenty-five words in block letters. A week later the September people were singled out and marched to the adjoining Quarantine Camp. During the day they were allowed to move about and shout messages to their friends on the other side of the electrified fence. In the evening they were locked up in the barracks and at night loaded onto huge military trucks and driven away.

That terrible night none of the December people slept. Alex Ehren watched the Quarantine Camp through a crack in the wall with fellow prisoners Fabian and Beran, crouching on his hands and knees like an animal. Up to that night it was the September people who were in command: they were the block seniors, the scribes, the Capos, the cooks and the foremen of the various labour gangs while the newcomers worked on the road or dredged the ditches. There was a rumour that the prisoners in the Quarantine Camp would be sent to a labour camp in Germany, but at the same time there was a whisper, dark and frightening, that they would be put to death. There were always rumours. Like the tides of the sea, they came in and went out with each morning. They spread from mouth to ear until they died and were replaced by others.

'A man at the guardhouse overheard the German sentries.'

'What did they say?'

'That they'll go to Heydebreck. A labour camp.'

'Mietek the Pole says there is no train. And no prison uniforms. They wouldn't send a transport in rags.'

'They'll give them clothes when they arrive at the new camp.'

'Why the postcards?'

'To prove that the dead are still alive,' said Fabian. 'Why else did they order us to date the cards a week ahead?'

'It's because the mail goes through a censor.'

'Some time ago a German officer made Fredy Hirsch, the Children's Block Senior, write a report. Why would an SS officer travel all the way from Berlin to learn about Jewish brats?'

'An officer?'

'Obersturmbannfuehrer Eichmann, they say. Spoke to Miriam and took a letter to Edelstein, the former Ghetto Elder. Maybe the children are to be exchanged.'

'For what?'

'For German prisoners of war. For trucks. Weren't we allowed to keep our hair? And we don't wear the striped prison uniforms.'

Fabian pursed his mouth. 'We wear rags with a red oil paint stripe down our backs.'

'They haven't separated the families.'

'So they can send us up the chimney together.'

Sometimes Alex Ehren got tired of Fabian and his black predictions. Fabian was a small man with a sharp nose and spectacles, which he had saved through the showers. One of the lenses was cracked and he polished the glass as if he could mend the crack. They tried to shut him up, to avoid his company, but the bunk was crowded and they had to bear with him as one bears with an aching tooth.

There were hours of chaos after the September prisoners were corralled in the Quarantine Camp, but towards noon, Willy, the German Camp Senior, nominated new 'dignitaries' from among the remaining December contingent. The previous Sunday Willy had arranged a soccer match on the muddy camp road and now he appointed the players and their wives as the new Block Seniors, the cooks and the labour commando foremen. Alex Ehren watched his new Block Senior climb on the horizontal chimney stack and walk up and down, swishing his cane left and right. He was an outstanding soccer player, a hulking boy with a shock of yellow hair that fell on his forehead.

'Anybody caught outside the block will be shot.'

He wasn't used to his new authority and his voice was pitched and strained. Beat or be beaten, he thought, looking at the faces in the hollows of their bunks. He was barely eighteen and had he not landed his new job, he would have died on the ditch duty. He looked at his wooden clogs, which he would soon exchange for proper shoes. He was rich now because his orderly skimmed the soup before the prisoners got their rations. And for a bowl of soup he could have a woman. He was still a virgin and when he thought about a girl he didn't see a face or hear a voice, but concentrated on her breasts and private parts. And the longer he thought about women the higher and more feverish his voice grew.

They weren't allowed to leave the barracks but through his crevice in the wall Alex Ehren saw the blue smoke of the trucks in the Quarantine Camp. The SS soldiers moved in knots and the striped Capos beat on the barracks doors.

'Look,' said Beran, in a voice harsh with fear, 'they are leaving.' In the pools of light the Capos herded the prisoners toward the trucks. It wasn't an orderly departure but a flight from the canes and from the teeth of the German shepherds. The prisoners stumbled in the sudden glare and turned left and right in an attempt to hold on to their friends. The Capos beat them to pack them tighter together and when a truck was solid with men, women and children, they snapped the back shut and flailed the rest into another vehicle. It was a scene of chaos and despair, and Alex Ehren felt his heart in his throat. There was a child left alone on the road and a Capo lifted it up to its mother. A woman with hair streaming like a dark halo tried to break the circle of sentries but a soldier struck her with a rifle butt and her face turned crimson with blood. There was a din and a tumult that carried to the barracks where Alex Ehren was pressing his eye to the crack. It was a sound of disintegration and bedlam, of trucks straining to break loose from the silt, of the Capos shouting, of a Babel of languages, of German commands and of the dogs, which had grown wild with excitement. Yet above all it was the sound of people, a sound, which, like water falling from a cliff, was full of terror and dissonance. The trucks were on the move and the Quarantine Camp, lit by the projectors, grew deserted. Yet the ground was still strewn with their presence, with torn hats and shoes and coats, mess bowls and a toy left behind by a child.

'Listen,' said Beran and lifted his chin. 'They sing.'

And indeed, from the trucks packed with people under grey tarpaulin, came the sound of singing. It was not one tune but three different anthems – the Czech '*Kde domov můj*', the Jewish '*Hatikva*' and the communist 'Internationale'. The three songs carried different melodies, they were in different keys and had divergent rhythm, but to Dezo Kovac, who was a musician, they were like a fugue, intertwining and merging and creating a rising helix of sound. The trucks were so far away now that Alex Ehren couldn't hear the engines. Yet the sound of singing was still there, though like the buzz of a mosquito, it grew higher and fainter as if coming from an immense distance. And then there was only its echo and its memory, as if the people hadn't sung with their voices but with their livers and hearts and souls that refused to be forgotten. When they die, Alex Ehren thought, they will leave nothing behind save their torn shoes and a doll in the mud of the camp road. Not a grave and not a tombstone because even we, the last to hear their singing, will follow. And those after us will die and turn to smoke as well, until there is nobody left to remember. He was overwhelmed by the terror of non-being, by the void of death, by utter oblivion, and he said: 'I will not sing.'

It was at that moment that the idea of the uprising was born in Alex Ehren's mind. They had no weapons, no organisation, no leaders and he was starved and exhausted from the cold and from lugging big rocks. Yet he repeated again and again: 'I will not sing.'

'Nonsense,' said Fabian, and moved away from the crack. 'At the end everybody sings. Some sooner and some later, but when your number is up, you have to go. Look at history. I haven't heard of anybody who didn't die. Sooner or later. It doesn't make much difference.'

Beran, who knew mathematics and whose thinking was orderly and deliberate, lay back on his bunk.

'The Germans are no fools. Why kill cheap labour if they can put us to work? They have a war to fight and they need hands for their factories. Or in the fields. They wouldn't feed prisoners for six months and then send them up the chimney. It doesn't make sense.'

Beran turned his back and closed his eyes. He thought about his wife, her neck and her belly and the few times they had been together. They married in haste when he was summoned because there was no other way Sonia could join the transport. They weren't on the same block but they met after work on the camp road. He thought about her with tenderness and when she brought him a bowl of soup, which she carried under her coat, they spoke about the future. What kind of apartment they would rent, what pictures they would hang on the wall and what meals she would prepare. She waited, bending her head in the drizzle, until Beran finished eating. She was a food carrier and was allowed to scrape the barrels before she returned them to the kitchen. It was hard work because the carriers were hitched into a canvas harness and lifted the barrels on wooden poles. They trudged through the mire of the road from one barracks to the next to deliver the tea and the midday soup and in the evening the ersatz tea again. It was cold and Sonia's clogs were caked with mud. She was often aching and weary but she always looked forward to the evening when Beran ate her bowl of cold mush.

Sometimes on a good day, she found a piece of potato at the bottom, but some women were like birds of prey and had always grabbed the beetroot before she could secure it for herself. Beran ate his soup sheltered by her body, and, in the intimacy of the barracks' wall, she laid her hand on his wrist. She knew that she was plain, that her hair was coarse and she had a thick nose, but at that moment she felt almost beautiful, for the touch of their hands was a bond of love. It was only a light touch, a touch of a butterfly, because in the camp men and women were not allowed to be intimate. And yet she felt comforted as if his strength had flowed into her blood. 'One day,' he said in his slow voice, 'the war will be over. There is a rumour that the Germans were defeated at Stalingrad.'

She never ate the soup, which she scraped from the barrel bottom, but brought it to Beran. Sometimes, when there was not enough to fill the bowl, she added from her own ration. She loved to watch him eat, because then he was only and exquisitely hers.

The night of the trucks brought windfalls to the December transport people. They didn't know how many prisoners were marched away but Rudi, the Slovakian Quarantine Camp Registrar, claimed that he had seen the lists.

'There is always a number,' he said. 'The Germans are sticklers for detail and everything is written down. There were 3,792 prisoners that left for Heydebreck.'

He twisted his mouth into a sneer.

'Heydebreck, they say, but who would believe the SS.'

He was a young man with a strong neck and shoulders and he thought about the girl who tried to attack a soldier before she was killed. Only a handful of prisoners had stood up against the sentries and they were all beaten to death.

'No use fighting them,' he said. 'One has to run.'

'How do you run away from here?' Alex Ehren looked at the fence, the ditch and the soldiers in the watchtowers.

'Watch me,' said Rudi and grimaced.

Suddenly there was enough space on the blocks. Alex Ehren moved with Fabian and Beran to an empty bunk with a pile of abandoned blankets. He wrapped one around himself and lay under the soft fabric, warm, comfortable and complacent, not caring that the wool still held the breath of its previous owner. The man might live, he thought, come back the next morning and claim the blanket. He held the cover to his chest, reluctant to part with it. He felt no compunction, no pain, no compassion for the dead man. What am I, he thought, a man, a monster, a stone? How would I speak to the man if he suddenly stood at the bunk?

'He won't. Once dead always dead,' said Fabian.

For about a week there was a climate of abandon in the camp. It took time to get accustomed to the space on the bunks, the warmth of the Dutch blankets, the new Block Senior, and even the half-empty latrine block, where Alex Ehren used to wait in a painful queue for a vacant seat.

'Grab it for as long as you can,' said Fabian, 'A piece of bread, a blanket, a better job. How long will I live? A week, a month, a year? Whatever it is, life is too short to be wasted on qualms. Why look for your better self? There is no better or worse you, because there is only one self that deserves to be pampered like a child. As long as it lasts. Why fuss about a dead man's blanket? What matters is to stay alive because that's what it's all about. What's wrong with being a crook and staying alive? When you are dead nobody gives a hoot whether you were an angel or a rogue. Conscience? Morality? My foot. Look at Mother Nature. Show me an honest rat, a merciful wolf, a good-natured bird of prey. Or a tree. Trees grow and choke the daisies at their feet. Consideration and honesty are an invention of the weak. Have you never walked in a forest? Green tops and a graveyard underneath. Why should I be different from a tree?

It's life or death and whoever is stronger prevails. I'd rather be a tree than a dead lily of the valley. Honest, modest and dead.'

Fabian thought about his father who had died when he was a child … four or five years old, he himself didn't remember. He had grown up in an orphanage where he learned the tricks of survival. He leaned forward as if he were revealing a secret.

'Take advantage of what there is. It's a rotten place but in a way better than the world outside. At least the Germans have made us all equal. The smoke from the rich stinks the same as that of a beggar.'

It was a long speech and Fabian felt embarrassed by telling too much. He took off his spectacles and rubbed the cracked lens.

'Everybody hates one's father sometimes,' said Beran. He was tall and gawky and he walked as if his head were a step ahead of his body. Yet he was gentle and knew how to listen.

Next day at noon Fabian caught Alex Ehren by the sleeve. 'Most of the instructors are gone and they need new people at the Children's Block. I may be a crook but I won't forget a friend. After all it was you who found the abandoned blankets.' And he laughed.

It was the only Children's Block of its kind in Auschwitz. There was none similar to it in Buna or Monowitz or even in the Central Camp, where the barracks were built of solid red bricks and had real windows. There were other camps, the Gypsy Camp or the Women's Camp where the children slept in special barracks before they were sent to their deaths. But there was none similar to the Children's Block in the Czech Family

Camp, where the children spent their days with their teachers and matrons.

Mietek, who had been in prison camps since the Polish war, claimed that there was no such block anywhere within the German conquest, from the vast spaces of the Soviet Union to the deserts of Libya in Africa, to Estonia and Latvia at the Baltic Sea. The Children's Block was started in October, three months before Alex Ehren arrived at the Family Camp. Dr Mengele, the SS physician, commandeered the furthermost barracks in the row and nominated Fredy Hirsch to run it. Arno Boehm, who wore the green triangle of a convicted murderer, came to the Block, looked at the stalls and clicked his tongue.

'Why give the Jews privileges?' He ran his hand over his shaven skull and pondered why the Czech transport was treated differently. As a German he had the confidence of the soldiers, but even they didn't know why the Theresienstadt Jews were allowed to keep their hair, wore civilian rags and underwent no selection.

Mietek, the Polish roof repairman, became friendly with Magdalena, one of the matrons and came to the Block every second day. He sat on the horizontal chimney with his striped beret at the back of his head and watched the children. They reminded him of his village and his eyes grew soft.

'You don't see many of them here.'

He too pondered the mystery and shook his head. He was an old hand at camp life and knew that all other children – the Poles, the Russians, the French and the Greeks – were put to death immediately on arrival. There must be a reason, he concluded, why the Germans allowed the Czech children to live. Yet what the reason was he didn't know.

Sometimes he repaired a roof in the Kanada Camp, where the newly arrived transports' luggage was looted and he brought the children an egg, an apple or a tattered book.

'Sure,' he said to Fredy, 'there is a scheme. One day they will barter them for gold or butter or sardines. Who knows? Today here, tomorrow on your way to Switzerland.'

Sometimes German officers came to see the Children's Block and once even Dr Mengele spoke to a child.

He touched the little girl's head with his pigskin glove.

'Call me Uncle Joseph,' he said in his thin voice and walked a step in front of Fredy, the Children's Block Senior. He got on well with the gym teacher who had been born in Aachen, spoke like a native German and clicked his heels.

A Jew, thought Dr Mengele, but certainly more human than the Polish convicts or the Gypsies in the D Camp. He looked at the man's shoulders, his sharp nose and strong neck. He may even have some Aryan blood in his veins. A pity I can't trace his family tree. One day, he thought, I could take his measurements. The long head, the spine, the proportions of the limbs were not Jewish. Yet he dismissed the idea because he didn't want to digress from his fertility research. It would be embarrassing, he thought, to ask the Children's Senior to strip and let him inspect his cranium, ears and private parts. For a while he contemplated reclaiming him from the death-bound contingent, but then he decided against it. There were other prisoners to take over the Block. It was enough that he would save the three physicians and the pharmacist for whom he had no replacement.

After the death of the September transport, Himmelblau, the new Children's Block Senior, took on Fabian and Beran and Alex Ehren whom he knew from the ghetto as teachers. He lectured them in his atrocious Czech, moving his head like a St Bernard dog.

'There are do's and there are don'ts,' he said. 'We don't speak about death and the chimney. We pretend that we'll stay here until the war ends and then return home. The Germans don't allow Jewish children to attend school—' he lifted his finger in the air '—and so we don't teach.'

'If I don't teach,' said Marta Felix, 'what shall I do with the children?'

She was forty and Himmelblau employed her because she had been a lecturer at the university and spoke French and Russian.

'Ah,' he said, 'I say to you so many things.' One corner of his mouth turned up in a smile while the other remained low and sad.

'How can you remember all the regulations? And who can tell the difference between play and learning? Sometimes play is the best learning and the best learning is play.'

Himmelblau got entangled in the Czech feminine and masculine genders and what was neuter he mixed up with both.

'What an awful language,' he sighed. 'How can anybody speak it? No wonder you can't remember about the difference between the learning and the play.'

When Fredy was still alive, Himmelblau had been his second, Deputy Children's Senior. He was different from the gym teacher, who was neat and elegant even in his prison clothes and who charmed little boys and clicked his heels when SS Obersturmbannfuehrer Eichmann came for a visit. Fredy sparkled and impressed, but it was Himmelblau who bore the burden of the daily routine. It was he who was in charge of the youth assistants, cut the bread rations, kept records and counted the children before the roll call.

There was a man, Felsen, among the instructors, a communist and conspirator, who seldom spoke to the other teachers.

'Fredy?' said Felsen and looked over his shoulder. 'He is like soap that produces foam but doesn't wash out the dirt.'

'And Himmelblau?'

'Who knows?' Felsen was careful not to enter into an argument, for he had secrets which he carried like an unborn child.

He drew his neck into his collar until he resembled a turtle and turned away. He had no group of his own but perambulated among the classes and talked about history and politics. On Mondays he huddled with a cabal of pupils with whom he produced a clandestine newspaper. They hung it on the wall and the children crowded around the sheet and read it as eagerly as if it were printed and published in earnest.

Alex Ehren had no doubt that Fredy was dead. There was a witness, a male nurse, who was one of the few whom Dr Mengele had reclaimed from the death transport.

'He took too many pills,' said the male nurse, 'and they carried him to the truck on a stretcher.'

'There is only one way to stay alive,' Rudi the Slovakian had urged Fredy, as they'd talked in his white-washed cubicle in the Quarantine Camp. He had friends in the Main Camp in Auschwitz and he'd known that the transport was condemned to die.

'What way?'

'Attack the sentries and take away their guns. Cut through the gate and run for your life. You are the man to give the word.'

'They will shoot at us from the watchtowers.'

'Not if you take them first.'

'How many children will die if we fight?' Fredy had fingered the whistle on his neck.

'Some may escape into the woods. But without a fight there is no hope for anybody.'

The Registrar had a girlfriend in one of the barracks and he was eager to save her life. He'd looked at the Children's Senior and at the whistle, which was the symbol of his authority. He was the only man whom people would follow.

'Other camps may join in,' Rudi had continued, 'the Men's Camp, the Gypsies, perhaps even the Buna prisoners. There might be a general revolt. Who knows where it might end.'

'I need time,' Fredy had said. 'Come back later. In an hour, in two. Before it is dark.'

He had been of two minds. He had little doubt that the transport would die but at the same time he'd hoped that he would be saved. He would be exempt from death because Obersturmbannfuehrer Eichmann, the SS officer from Berlin, needed him. He'd known that the Family Camp had existed for a reason. Some of the prisoners might be executed, but the camp would prevail. And as long as the camp existed the Germans would need him. Hadn't he written a report about the children for Eichmann? About their better rations, their sport lessons behind the barracks, their adequate clothing? Eichmann had folded the document, put it in his briefcase and nodded in approval.

'Good work, Youth Senior.' The SS man had taken the paper, but he had been careful not to step too close or touch Fredy's clothes. 'You will be rewarded.'

What reward was there other than life, Fredy had wondered as he'd lain on his pallet. Outside somebody had called out the numbers of those who were exempt from the transport and would return to the Family Camp. Mengele's twins, the hospital staff, the Camp Senior's lover. He had left his room and stood on the camp road craning his neck for a messenger with his name. The message was late but it must, it certainly would arrive. Hadn't Eichmann, the SS officer with the face of an accountant, promised? 'You will be rewarded.' But would he keep his word to a Jew? Fredy had known that the Germans had a twisted sense of humour and they thrived on deceit and cruelty. He had known them well, for he had attended the same schools with them and had been weaned on the same myths and fairy tales full of blood and terror. Eichmann was in Berlin and might have forgotten, he'd thought. Or was it a practical joke? Would he promise and then let him die after he had used him? His hope had become the father of his despair and he had lain on his bunk motionless and wrapped in his frustration like in a cloak.

Should he listen to the Slovak Registrar and start a mutiny? He'd mulled it over: the children loved him, and if he blew the whistle the older boys would attack the Germans and so would some of the grown-ups. But what was the use of fighting against an army that had guns and armoured vehicles? He had heard a rumour about an uprising in Warsaw. But weren't they all killed or burned like vermin in their cellars? Fredy felt sorry for the children who would die, but he felt even more pity for himself, for his youth, for his perfect body, for the days he would not live. He had got up from his bunk and walked to the gate. He'd asked a registrar about a message but there had not been one. He had returned to his cubicle confused by his fear and frustration.

After an hour he had got up from his bed to find one of the physicians.

'I've decided,' he had said, 'as soon as it grows dark I'll give the word. I need a pill to steady my nerves.'

During the day everything had seemed normal in the Quarantine Camp; people met outside the blocks and the instructors played a game with the children. They had been served their midday soup and some of the prisoners had waved to their friends in the Family Camp. The three Jewish doctors and the pharmacist had kept themselves apart. Dr Mengele had promised that they would be reclaimed from the transport. Their numbers were already at the Registrar's office and they would return to the Hospital Block before nightfall. The physician had looked at Fredy's eyes, at his trembling hands and his twitching mouth.

The Children's Senior had been in distress and could blow his whistle any moment, the physician had realised.

A mutiny against the Germans was lunacy; it was the death of all – of the doomed transport, of the prisoners in the Family Camp and even the reclaimed hospital staff. If Fredy started an uprising, there was no chance for anybody. The man was crazed, obviously out of his mind, and if he wasn't stopped, the Jewish doctors would perish with the rest.

'I'll give you something, a sedative,' the physician had said and turned to the pharmacist.

They had been sorely short of medicines, but they did have a small stock of painkillers. The druggist had handed him a bottle of sleeping pills. The doctor had poured out its contents and had closed his hand in a fast movement. He had some cold tea in his mess bowl and he swilled the tablets round its bottom until they dissolved in the murky liquid.

Through the mist of his slumber Fredy had seen his errand boy at the door. The child was like a dog eager to obey. Fredy had motioned him nearer and had lain his hand on his thin shoulder. He had tried to retch but his stomach hadn't responded.

'Tell Himmelblau I need some food.'

The boy had been barely able to understand him. Fredy had felt desperately heavy with sleep but there was a thing he had to do before he would rest. It was late afternoon and there was still enough time to blow the whistle.

There was always some food on the Children's Block. The children got the parcels of those that had died, had starved or been killed by dysentery or one of the infections that bloomed in the camp. Miriam, the new matron, took the crumbs and cooked them into a thick mush, which she handed out to the children. They loved the sweet soup and licked their mess bowls until they shone. It had taken the errand boy three attempts to pass on Fredy's message.

The soldier had shooed him away from the fence and aimed his gun at him, but the child had always came back, each time from behind a different block. The sentry saw him but didn't shoot. He knew about the planned execution and he had orders not to frighten the Jews into a frenzied crowd.

The matron had stirred the mush in a pot until it thickened. She hadn't seen Fredy outside the barracks and she felt that he needed the food for some urgent reason but what it was she didn't know. Himmelblau chose Neugeboren, and the child had crept into the ditch and had slowly pushed the pot towards Fredy's errand boy on the other side of the fence. They had watched him as he had manoeuvred the bowl, once to the right and then to the left and then forward. It was a dangerous task because the wires were electrically charged and had he touched them he would have crumpled and remained on the barbs, dark and warped and charred.

Fredy had been too dazed to eat. He had managed to swallow only two spoonfuls of the mush.

'You eat the rest,' he'd said to the child and he had turned to the wooden wall. But the boy wouldn't eat and the pot remained by the bed, slowly setting into a sweet solid cake.

The Slovakian Registrar had returned early in the afternoon. It was the 7th of March and he'd known that the SS would call a curfew at dusk, as soon as the sun had begun to set.

'Wake up.' He had shaken Fredy by his shoulder. 'I've spoken to the underground people. There is no train and the

Special Commando is preparing the gas chambers. The only way is to fight. Blow the whistle before it gets dark.'

He had bent over the sleeper but the man had been in a deep swoon. His mouth was open and his breath shallow and laborious. For a moment the Registrar had been tempted to take the whistle himself, but he had drawn back because it wasn't his turn to die. He had sent the errand boy for a doctor who had taken Fredy's pulse and lifted his eyelid with his finger.

'What's the use? Why not let him sleep?'

He had been about to leave the Quarantine Camp any minute now and he was impatient with the Registrar; the Germans might call a curfew in a moment and he didn't want to be caught in the hubbub.

'What is it?'

'Some kind of poison perhaps. Who knows? In normal circumstances I might try to save him, but what sense does it make here?' He had shrugged and he'd turned to go.

'He had a task to do.'

The physician had looked down at the strained face.

'They'll take him on a stretcher.' He had paused and then went on. 'I have been trained to save the living.'

Somebody outside had called out the doctor's number and he and the Registrar had left in a hurry. The child had squatted on the floor for a long time and then eaten the cold mush.

# 2.

THE CHILDREN WERE SMALL FOR THEIR AGE. THEY WERE white and undernourished because they had been in the camps for a long time – some of them, like Adam Landau, Bubenik or Majda, for as long as three years. Half of Alex Ehren's wards went to Heydebreck, or wherever the transport had been sent, so only twelve children remained. They had so many wooden stools now that each child had one for itself and could use another one as a table to write on, to draw a picture or eat his soup from his bowl. In the past, when the block was still crowded, some of the children had to sit on the earthen floor, where they squatted like frogs in the dim light that fell through the window slits. They had no pockets because the lining of their clothes had been ripped out and the holes sewn fast. They tied their food bowls to their waist and threaded the spoon through a buttonhole. The rest of their possessions – a crust of bread, a broken comb or a glass shard – they wrapped in a rag and hid in their shirts. At the beginning, the children laughed at each other's looks because the boys wore men's hats whose brims had been cut like shovels, and the girls trailed their coats, which were far too long for their legs. They looked as if they were standing in front of a crooked mirror, for each of them was a joke, a caricature of their previous self.

However, as they were all equally grotesque, they grew accustomed to their appearance and laughed no more.

Sometimes they traded a piece of clothing among themselves, swapped a jacket, a shirt or even a foot rag for their clogs. Yet the boys took care not to lose their shovel hats because at dawn and in the evening Himmelblau taught them to take off their hats and put them on again. He stood in front of the row and repeated the drill, again and again, until they were like one body and their hands rose and fell in one sharp sweep. Yet even then he kept them drilling because whenever an SS Block Senior appeared at the entrance all the boys, from the first graders to those who were almost fourteen, tore off their hats and stood at attention.

There were two roll calls, one at dawn and another at dusk, but the evening call was the worst because the inmates were exhausted from a day of labour, and some of the sick or elderly toppled over and died. There was a piece of rail on a chain, which the Camp Capo beat with an iron pipe, and the prisoners, driven by the wardens, scuttled and formed a five-row formation. On the days of the fiercest cold, the children took their roll call inside the block, where they were sheltered from the rain and wind. Sometimes a child failed to obey the bell because he had fallen asleep or was playing in a corner.

Himmelblau was responsible for the correct number of children and he suffered from stomach cramps before every roll call. He kept counting the children even during the day but each time the number changed and he had either two too many or one not enough, and he started counting again. He woke up at night in a cold sweat and next morning sold his bread ration to Julius Abeles for a pinch of tobacco. He rolled a cigarette vowing that it would be his last and that starting from tomorrow he would abstain from his vice. Yet at the same time he knew that his craving for tobacco was stronger than his will and that without a cigarette he couldn't go through another roll call.

Alex Ehren's children were barely eight, but they were unruly and wild and he had difficulty keeping them together. He took them for a walk but they scattered like water drops, peeped into barracks, fought and shouted until the hunch-backed Camp Capo limped from his room and waved his cane.

'Whoah,' he said in his croaking voice. 'What's going on? Can't you make the brats behave? Should I use the cane and thrash one or two?' Yet he laughed at their pranks because he had a weak spot for Adam Landau, one of the boys.

To hold their attention Alex Ehren invented a memory game. They were explorers and traveled in the jungles of the Amazon, to the North Pole or in the forests of Africa.

'When we come back we'll draw a map,' he said. 'Remember, never before has man visited these parts so be careful to remember.'

He split his explorers into three parties and those who came up with the most details won the competition. They loved the game and Alex Ehren soon had a map with good measurements of the camp.

'Save it,' said Felsen the communist as he looked at the paper. 'One day it may come in handy.'

'Handy for what?'

But Felsen drew his head deep into his coat and wouldn't answer. He often left the Children's Block and Himmelblau had to ask Lisa Pomnenka, the handicraft instructor, to fill in for the history teacher.

The BIIb Czech Camp, like other Birkenau compounds, was 600 metres long and 130 metres wide. There were thirty-two wooden stables along the camp road, the even numbers on the right and the odd on the left. One of the blocks was used as a kitchen, another as the Registrar's office, another one as the clothes storeroom and at the far end of the camp was the hospital and the Children's Block. There were three latrines, each with 396 holes, and two washrooms with four corrugated iron troughs. The two rows of barracks were separated by the road and two parallel ditches, which drained the muddy grounds. Around the compound ran the electrically charged fence, dotted with projectors on concrete pillars that bent forward like the tentacles of an octopus.

Each barracks was 40 metres long, 9 metres wide and 2.5 metres high, which added up to 1,000 metres. With an average occupation of 500 prisoners, each inmate was allotted 2 cubic metres of living space. A horizontal chimney stack cut through the length of the barracks. At the front end there was a space where soup was distributed at noon. There was a similar space at the rear, where during the night latrine containers were placed and corpses stacked before they were taken away by the Cart Commando next morning. To the left and to the right of the entrance were two whitewashed cubicles, one for the Block Senior and the other for the Deputy Block Senior and the Block Registrar.

The children added and subtracted the figures and Neugeboren, who was the sharpest of the group, came up with the result.

'Less than a metre of floor space for each person,' said the boy but he wasn't surprised or taken aback, because he had forgotten the world outside. He had an intimation, like a shadow moving in the dark, of a window with flowing curtains, of a bed with a bright cover and the fragrance of a flower. Yet all that was deep in the past and the boy didn't know whether it was a memory or a tale told by the instructor.

Adam Landau was the worst of the boys and Alex Ehren would have beaten him had he dared to break the rules.

'You beat once and it helps,' Himmelblau had told him, 'but when you beat again it doesn't help so much and you beat more and longer. Where is the end of beating? Think where the children live and what they see. On the camp road, behind the fence, in the barracks. Horrible things. They see cruelty and pain. And death. These have become commonplace. Will Adam be better if I give him a slap on his bottom? Or pull his ear? Or will he become worse?' He spoke fast and had to pause for breath.

'In the camp our rules look foolish. But what harm can a little foolishness do in a world of insanity? Maybe in a world of insanity our foolishness is reason. We do not beat them and we do not make the children fear. We do not speak about the future; we live only for the here and now. We make an island in the sea. We pretend that we are not in the camp. We make them forget the chimney, their hunger and the Germans. We create a world of make-believe.'

It was an inspired speech and Himmelblau had meant every word of it. But when he returned to his cubicle he rolled himself a cigarette, the third this morning, and felt afraid of things to come.

It was all right in theory, thought Alex Ehren, but Himmelblau didn't have to deal with the brat day after day, didn't have to make him sit or write and prevent him from kicking Bubenik on the shin. He was lucky, he decided, that Adam often played hooky for days at a stretch.

'Where have you been?' he asked the child.

'None of your business. Had more important things to do.'

'What things?'

'Don't remember.' The boy was as hard as a pebble.

There were others who disturbed the lesson but none was as malicious as Adam. He was tiny, almost a dwarf, with the face of an angel but with a temper of a wildcat. The smaller boys lived with their mothers but the older ones slept in the Men's Block. However, there were children like Adam Landau, who had come to the camp without their parents and had to fend for themselves in the murky world of the barracks.

Alex Ehren woke the children an hour before the roll call and they marched through the shivering dawn to the washroom. It was so cold that the puddles turned brittle with ice, which the children broke with their wooden clogs. They stripped to their waists and washed in a trickle of water, so thick and ill-smelling that the SS were forbidden to rinse their plates in it. It was cold at night and the taps were furry with frost. The children flapped their arms and blew on their fists as they waited their turn for the one towel they shared. Alex kept a list of who would use the towel first and who came later, when the cloth was soaked and limp with water.

'I won't wash. Not today,' Adam hid his hands in his ancient overcoat. 'Washed yesterday and that's enough.'

'No exceptions.' Alex Ehren held out a piece of rough soap.

'We'll go up the chimney clean or dirty.' Adam spat on the ground in imitation of Jagger, the Camp Capo, who was his friend. 'I don't give a fart about your rules.' He looked up with his eyebrows knitted and his mouth puckered in a sulk.

Sometimes the hunchbacked Capo came to the Children's Block and went off with Adam.

'Let's go and check what's cooking,' he would say and they would walk to the Kitchen Block where he ordered Otto, the Kitchen Capo, to let Adam suck on a marrow bone.

On such days the boy missed his portion of soup, which Alex dealt out to the other children. Adam didn't mind foregoing his ration because the Capo would give him an apple, another time a piece of cheese and sometimes a sugar cube from a dead man's pocket.

The children were not supposed to mention the chimney or use foul language. Their life was full of regulations – there was a way to get up, to dress and to wash in the morning, and another rule about visiting their parents. There were things that were done and others that weren't, and as long as they followed the rules, they were sheltered in the womb of the Children's Block. True, the regulations restricted their freedom and some rebelled and tried to break out. Yet once they pierced the balloon of make-believe they were exposed to the horrors of the day.

'For the last time,' said Alex Ehren, locked in a battle of wills, 'take off your jacket and wash.'

Adam looked at his mates, at Neugeboren who had pushed Fredy's pudding under the fence, at Bubenik, his rival, and at the thin girls in their coats, with their kerchiefs over their hair.

'Damn you,' he said and tore at his jacket.

He ducked and cursed but he did strip and take off his six shirts, which he wore onion fashion, one over the other. He stretched his arm and drew back at the touch of cold water. He rubbed his eyes, his ears and his neck with his hand and started to dress.

'You have to use soap,' said Alex Ehren.

The others watched in a circle with their eyes alive and excited. They weren't Bubenik and Neugeboren and Eva and Hanka any more, but a bunch of savages eager to kill.

Once, when Adam had dodged his wash three times in a row, Alex Ehren had let the children grab his arms and legs and strip him. 'One,' they'd chanted and took off his first shirt. 'Two and three,' they'd triumphed over the next layer. 'Four!' Majda, who was a timid girl with ash-blonde braids tied with a piece of string, had exclaimed. Adam had scratched and twisted like a weasel and pelted them with foul language. He'd cursed Alex Ehren, his mates, Himmelblau and the Block.

'The Capo,' he'd said, 'he'll beat the shit out of you.'

They'd rolled him, small and naked, into the slimy trough and scrubbed his back with a twig broom and a piece of jute, which they had torn from a straw mattress. It had been fun and when they'd finished they were as wet as the boy, but they hadn't seemed to mind. It had been good to vent their fear on their mate and comrade.

For some time afterwards Alex Ehren was afraid to meet Jagger, the Camp Capo, but the hunchback didn't bear Alex Ehren a grudge.

'I am taking the child for an outing,' Jagger had said in his deep voice. 'He is too small to read and write and work on sums. Plenty of time to catch up later,' and he'd winked, laughing at his morbid joke.

Alex Ehren hated the regulation soap and had it not been for the children, he wouldn't have used it on his hands, his chest and his face. In the evening when the children left the Block to see their parents, the instructors sat on the horizontal chimney and ate their bread rations. They ate their slice slowly, holding it in their cupped palms, anxious not to let even one morsel fall on the ground. It was all the bread they got for a day and some preferred to save a part of it, the crumb or the crust, for breakfast. The bread was dark and heavy and came in small square loaves of which each prisoner received one quarter. Sometimes they got with it five grams of margarine or a piece of cheese or dollop of beetroot jam, and on Sundays a slice of substitute sausage.

They chewed each mouthful at least seven times to savour its flavour and the life-giving strength. They swallowed the bread with remorse because once the food had left the tongue and palate, it was irreversibly gone. One evening Fabian stood up and held up a piece of soap.

'In our world nothing gets lost. Where does the bread go? It goes down into my stomach and from there to my hands and head and body and makes me live. But what happens when I die?' He tried to catch their eyes. 'I did some research,' he said, 'and found the answer.

'This, my learned friends, is a cake of soap, which helps us to stay alive. Isn't it written—' he motioned to the slogan painted on the rafters '—one louse, thy death. Imagine, a small, almost microscopic creature and so deadly. How about man who is a thousand times bigger than a louse? Let alone an SS officer who looms even higher?' He paused, allowing the instructors time to laugh.

He turned the soap in his fingers and brought it close to his broken glasses.

'Look, there is something written on the soap. There are three letters: R J F. I wonder what these letters stand for.'

'Probably the name of the factory,' said Himmelblau.

'Not so.' Fabian grimaced and held the soap away from his face. 'The Germans burn the dead and use their ashes as fertiliser. One day a Jew and next day a cabbage. Though I would prefer a cherry tree or a rosebush. Anything but a concentration camp. But what do they do with the little fat that remains?'

'Enough,' said Marta Felix, frowning. 'The joke has gone far enough.'

'What joke? R J F. Real Jewish Fat ... that's what the letters mean. This is what I have been told by a man from Monowitz.'

It was Fabian's fear that made him speak of their death. He flouted his death, hoisted it like a banner and came back to it like a thief to the scene of his crime. He cracked jokes about his own death to assuage his terror. At the beginning, every time Alex Ehren thought of his death, his heart missed a beat. It happened once or twice, but then his rage welled up from his stomach and rose to his head and his anger became stronger than his terror.

'I will not,' he said, 'I will not go meekly to the slaughter. I will not be burned to fertilise German fields and I will not be made into a cake of soap. I may die, but I will take some of them with me.'

He sat on the tepid chimney with his eyes to the ground, but with his fists clenched so tight that his palms hurt.

The instructors were silent but after a while they took up another theme. At the beginning they were timid but then their voices grew louder, as if they were trying to drown out the words that would have been better left unsaid.

In the evening, when most of the prisoners were asleep on their pallets, Felsen tapped Alex Ehren's arm and led him to a corner.

'You brag,' said Felsen, 'and you don't know who is listening.'

'Who is listening?'

'The walls. The floor and the rafters. Those who speak are dangerous.'

He contemplated Alex Ehren in the light of the dim bulb and ran his hand over his face. 'There are talkers and there are doers. But they don't brag about what they do.'

'What do they do?'

'They are ready to fight for their lives.'

'I didn't know.'

'Of course you didn't. They don't advertise, but there is an underground organisation.'

Where?'

'Here and in other camps. All over Auschwitz.'

Alex Ehren was overwhelmed. He had found a group of people who, like him, wouldn't accept their ordeal.

'How do I join? I'll do anything they ask.'

'First of all, shut up. Don't trumpet into the world what a hero you are. Someday they will give you a task.'

'When?'

'I don't know. Not before the time is ripe.'

Alex Ehren lay on his bunk afraid and excited. He imagined the chaos, the fight, the dying people among the barracks. But for the first time in his Birkenau existence there was a flicker of hope. He knew that most of them would perish, but why shouldn't he make it to the woods and join the partisans? In his mind he saw the mountains and the rugged men who ambushed German convoys and blew up bridges. He knew nothing of the place where he was being held, which Polish town was nearest, or how far it was to the Slovakian border. He had no idea of the German security installations outside the fence, the number of garrisons or how to cross the river Sola. And yet at night he dreamt about the mutiny, the struggle and his escape. For within the slavery of the camp the convicts had one freedom of which nobody could rob them – the freedom to dream.

There was no paper on the Block because the children were not supposed to learn how to read and write. Alex Ehren took them to the Registrar's Block where the children stole used sheets from garbage bins. The scribes compiled daily lists of how many men and women were on each block and who had died during the night. There was the weaving workshop and the spinning shop and the mica plant for women where the workers produced military equipment. The foremen kept records of the workers, of the used materials and the finished products. The children went through the bins until they collected enough scraps for the day. They had no pencils except the one stub Alex Ehren saved for the postcards on which they could ask for food parcels.

There was a man on the Children's Block who was good with his hands. He had only a broken knife, a file and a rusty screwdriver, but he knew how to repair a door, fix the smoking oven or build a small stage on the horizontal chimney. Sometimes he even produced toy soldiers from a piece of wood and some bent wire. They called him Shashek, which means clown, because his mouth was frozen into an eternal smile. He was a whim of nature and his laughing countenance was often his misfortune. In the first months he worked together with Alex Ehren on the road, where they carried boulders from a pile, split them with a hammer and built a pavement. It was a frustrating task because as soon as they finished a stretch the silt swallowed the stones and they had to start from the beginning. The SS sentry beat Shashek more often than the others because the sentry thought that Shashek was laughing at him.

'Stop grinning,' said the German soldier and lashed out at Shashek.

'I can't. It's my face that grins.'

He was scared of the sentry and of his rubber hose. Yet his mouth was turned into a smile and the more frantic he grew the worse the sneer on his face became.

The sentry caned him until he cried but even the tears that rolled down his cheeks didn't change the laughing grimace of his face.

Himmelblau never regretted that he took Shashek onto the Block, because his ingenuity brightened the children's lives. He had a shelf at the rear end of the barracks where he hoarded twisted wires, pieces of wood, a broken spade and half a dozen beer bottles, which he found behind the German guardhouse.

'Why all that junk?'

'One day it will come in handy. To throw away is easy but to find is difficult.'

He rummaged in a trash box and shook his head. 'No pencils. Why don't you try charred splinters?'

They had no knives to peel off splinters but Bubenik had a sharpened spoon.

'I rubbed it on a brick,' he said and ran his finger over the edge. 'Cuts even bread. No problem to peel off a splinter from my bunk.'

They spent the afternoon grinding their spoons on a stone and when Bass started the fire in the oven, he charred both ends of the children's splinters. With each end they wrote three words and sometimes even four. Alex Ehren's wards were still poor writers but the older boys ran back and forth to the oven and watched their wooden pencils flicker in the flames.

Adam Landau had the sharpest spoon of all. He worked on his knife for several days until it looked like a dagger, thin and sharp on both sides, honed into a dangerous point.

One day, thought Alex Ehren, he will stab to kill. He felt that he ought to take away the weapon from the child but he never did.

The children unravelled yarn from their straw mattresses. They ripped open the jute and wound the thread into skeins until the straw spilled on the ground. Lisa Pomnenka had taught them to produce macramé patterns and they wove strings and belts even during writing lesson. The macramé work turned into an obsession and for some time everybody, even the boys, sat and twisted the strands into an ornament or a rough mitten. The instructor was young and when she got up from sleep she looked as if she were a girl in Beran's group of older children. Sometimes, especially after an unruly lesson, Alex Ehren watched her work with his children and envied the ease with which she handled her pupils. He left her with a bunch of urchins, excited and fighting among themselves but when Lisa Pomnenka entered the circle they turned into lambs. The girl had dark hair and blue eyes, which were like two pools of water. She was inconspicuous, moved with bird-like movements, and at first Alex Ehren hardly noticed her presence.

During the first months in Birkenau, Alex Ehren felt no desire. He worked on the road, and in the evening sank heavily into sleep. He had no dreams because his life was in his hands and feet, and his stomach was aching for bread. There was also the fear of blows, of the cold and of sudden death, all of which rendered his existence entirely physical. He was so burdened with his body that he didn't look up towards the sky, until he was like an animal, a dog or a lizard.

Neither was there love. He slept on a bunk with seven prisoners and in the evening he met an uncle of his, but he was numb inside and felt nothing, neither affection for his friends nor hatred for his torturers. He listened to words but they had little meaning beyond their sound. He was like a house gutted by fire or like a stone cast into the universe. He was deprived of familiar road signs and his life crumbled and fell apart. His state of shock grew and deepened and had he not moved to the Children's Block, he would have turned skeletal and apathetic and, like many others, would have died on the road or in his sleep.

After two weeks on the Children's Block he recovered. He watched the blue-eyed girl and something within him stirred. In the evening he sat next to Lisa Pomnenka and when she turned her head he smelled her young and feminine hair. He grew stronger because he ate the thick children's soup and occasionally received a share of Pavel Hoch's parcels. At the beginning of March the prisoners had written postcards and now some of them received bread parcels. The mail was searched for contraband, for matches, candles, torches, money or a letter. The parcels were looted of the better foodstuffs and often arrived with the bread mouldy and spoiled. The inmates roasted it on the stove and this burned away the mildew and made it edible.

'How lucky you are,' said Alex Ehren to Pavel Hoch, looking at the neat lettering on the wrapping paper.

'Aninka and I were born in the same small town,' said Pavel Hoch. 'We have known each other since we were kids. Went to the same class. We were friends at first and later became lovers. When I get back we'll marry.'

His words sounded as simple as spring water and Alex Ehren envied his friend his faith. Pavel Hoch's parcels often arrived half empty, but at times they slipped through undamaged. This shoebox had been packed with love, each article in a napkin, a loaf of bread, an onion, a seed cake and dried apples in a paper bag. The food smelled of a kitchen, a tablecloth and clover.

'Why do you share with me?' Alex Ehren asked.

'There will be another parcel. In the country it is easy to get food.'

'How long would a woman wait? A year, two? What if you die?'

He ate the bread, which was half spoiled by its long journey. It was hard and stale, but it still held the taste of the field in which it had grown. Why does he share his bread, wondered Alex Ehren; I have nothing to give him in return.

They slept on the same bunk and sometimes spoke about the books they had read and their friendship helped them carry their fear.

One evening Alex Ehren sat next to Lisa Pomnenka and his arm touched her elbow. He felt her warm skin and there was pleasure in the accidental encounter. The girl looked up from her bowl and smiled. Yet Alex Ehren was too shy to say a word or look in her face.

Lisa Pomnenka, whose name meant 'forget-me-not' was even better with a pencil than with the patterns of macramé, which she taught Majda and Eva and Neugeboren. Sometimes she drew a house, a garden and a tree for the children. She also produced animals they had never seen – a cat, a cow, a hen with a brood of small chicks and even a monkey. Alex Ehren wrote out the names of the animals and the children learned to spell the words.

Sometimes he touched her wrist and, although Fabian made fun of him, they soon sat holding hands like children. In the following days Alex Ehren woke with a thrill and an expectation that he would meet the girl and watch her draw her little pictures on scraps of paper. She was neither beautiful nor clever, but there was sweetness in her movements and he loved the fall of her voice.

She spoke to him about her father, who suffered from a strange illness. He hovered between waking and sleeping and wouldn't get up to receive his bread ration. There were many diseases in the camp – erysipelas, jaundice and inflammation of the brain – and when her father grew worse, the Block Warden sent him to the hospital opposite the Children's Block. Lisa Pomnenka saved her soup and the orderly agreed to take it to her father. They tried to talk to him through the wooden wall, but he was indifferent and wouldn't answer.

She tapped on the wood with a piece of stone, not noticing Dr Mengele, the SS physician.

'You'll spread the infection. Go away.'

'He's my father,' she said and her voice was shaky with fear because there were rumours of horrible operations the SS doctor conducted on young women. She looked at his face and thought about the twins on the Children's Block, the two thirteen-year-old boys and the two girls, Eva and Hanka, whom he occasionally summoned to the Hospital Block for examinations. Mietek the Pole, who came to visit Magdalena, spoke about the experiments conducted in the Hospital Camp. The victims were wheeled in and after some time carried out dead, covered in blood. The twins, however, returned safely and with a piece of bread in their hands. And yet the evil rumours persisted, and Lisa Pomnenka was frightened and drew her coat tight over her chest.

'I've seen you before,' said the SS physician and looked at the girl with interest. 'You work with the children. What do you do there?'

'I am a painter,' she said in a surge of courage.

'A house painter or a portrait painter?' He laughed.

'Portrait painter,' she said.

'Could you paint my face?'

'I could.'

'Maybe some day.' He was amused by the blue eyes and the trembling mouth. 'What would you like to paint?'

'The Block wall. Make it a green meadow with flowers.'

'Why don't you?'

'I have no brushes,' she said. 'No brushes and no paint.'

'We'll see about that.' He turned abruptly and stepped into his office.

That night Lisa Pomnenka's father died. In the morning the male nurse handed her a bundle with his belongings, a chipped bowl, a spoon and a ration of bread. Usually the orderly took the bread for himself, but as he had seen Mengele talk to the girl, he didn't steal it.

She didn't get her father's clothes because as he died on the infection ward, his rags were burned on a smouldering fire behind the washroom.

The girl didn't cry. She knew that she should be sad and feel pain but she felt nothing and had no tears.

'Why can't I be like others?' she asked. 'I loved my father and I visited him every day and even washed his shirt. But now, when he is dead, I feel no pain. Am I a monster? Don't I have a heart?' She punished herself and wouldn't sit with Alex Ehren and hold hands and touch. She worked with the children on their macramé patterns but after the lesson she kept herself apart. 'There is so much death around,' Alex Ehren said, 'that it has drowned our sadness.'

A day later Dr Mengele sent Lisa Pomnenka a box of paints and an assortment of brushes.

Death had been with them from the very beginning. Three months before, Alex Ehren arrived at Birkenau in the small hours of Christmas Eve. It had been an agonising passage for the fifty people in the boxcar – men, women and even children – who had little space and only one bucket for their needs. In the first hours of the journey they joked about the lack of privacy and took turns holding up a blanket, but soon the bucket was full and spilled on the floor. They were so crowded that only half of them could sit, while the rest slept leaning against one another. They still had some luggage, a rolled up blanket, a pillow, an extra pair of shoes and an overcoat. They piled their bundles in one corner and let the children rest on top of the heap. They were thirsty and licked the sooty icicles that Alex Ehren broke off the roof. The third day was the worst because they were too ashamed to relieve themselves on the floor and suffered from pain in their guts and bladders. There was only a narrow window at the back of the car and the prisoners had no air to breathe, no water and no space to stretch their legs.

When the doors were thrown open, the men were separated from their women and herded into a snowy rut along the fence. Some of the prisoners managed to relieve themselves behind the cars, but most of them were driven on with their guts full and painful. Alex Ehren saw Beran and his wife Sonia squat on the rails and hold hands in a moment of blissful relief. They moved their bowels until a Capo drove them apart into separate columns. 'The happiest hour of my married life,' said Beran and turned his head to look at the marching women.

The deportees were confused by the night, the shouting, the lights, the transition from one world to another. They were bewildered by the men in striped uniforms, the sudden separation from their families and, above all, by their utter helplessness. Alex Ehren had seen the names of towns they were passing and he knew that they were being shipped east, but where they were he didn't know. They waited in the cold snowdrift until they felt like trapped animals. Finally the column moved and Alex Ehren struggled against the wind, which hissed over the ground. He closed his eyes because the frozen flakes of snow stung like needles into his face.

At first he didn't notice the corpses that lined the track, but when he opened his eyes he was appalled by the gallery of dead bodies. They were men and women, some of them his friends, some of them strangers and others he had known by sight from the ghetto. The bodies were frozen to stone in an indecent gesture with their blood glistening in ruby crystals on the snow. They sprawled, grotesque, uncouth, their eyes open and their mouths grinning horribly in an arrested shriek. The men lay with their genitals exposed, some clutching their crotch, the women with skirts lifted like dancers, exhibiting their naked bellies and thighs and the hair of their shame. It was a spectacle – lewd and obscene – and at the same time unspeakably horrible, because the dead were so similar to the living – their shoes, their clothes, their faces.

How easily, Alex Ehren thought, they could have been Sonia or Beran or himself. Like them they had been plagued by their bladder and their gut and when they left the column to relieve themselves the soldiers shot them. Alex Ehren walked along the obscene exhibition and when he was unable to restrain himself any longer he let his water flow. He felt no shame as it spread warmly from his crotch to his leg and into his shoe.

For the rest of the night and the following day the prisoners were kept in the sauna. They fell asleep one across the other on the concrete floor. When they awoke Dezo Kovac lit the Chanukah candles. They had been robbed of their luggage but some of them had hidden some food under their shirts and Shashek found a candle in his pocket. They sat in the corner,

Alex Ehren, Beran and Fabian. Kovac broke the candle into two pieces and stuck them on the concrete floor. They kept together in a circle to screen the candles from the SS sentry at the door.

'These candles we light in memory of the miracles thou hast made for our fathers and for us in days past and in the present time.' Dezo Kovac was the only one who knew the Hebrew blessing, but they did remember the Chanukah song and watched the flames move with their breath.

There was a man, a musician and composer, with whom Dezo Kovac used to play the violin. He sat on the ground with his head hanging over his knees and his hair wild and dishevelled. He was an artist and the journey and walk among the dead had unsettled his mind.

'I'll sing for you,' he said and stood up. He put up his hands and sang in a thin feminine voice, moving his hips and dancing in small dainty steps.

'These candles,' he sang, 'we light in memory of thy miracles.' There was little space for his dancing and he stepped on the lying men. The German sentry, a pale-faced SS Rottenfuehrer, noticed the commotion.

'Silence,' he ordered. 'Shut up and sit down.'

But the musician wouldn't stop and when the soldier came closer he clawed his fingers into the sentry's face like a bird of prey. The soldier fired a shot and the musician fell to the floor bleeding from his mouth. They added his corpse to the pile of the dead outside the barracks.

'Miracles?' said Fabian. 'There are no miracles.'

He thought about the frozen corpses along the ditch and shook his head. He spat on two fingers of his hand and snuffed out one of the flames.

'Neither for us nor for our forefathers.' And he extinguished the second candle and said doggedly, 'No miracles and no God.'

Later a gang of Polish prisoners with shaven heads tattooed a number on their left forearm. Some of the children struggled and cried, but others, like Adam Landau, were defiant and silent.

After three months they had learned to live with death.

# 3.

BY THE END OF MARCH THE EVENINGS GREW LONGER. IT still rained most of the time and sometimes there was even snow, which the children formed into snowmen or into balls, which Adam threw at their faces. Towards noon the snow melted and the Polish workers spoke about the flooded Sola, a river the prisoners had never seen. The men who worked in the ditches suffered most because their rags froze stiff and the wind chilled their bones. Many of them died, and it took the Cart Commando all morning to collect the bodies from behind the barracks.

Whenever there was a break in the rain, Magdalena took the children behind the Block to play games, to stretch and to run in a circle. The Children's Block was the last barracks in the row and through the fence the children saw the railway and the platform.

There were days without a single train but then two came in succession, with cars clanging and screeching as the engine manoeuvred back and forth to a halt. They watched a column of men and women in their ill-fitting Sunday clothes being marched away and there was another procession and then another until the train was empty and the locomotive depart-ed with a whistle. A commando loaded the orphaned luggage onto wooden carts – the suitcases and the bundles and even the abandoned rolled-up bedding – and drove them in the opposite direction.

Whenever there was a transport, Magdalena was unable to conduct a lesson because the children were fascinated by the train, the people on the ramp, the SS men and the barking dogs. They didn't ask questions but instead watched and pointed their fingers at this and at that, and even laughed at a man who stumbled and fell. Magdalena wondered how much the children knew and whether they spoke among themselves about the people that walked away and vanished. She was glad they didn't ask her because she didn't know what to answer; whether she would be able to hide her own fear and lie about a labour camp, a factory or woods where the prisoners cut timber. What would she say about the chimney, the smoke, the red glow that lit their nights? Sometimes she caught wisps of their words and phrases, but the children sounded less scared than the adults. They didn't know the meaning of death, she thought, and was relieved by her conclusion.

In her earlier days the dance teacher had liked trains because there was magic in the distances, in the new faces, in the little gifts people brought and in the sadness of parting. The children were intent on the arriving people, but they were thrilled even more by the food that grew into pyramids after the transport was taken away. For the children were hungry. It wasn't a hunger that could be stilled by a piece of bread, because they suffered from a need that grew out of many months of starvation, of a deprivation so deep that it encompassed not only their stomachs but their whole beings, their minds, their eyes, their hearts and their limbs. True, the children ate better than ordinary prisoners, and yet their hunger was an obsession and a craze, so that they were unable to think of anything else but the food that piled up behind the electric fence.

The people on the train didn't know where they were being taken. They had been told about a labour camp or farm work, and they had packed into their luggage a blanket and a pillow, warm clothes, a spare pair of shoes and a bottle of cold medicine. They sold their last silver and their wedding rings to buy food for the days before they would find work.

When they were gone, the commandos piled up the food, each kind on a separate mound. There were loaves of farm bread, deep brown and round, built like a house of cards. There were winter apples that kept their fragrance for many months, black-rinded cheese, sausages and wreaths of garlic and hot pepper. It was an agonising sight, and the hungry children called their friends from the Block to see the riches. They left their stalls and stood at the fence – the instructors, the youth assistants, the matrons and even Himmelblau, the bespectacled Children's Senior – and their mouths filled with bitter water.

Towards noon most of the food had been put into crates and loaded on the returning train. The broken loaves, the sacks that tore and spilled on the ground and the meat no longer fresh were not shipped back to Germany, but were cooked into a soup for the children.

Sometimes Alex Ehren met a friend on the camp road, but he didn't stay long because he was impatient to go and sit with the girl. They cut their bread ration into thin slices and laid them out on a piece of paper. He loved their shared meals, which made them almost a family, and the stall, intended for three horses, became their home. They had, as she once said, a bubble within a bubble, a private world of make-believe on the Children's Block island. They spoke about insignificant things, which, in the light of their affection, became matters of beauty. They laughed at the ever-falling rain, the mouse that lived in a hole under the wall and at the old man who burned infected clothes behind the latrines. Yet above all they touched.

There were no secrets and no privacy among the deportees. They lived so close that they were unable to conceal a rag, a piece of string, a quarrel or a romance. The instructors didn't deride the lovers who held hands and even Fabian, who used to rail at matters holy and profane, turned his head and pretended not to see. Sometimes Alex Ehren put his hand on the girl's small breast and they sat locked in contentment, unaware of their surroundings.

Once they kissed and his stool tipped over and they tumbled to the ground. It was droll and they laughed, but the next time he tried to kiss her, she shook her head.

He was grateful that his bunk-mates didn't make fun of him and the girl, though after their kiss and fall Fabian rubbed his nose and scoffed: 'Only swallows make love on the wing. Did you think you are a bird, Alex?'

By then they already knew the day of their death. There was a woman Registrar in the Main Camp, one Katherine Singer, who had seen the lists and told them.

'There is an "SB 6" written next to your number,' she said. 'You'll get special treatment in six months.' She was blunt because there was no reason for sentiment in the lunar landscape of death. 'It's better to know than to be blind. No time for solicitude. The truth narrows your choice and helps you decide.'

She was a member of the organisation, a friend of the seamstress at the Clothes Storeroom and a believer in an uprising.

It was frightening to know that they were going to die. But it was seven times more difficult to know the date of one's own execution. Time heals, thought Alex Ehren bitterly, but my time has become my curse. In the past he wasn't aware of time. It flowed leisurely like water, day after day and year after year and was only occasionally dotted by a memorable event.

Now time became a commodity, a tangible object, a treasure, which had to be hoarded and saved. He counted his minutes like a miser who counts his gold and he mourned for each morning and each night that had passed. He was reluctant to sleep because sleep shortened his time to live. Time was like a river, which he craved to arrest, to stem with a dam, or like a fish become one with the current.

It was a losing battle because his hours ticked away hopelessly and horribly and left him in a state of prostration. He started with a trove of days, seventy or eighty, and at the beginning he still had time to spare on small, trivial matters. Yet as the days unravelled from the skein of time, he regretted events he had missed, a book he hadn't read, a place he hadn't visited, a girl he hadn't loved, for he knew that all these were irretrievably lost. Sometimes he wished he were like Beran, who had come to terms with his mortality.

'Time is my enemy,' said Alex Ehren. 'It is like an animal that devours me from within.'

'Rubbish,' said Beran. 'Time is a human invention. Like the clock. If you don't worry about it, it won't bother you. Time is like breathing. When you start counting your breaths they'll choke you.'

The gawky instructor still met Sonia on the camp road where they stood until the free hour was up. Sometimes they remembered poems they had read and they recited them together, helping each other out where they forgot a word or a line. Beran found pleasure in small things, in a new shoe-lace Pavel Hoch had stolen for him at the Clothes Storeroom, in a piece of potato he found in his soup, and in an ant he watched with his pupils. There was no anger in him, which Alex Ehren was unable to understand. Alex Ehren rebelled against the transience of life and sometimes tried to speak about it with the girl. Yet Lisa Pomnenka refused to talk about time.

'I'm too stupid for philosophy. We'll wait and see what happens. Today is today and tomorrow will take care of itself.'

She went on with the simple acts of living, her shared meals with Alex Ehren, the macramé lessons and her painting of flowers and animals, which the children pinned on their bunks.

'Why worry about things that I can't change? Of course I am scared of the chimney, but most of the time I don't think about it and that helps.'

She unravelled an old sweater and knitted Alex Ehren a vest, which he wore under his shirt.

'How long will I wear it?' he asked, and she shook her head and laughed.

'A month, a year, who knows. When it gets too old I'll knit another. There are more important things than that.'

'Like what?'

'Painting the wall,' she said, and looked at the dark cavern of the Block.

Shashek, the handyman with the grinning face, hammered together a ladder on which the girl worked. She started at the entrance door, where the kindergarten children had their stall, and drew grass and flowers until the wall looked like a window into a different world. She was meticulous about every blade and each petal and her picture was clear and simple. Each day there was more of it and in the morning, when the children arrived at the Block, they looked at the wall and counted the new daisies above their heads.

Alex Ehren knew that the girl wasn't an accomplished painter; her pictures were groping, artless and outspoken. The charm was in their simplicity. Shashek watched her from his workbench, and though his face smiled, he was jealous whenever Alex Ehren sat with Lisa Pomnenka.

By the end of March Alex Ehren was in love with the girl. He felt less scared, as if the touching of hands and the meetings of skin against skin helped him overcome the horror of time. There were still three months till the 20th of June, which was the day of their execution.

The children didn't seem to be afraid of dying. They feared the night, the SS soldiers, the dogs, the beatings and hunger but they were not scared of death. The smaller ones, Alex Ehren thought, were like plants or animals who are unaware of past and future, and thus they didn't fear time. However, fear was like a contagious disease and as they lived with their mothers, they became infected. Their fear was often shapeless but it showed in the small drawings on paper scraps for which they rummaged in garbage bins. They drew the barracks, the fence, the SS sentries and a dog so huge that it filled most of the picture. Their drawings were full of angular strokes and their sun was like a spider suspended from a cloud. Yet Eva drew a family in a house under a tree and on the table there was a dish of steaming soup.

Sometimes Majda's mother, Agnes, came to the Block to ask about her child.

She carried food barrels and shared a bunk with Sonia. Her coat was bespattered by soup, but she looked elegant even in her rags. She talked with Alex Ehren about Majda's reading and writing and was pleased by the macramé, which the child had made for her birthday.

Agnes looked at the teacher and wondered how old he was, perhaps not more than twenty. He might easily be her son, she thought, and he was certainly too young to understand. The camp was a place for the very young because men of forty, who had been lawyers, merchants and educators, grew prematurely old. They spoke about their past and shuffled about, unwashed, smelly, wrapped in their blankets, with their trousers trailing. There were women who had turned grey within three months, were wrinkled and bent and had lost their monthly cycle.

It was, Agnes thought with horror, as if each day carried the weight of a year. Agnes looked at Alex Ehren and was suddenly afraid that she too would one day wake up old, toothless, with her flesh sagging. Yet she was also worried about the child and would have liked to talk with somebody experienced.

There were things on the Women's Block of which nobody spoke. How could she tell Alex Ehren about the strange men that visited women on their bunks? It was a secret that everybody on the women's barracks knew and which she couldn't hide from Majda. There were, on the one hand, the days on the Children's Block, with its make-believe painted wall, and on the other, the nights on the Women's Block, which like spoiled food, the girl couldn't digest. What other reason could have made the child a bed-wetter?

Her disorder was an annoyance because the women complained about the smell and discomfort. They pestered Agnes to move with the child to another bunk, to the back of the block next to the night latrines. She aired their straw mattresses and turned them upside down and at night put a motley collection of rags under the child. Yet the straw never dried out and the smell lingered, not only on their bed but also on their clothes. At dawn she rinsed her rags under a tap, but as she had nowhere to dry them, she hurried back between her shift of the morning barrels of tea and the midday soup, held the clothes in the wind and spread them out over their blankets.

She was lucky that she worked as a barrel carrier and so could bribe the Room Warden. She spoke to the child, woke her in the middle of the night and wouldn't let her drink her evening tea. Yet each morning the bed was soaked and she had to clean up and wash and hold up the blanket to dry in the wind. There was a bond of love between her and the girl with the ash-blonde braids, yet after some time she grew tired of the barrels, the child's trouble and the complaints of her bunk-mates. She was still a beautiful woman with large eyes and the gait of a queen, elegant and ladylike, and each time Jagger, the hunchbacked Capo, saw her labouring up the camp road, he took off his striped beret and bowed.

'There could be another job for the gracious lady. Just say the word. The Capo is willing.'

She turned her head and didn't answer, but she thought about the other job and the heavier her burden grew the more she was tempted to give in to the Capo's offer.

The women in the Family Camp lived apart from their men. They met on the camp road before the evening roll call. The women, who were stronger than the men, handed their husbands and sons a morsel of bread or a spoonful of their soup, which they had saved from their rations. It was as if in the camp world the women had turned into mothers and the men into their sons or aged fathers.

In the middle of March, the old Camp Senior, a German convict with the green triangle of a murderer, was allowed to join the SS and volunteer for the East Front. Willy, the German prisoner who replaced him, took a Jewish concubine. Their liaison loosened the discipline and some women slept with the cooks or Block Seniors who paid them with a bowl of soup or a bread ration.

Alex Ehren knew that there were two kinds of convicts. On the one hand there were the camp officials, the Capos, the Registrars, the Block Seniors and the potato peelers who had enough food and were thus less exposed to death. Then there were the common prisoners, the labourers on the camp road, in the ditch and in the sweatshops, who lived on starvation rations and froze in the icy rain. They were unshaved and filthy, and finally succumbed to diarrhoea and to their lack of will to live.

There were also the Polish craftsmen, like Mietek, the roof repairman, who visited the Czech Camp to meet the long-haired women. It was dangerous to have sex in the camp because if a convict was caught he was punished terribly. The Capos, the Block Seniors and the artisans paid the women with bread and stolen goods and slept with them in the Block Senior's cubicle at the barracks entrance. When a German sentry entered the camp the first prisoner who saw him exclaimed, 'Attention, attention', which was repeated by the guard at the next block and then at the next, until the whole length of the camp reverberated with the warning. The lover left by the back door and the woman hurried back to her workshop, clutching the piece of bread under her apron.

When Dasha, the girl librarian on the Children's Block, heard the warning, she hid the seven books among Shashek's junk and sat with the other children. They switched to a song or a game or repeated German sentences, because teaching, like sex, was a forbidden activity.

One day an SS Block Senior caught a couple lying together on a bunk. He had slipped into the camp unobserved and walked along the fence where there were no guards. He was a man with pale-blue eyes and hair the colour of straw. The convicts called him the Priest because he carried his hands in his sleeves and gave orders in a whisper, but they were afraid of him because he had a cruel mind and enjoyed seeing people suffer.

A bench was set up and the culprits were stripped and spread-eagled over the planks. The man was tall and well built, and, because he worked in the potato-peeling commando, his body was vigorous and strong. Alex Ehren watched the young woman whose copper hair had kept its sheen despite the squalor of the camp. Her face was contorted with fear and yet the head with its red mane was wild like that of Medusa. The Block Senior cut the air with his cane, which produced a sharp and menacing sound.

'Thirty lashes,' said the Priest, and Alex Ehren watched the woman's body quiver at each blow. There was life and passion under her luminous skin and as she tried to lift herself from the bench he saw her lovely breasts, smooth and shaped to perfection. The cane broke the delicate blue veins and her blood ran in tiny brooks into the parting of her back. Alex Ehren was ashamed that his pity was spiced with desire but he didn't look away from the naked body, from the red hair and the wounds that opened like lips.

The lovers were carried to the Hospital Block, but even in her swoon the girl was exquisitely beautiful. The man died several days later of infection but the girl recovered and returned to her bunk, limping, pale and with her head shaven clean. The women at her bunk gave up part of their bread and nursed her back to strength.

'We have two lives,' said Marta Felix, who was the oldest of the teachers on the Children's Block, 'one dressed and the other one naked. We try to keep them apart but sometimes they intertwine and meet.'

It was a terrible thing that the children watched the flogging and Himmelblau felt guilty that he didn't refuse to let them attend. He braced himself to face the SS soldier, the Priest, but he was scared that he too would be caned. He feared the bench and the blood and did nothing.

In the evening he locked himself in his cubicle and lit a cigarette. The matter was all over the camp, he mused, and even if the children hadn't seen the flogging and the naked bodies, they would have heard about them anyway. It was always the same, Himmelblau thought unhappily; he was full of good intentions but at the end he bowed to the inevitable, his common sense or his fear. He blamed himself for his weakness and thought about Fredy, who had failed in his moment of truth. He drew smoke into his lungs and consoled himself that he was like the grass that bends in the wind but survives the storm. One day, he assured himself, the war would come to an end and if he dodged, bowed and complied, some of the children might survive. He fingered the whistle on a string and thought about the uprising. He wasn't a brave man but neither was he a fool and he knew that unless there was a miracle, they would all die.

For several days Alex Ehren felt ashamed and wouldn't touch Lisa Pomnenka's hand, as if he had committed adultery with the copper-haired woman. Sometimes, especially after the children had eaten their soup and had no patience to learn, Fabian climbed on the chimney and conducted a sing-along.

He wasn't a musician like Dezo Kovac, who read notes and played the violin, but he was a performer and a clown. The children left their stalls and settled on the dirt floor like a flock of birds. The earth was bumpy and cold but the youth assistants swept the floor with rag brooms, which they had made from fine strands of jute.

'What shall we sing today?' He wrinkled his brow above his cracked spectacles.

'*Alouette*,' shouted Adam, and Bubenik and the girls joined in and they too cried, '*Alouette*', which they loved.

He opened his arms as if confounded by their choice. '"*Alouette*"? What? Which *Alouette*? I don't remember.'

'You do, you do.'

Fabian flicked his nose with his finger and nodded. 'Ah, it's *Alouette* you mean,' he said. 'Why didn't you say "*Alouette*" right away?'

He strode up and down the horizontal chimney and sang the first line about the bird's head. The children joined in and went on with other parts of the bird's body to be plucked, the ears, the neck, the eyes, the elbows and the feet. The song went on for a long time, wild and rowdy, though not entirely out of bounds, because Fabian conducted the voices with his hands, his head and with his whole body. Some of the children moved their arms in time together with him and others, like Bubenik, took a bin and beat out the rhythm with his fingers. They were so absorbed by the tune they forgot the time and place and the squalor of their existence. Fabian started a Czech folk song and then another and afterwards a popular tune about nine canaries and a laughing gull who survived the flood. They sang and as they sang they transcended their misery. They were one body, which sang with one strong voice, and as long as they sang they were not unhappy.

Sometimes the Camp Capo came to listen. Another time it was a convict craftsman from the Men's Camp or even an SS sentry who didn't understand the words but clapped his hands to the tune. Most of the children were Czech but even those who spoke German or Dutch followed the melody. At such times the Children's Block was like a ship in the wilderness of the ocean and the sing-along was like a taste of home.

In the evening Alex Ehren told the girl about his family.

'Towards winter all my seven uncles and aunts went on a pilgrimage to the village. It wasn't much of a village but rather a hamlet between a meadow and a forest. By that time my grandfather was dead but there were two old people, a brother and sister, who lived in the house with the thatched roof and earthen floor. The house had two rooms, one with a bed and the other with a trestle table and four ancient chairs. They were full of woodworm and so brittle that we weren't allowed to play hide and seek among them. Dry garlic hung from the beam and the kitchen ceiling was so low that even I could touch the wreaths.

'We drove to the hamlet before winter because the old people were too weak to walk in the snow to the grocery store in the next village. The highway ended a long distance from the house and our car struggled up the lane lined with blackberries, ferns and frightened rabbits. My seven aunts and uncles parked their cars at the duck pond and we carried the flour, butter and smoked meat inside the hut. Sometimes I stepped into goose droppings and the village urchins jeered and hooted at me from behind a linden tree. Up the stream the old people owned a stretch of meadow and I waded knee-high in the uncut grass. The old man didn't keep cows any more, but there were still bales of straw in the shed, and when Aunt Sofie ladled out coffee from an iron pot, it smelled of dung. Uncle Hugo broke pieces of cake into his mug and sucked them loudly. He had only a few teeth left and his cheeks were sunken and hollow. Yet he was still strong and tall and enjoyed his food.

'The family lived there for six hundred years. Sometimes we were chased away but we returned to the house and the pasture. Horse and cattle dealers, that's what we were. They left on Sunday morning and walked far, even beyond the German border. Nobody would stop a horse dealer because we catered to the nobility. Bought a sick horse and kept it in the meadow until it fetched a price. "Times were better then," Uncle Hugo said, "because a handshake was a man's word. No honesty among people today."

'He crumbled another piece of cake and I knew he would speak about his name. He always spoke about his name and I remembered every word of the story and every twist of his voice and yet we sat and listened, because he was so old that he had forgotten that he told us the same story a dozen times already. It was the most important thing he knew and he spoke the words as if he were laying bricks.

'"It was my grandfather," he said, "may he rest in peace, who was given the name. There was a war and the price of bread went up and up until people ate the bark of trees. 'I'll go and find out about the enemy,' my grandfather said to the general. 'How many men and how many horses and where they will attack. I will take a cow with me to cross the border.'"

'The old man drank some coffee and looked at the children.

'"It was a dangerous thing to spy on the Prussians. If they found out that my grandfather was spying they would hang him from a tree. But who would suspect a Jew with a cow on a string?" The old man laughed and ran his fingers through his beard. "The Empress sent two regiments to the border and the Prussians never came to Bohemia. Saved the Empire, he did, and Maria Theresa paid him three gold *talers* and gave him a new name. 'Ehren,' she said. 'From now on you will be called Ehren, which means honour, because you saved us from the Prussians.'"

'We never stayed there for a meal, because we wouldn't let old Sofie cook for so many people. But when we parted she touched my cheek and fingered the cloth of my coat and her voice was full of envy.

'"Such cloth," she said, "and such fat children." There was a hint of regret in her voice. "It is easy to marry if you are rich," she said.

'She had never travelled on a train or visited us in town because she was afraid of trains. It must have been difficult for the old people to go on a transport.'

They sat and were silent, and Alex Ehren thought about his own fears.

'I mustn't be afraid,' he said, 'because I am an Ehren,' and he and Lisa Pomnenka laughed at the notion that a name might save anybody from fear.

There were things that helped and there were others that grew on people like moss on a stone. Alex Ehren saw the skeletal prisoners wrapped in a blanket, bent and dragging their clogs in the mud. He knew some of them and he was surprised how old they had grown. Once he watched his teacher, a professor and scientist, wade through the muddy silt. At first he couldn't recognise him because the man, who had always been neat and well groomed, was now just another bedraggled prisoner. One of his clogs got stuck in the mire and he stood with his naked foot lifted like a bird. He groped for the clog and fell on his face in the dirt.

It was as if the three months in the Family Camp had added thirty years to the prisoners' age, twisting their backs and folding their faces into wrinkles. It was the hunger, the dirt and the exposure to death that rode through their time like the horses of the Apocalypse.

'I won't succumb,' Alex Ehren repeated stubbornly, 'and I will not go under.'

He was fortunate, he thought, that Himmelblau had taken him on the Block, that Pavel Hoch shared his parcels with him, and, above all, that he was in love with the girl. For love, more than anything else, was a remedy against corruption and decay.

And yet he was often desperate.

Six hundred years, he thought bitterly, six hundred years in the same village and a name of honour granted by an empress. What use are the name and the years, if I am a Jew and a stranger in my own country?

After work the instructors talked. They knew the time of their death but they argued as if there was a future and freedom of choice. And then there were the children, who were a duty and an obligation, who provided the meaning for their existence.

Most of them were like Alex Ehren, who, until the outbreak of the war, believed that he belonged. The fields, the rivers, the forests and the hills were his country because he read the same books, and laughed at the same jokes, as his Czech friends. The only difference, he thought, was their religion. Some of his classmates were Catholics, some Protestants and others Jews. They dated the same girls and some, like Pavel Hoch, who would marry his sweetheart Aninka, would have non-Jewish children. Yet with the German invasion and the New Order in Europe, they were set apart, robbed of their possessions and, at the end, taken to the camps.

Their neighbours were solicitous and bought them food, which the Jews were not allowed to purchase. But when the day of their departure arrived, the neighbours watched them leave from behind their curtains and hurried to take over their abandoned homes.

'It was like losing the ground under my feet,' said Alex Ehren. 'At first my schoolmates came to see me every day. They even brought me homework. "It can't last," they said. "In a couple of months you'll be back. What a stupid law that Jews can't attend school."

'I had to wear a yellow star and they wouldn't walk with me in the street and came less and less often, and when we had to move in with another Jewish family, they stopped visiting altogether. It was as if I were dead.'

'Being a Jew isn't a choice,' said Beran. 'There are things that cannot be changed. I am who I am, tall or short, a gentile or a Jew. And as I cannot change my identity, I have to live with it.'

'How do you live with it?' asked Fabian, gesturing with his hand to the stalls of the Block.

'We are not the first. There were the persecutions of the Middle Ages, the Crusades, the Inquisition and the pogroms of Kishinev. Yet some of us always survived to tell the story.'

'What story? About being the scapegoat for other peoples' misfortunes? When there was a plague, they claimed that we had poisoned the wells, and when there was no harvest they accused a Jew of murdering an infant. Aren't we always the cause of wars, famine and disaster, murder and arson?'

'It's because we carry a message,' said Beran.

'What message?'

'The Ten Commandments,' said Himmelblau, who had joined the group.

'And Christianity,' added Marta Felix, who had studied philosophy and history at university. 'The idea of justice.' She had been married to a German, a humanist and writer, who had divorced her rather than lose his tenure. 'Sometimes we were only the soil on which new ideas grew. We provided the beginning and the impulse. But whenever there was progress and improvement we were there.'

She stopped and shook her head.

'How strange that most of our ideas have turned against us. It was we who proclaimed that thou shalt not murder and we were the most murdered people on earth. The Jew Jesus Christ preached love among people but the history of the Church is one long record of torture, murder and burning of the Jews. The Jew Sigmund Freud opened the locked rooms of the human mind and another Jew Albert Einstein found the equation of the infinite, but their books are burnt in a Teutonic auto-da-fé. We are hated because we are the Rothschilds and the Marxes, though I don't think we are either. We are just like any other people, good and bad, clever and stupid, rich and poor, but as Jews we are punished for whatever we are.'

'We are not like other people,' said Shashek, who usually kept his mouth shut. 'We have no country, no government and no army.'

'After the war I'll go to Palestine,' said Beran slowly and there was something childish in his words, because from where he stood the Jewish country was far away and unattainable. Many of the teachers were Zionists while others, like Felsen, believed in a communist revolution, and Hynek Rind dreamt of living in a small Czech town. Yet all of them without exception had a vision that kept them above the waters of despair. They couldn't work with the children without a star, a flag or a dream to look up to. They were not more moral or better educated than other prisoners in the Family Camp; they were hungry and tattered and cold, but the community of the Children's Block made them transcend their misery and deal with matters beyond bare survival.

At the end of March Felsen gave Alex Ehren his assignment. They crossed the camp road to the Hospital Barracks. The storeroom was piled with beds, empty bottles and mattresses. Felsen bent under a bed and extricated an anchor of tangled pipes, which looked like a skein of snakes.

'You will throw the thing into the electric wires and cause a short circuit.'

'Yes,' said Alex Ehren, 'I've seen the wires; they run across the camp.' He touched the iron, which was cold and unwieldy. 'It's too heavy.'

'You'll cast it on a rope,' said Felsen, and he drew his head between his shoulders. He was suddenly uncertain of his choice.

'A rope?'

'The girl will make for you a macramé cord. Tell her you need it for the tug o' war.'

Everybody knew that Alex Ehren's group was good at the game because they often won against older and heavier rivals. The three boys, Adam, Neugeboren and Bubenik, were like cockerels; they dug their clogs into the muddy ground and pulled until their faces were puffed up and red from the strain. They gave a sudden tug, which made the other group slip and let go of the rope. Adam was a nuisance and often made Alex Ehren's life miserable, but when they won he loved even him. He thought about the children who would be caught in the uprising, the blackout, the fire, the chaos and the shooting. There is no choice, he said to himself and wondered if any of them – one or two or several – had a chance to cross the river and reach the Slovakian border.

'Yes,' he said, 'I'll throw the anchor. How will I know?'

'Somebody will tell you. There is enough time.'

Afterwards Alex Ehren was of two minds. He was glad that he was a part of the mutiny but at the same time he was scared of the terrors it would unleash. He was in love with the girl and their togetherness was a shelter against misery.

'There's no hurry with the rope,' he said to Lisa Pomnenka. 'We'll need it when the ground behind the Block dries out.'

# 4.

THERE WERE SEVEN BOOKS ON THE CHILDREN'S BLOCK. During the night they were locked in Himmelblau's cubicle, together with the can of medicine and the crushed cakes of the orphaned parcels. However, during the day they were shepherded by Dasha, one of the youth assistants. She was a thin girl with woollen stockings, and she kept the books in a row, arranging and shuffling their places according to a mysterious scheme.

There was H G Wells's *A Short History of the World* and *Elementary Geometry for High Schools*, a tattered French novel and a Russian dictionary, which Felsen studied in preparation for the arrival of the Soviet army. Dasha also had an outdated atlas showing empires that had long ago ceased to exist, and three-quarters of a nineteenth-century Czech village novel.

Himmelblau kept the twenty adolescents aged fourteen to sixteen on the Block to save them from slave labour in the open. There was Bass, the oven boy who fought about every piece of brown coal; there was Thomasina, the Dutch girl who assisted the kindergarten teacher; and Foltyn, the door boy, who wore a great coat that Himmelblau had got for him in the Clothes Storeroom. There was also a flock of girl sweepers, who cleaned the floor with brooms made by Shashek from old sacks. The earthen floor crumbled and the sweepers sprinkled it with water until it became soft and muddy. They swept the floor so many times that it sank and formed a step at the gate.

It wasn't easy to keep the children together because they played hooky and ran to the kitchen or the potato room where they scavenged for food. They were wild and even cruel, and Himmelblau would often call the culprit into his cubicle and threaten him in his poor Czech.

'I will you a box on the ear give, you horrible pest.' He waved his hand in the air, but he only beat Foltyn the door boy once.

In the mornings the Block was full of clandestine activity because Marta Felix and Felsen and even Beran taught forbidden geography, history and politics. They felt secure because Foltyn the guard would warn them at the approach of any SS sentry, so they would switch to a game or a story. That day, however, the boy left the gate unguarded. He was listening to Marta Felix's lesson and didn't notice that the Priest, the SS Blockfuehrer with the low voice and hands in his sleeves, had entered the Block.

He stopped here and there, inconspicuous as a grass snake, and listened to the children. He didn't understand the language and it took him some time to discover what they were doing. It was fortunate that Fabian noticed the soldier and called out: 'Attention, attention.' The children hid their charred splinters and scribbled-on papers and stood up before the SS man could see the reading and writing and the map of Europe that Felsen had drawn for his pupils.

The door boy was tall for his age, almost a man, and he begged for a different punishment.

'I'll take anything,' Foltyn said. 'Send me to a commando – I'm not afraid of work – but don't flog me in public.'

'You have done a terrible thing,' said Himmelblau,' and you'll take the consequences. I'll think about your punishment and tell you tomorrow.'

He waited a day to let his anger abate, but in the end decided that the culprit had to be punished. He locked the door of his cubicle and beat the boy with a piece of plywood until the youth was bruised and Himmelblau's hand tired.

'Sometimes,' he justified himself to Miriam the matron, 'there is no choice.'

He thought about the clandestine newspaper which Felsen the communist hung on the back wall, the books, the scraps of writing paper and the rehearsals for the approaching holiday. He thought about the many dangers and he was scared. The children were like quicksilver and always planning some mischief. He knew that the teachers spoke about an escape and a mutiny, but if anybody was caught, it would be he who would be held responsible and punished.

'The Germans,' he said, 'might dismantle the Block and send the children to work. The service boys will see Foltyn's face and be careful. The beating he will forget, but if I send him on the road he will die.'

He worried about the children but he was also scared for himself, because he knew he wouldn't live long on the road gang or in the ditch commando. At night he couldn't sleep and smoked a cigarette, because he was ashamed of his faintheartedness and he felt contrite for beating the boy.

*

As there were no stories, no adventure books and no fairy tales in Dasha's tattered pile, the instructors invented what Marta Felix called a walking library. The teachers recalled novels they had read before they were taken to the camps. They prepared a list of books, which they would tell the children in daily instalments. Magdalena was good at Nils Holgersson and his flight with the geese; Shashek told tales about Indians and adventure; and Dezo Kovac, who had attended a religious school, taught stories from the Bible.

Before the camps Alex Ehren had been a fervent reader. He was the kind of reader to forget the world and lose himself in a book, a trait which enabled him to recall the memories. However, the children preferred Fabian, whose voice rose and fell and turned into a whisper in accordance with the plot. There was a waiting list for his stories and while the children begged Fabian not to stop but go on, they chose Alex Ehren only when no other walking book was available. There were no partitions between the stalls and the children heard the voices on their left and on their right. Sometimes they even forgot to listen to Alex Ehren, because they were so intent on Fabian's voice from the adjoining group.

'What's wrong with learning two lessons at once?' Himmelblau winked. 'The more they hear the more clever they will be.'

Alex Ehren didn't know whether it was a joke or a comment on his inability to hold the children's attention, but he felt inferior and envied Fabian's popularity.

Himmelblau took Dezo Kovac onto the Block after the musician wasn't accepted into the camp orchestra. The new

Children's Senior loved music and before the war he and Heda, his wife, spent their evenings listening to records of Mozart and Beethoven and even modern composers like Bartók and Schoenberg. Once a month they would dress in their best clothes and travel to Prague to attend a concert. The whole next week they discussed the programme, the soloist and the conductor's interpretation of Brahms.

Himmelblau had dreamt of becoming a musician but he was unable to hold a melody and when he sang he was hopelessly out of tune. He went to the best teachers, learned to read notes and, to the dismay of his neighbours, spent much of his free time practising. He tried the piano and the flute, the trumpet and even the percussion instruments. He repeated the same piece a hundred times, but somehow the music never came out right – the tune, the rhythm, or the syncopation – and after a while he gave up entirely.

'Not every music lover can be a music maker,' one of his teachers had said and Himmelblau repeated these words to justify his inability to sing in tune.

'You can work on the Block,' he told the violinist.

He remembered how sad he'd been when he had to hand over his records and the gramophone. Under German rule, Jews were not supposed to listen to music. He was lucky, he thought, that his gentile friends had formed a string quartet to which he and his wife were invited.

He listened to Dezo Kovac and his heart went out to the violinist.

'Never mind the audition,' he said to Dezo. 'What we need is a music teacher.'

The camp orchestra that wouldn't take Dezo Kovac rehearsed on the Women's Block. The musicians sat on a wooden platform and played the same music over and over until the women complained and asked to be moved elsewhere. At the beginning all the musicians were prisoners from the September transport, but when they were put to death in the gas chambers, Jagger the Capo locked the three trumpets, the cello, the saxophones, the drum and the violins in his room. A week later the hunchback found a composer of international fame among the December transport people and appointed him bandleader.

'Start a new orchestra,' he said, 'and I'll get the players a second helping of soup.'

The musicians stood in the cold and waited for their audition. They were desperate to join the orchestra where they would not only be sheltered from the rain but would also get an extra portion of soup. There was a rumour that at the Camp Senior's parties the conductor and the Capo drank wine and danced with naked women. They needed music and paid the fiddlers with bread and sausage, which they stole from the prisoners' rations. Some of the inmates in the queue were dabblers who had played the violin for a year or two during their school days, but others were genuine artists. All of them, however – the dilettantes and those with the soul of a musician – jostled in the mud of the camp road. Never before had there been a more serious competition, because the prize wasn't mere fame or money but half a bowl of beetroot soup. In the past the pianists, the concert violinists and the cello players would have laughed at such a competition. But nobody laughed now, because in the camp trifles grew out of proportion and turned into absolutes. They were more intent on winning a place in the orchestra than ever before, because a second helping and a workplace under a roof were a watershed between life and death. The auditions lasted two days and at the end the orderly sent the rest of them away.

'No more,' he shouted. 'No more musicians for the orchestra; all the places are taken.'

There were still many, perhaps fifty more applicants, to whom the conductor hadn't listened.

He couldn't take all, thought Dezo Kovac, because there were only fifteen instruments.

'An audition wouldn't have made much difference,' said Fabian. 'He wasn't looking for a virtuoso. He chose the musicians from among his friends and relatives.'

The orchestra played only three tunes because these were all the Camp Senior knew and he refused to change the repertoire.

And thus it was 'Marinarella', and 'Roll Out the Barrel' and 'The Blue Danube' again and again until everybody in the camp knew the melodies by heart.

Alex Ehren stopped with his children in front of the Women's Block to listen, and Bubenik, who had a gift for rhythm, drummed the beat on his soup bowl. Sometimes Eva climbed on a crate and moved her hands in imitation of the conductor, and then they marched in time with the music back and forth in front of the women's barracks. The children were full of energy and, though they got up very early, they never seemed tired. There was no place to play or be alone without supervision. Sometimes Alex Ehren ran out of ideas for how to keep them occupied, and with no new and exciting activities they got bored and ran out on the road.

The camp orchestra performed twice a day. They stood next to the camp gate and when the inmates marched to work they fiddled away at their pieces. When the prisoners returned, carrying their dead among them, they played the same tunes again. The mating of death and music was obscene, and Alex Ehren wondered at the mind that had spawned such an idea.

Lisa Pomnenka painted the wall and as the children followed the colours grow and merge into a shape, they felt as if they really saw a meadow and a copse of birches. The painter added flowerpots with red geraniums that spilled over, alive and blooming, towards the ground. The two girls Eva and Hanka asked her to paint Snow White and Dopey, one of the dwarfs, but the figures were out of proportion because she had never painted on a perpendicular surface before.

There were no birds to see in the camp, not even common sparrows that can live on nothing and are usually everywhere. Neither were there stars because in their first weeks the prisoners were not allowed outside the barracks after dark.

Later when Alex Ehren marched the children to the washroom, they lifted their heads and did see the morning star among the clouds. Yet there were certainly no birds. At first he thought that they had moved elsewhere where they could find food, but then he noticed that they died on the electrically charged fences. He had seen a bird once, a blackbird or a starling, which flew in over the roofs and touched two wires.

There was a spark, blue and fleeting like a whisper, and the bird fluttered and fell to the ground.

I'll paint the things that we miss, Lisa Pomnenka thought, and on the birches she drew pigeons and larks and even a stork in flight. The children stood in front of the wall and counted the birds one by one, in the sky and on the pines, on the birches and in the hazelnut bush. The coloured wall spread and grew and transformed the Block into a place bright with make-believe trees and flowers and birds.

She spent her free time with Alex Ehren. They stole a quarter of an hour in the morning before the groups gathered in their stalls and they sat together at noon when the children were eating their soup. Yet above all they looked forward to the late afternoons, the free hour before the evening roll call, when the Block was dark and half empty. They were never alone because even when the children left to meet with their parents, the instructors argued about politics and the world after the war.

The lovers were happy when they sat next to each other in their open stall, ate their bread and drank the bitter brew they called tea. Sometimes they talked little because there was no need to say insignificant things or be romantic. But when they held hands or when he brushed his face against her cheek they almost forgot where they were.

One day the German doctor summoned the girl. 'You said you could paint a portrait.'

'You see I can.' She pointed with her chin at Snow White and the lopsided dwarf.

'You'd better,' he said. 'Tomorrow I need you in the Gypsy Camp.'

Next morning a sentry took her away to paint a Gypsy girl with strange spots on her skin.

'She is very beautiful,' Lisa Pomnenka told Alex Ehren later that day. 'Smooth and wild like a cat. She was totally nude but she wasn't ashamed in front of the doctor or the pockmarked SS sentry who brought me in.'

She worked on the Gypsy painting for three days and each evening returned with a loaf of bread and some sausage. It was good to sit close to each other with a full stomach, and they felt richer and happier and more content than they'd felt for a long time. Yet even in their closeness she wouldn't speak anything else about the secrets of the Gypsy Camp and kept her knowledge to herself.

Twice a week, on Mondays and Wednesdays, the children produced a show. They prepared a play, a charade, a dance or a song, and, at the end of the performance, Miriam, the head matron, distributed cake crumbs from the abandoned parcels. Wednesdays were more important than Mondays, because there was also a competition and Himmelblau handed out prizes to the winners.

The competition was a game but then everything on the Block was disguised as a game, even the things that mattered and were of great importance. It was difficult to fight filth and vermin. The sweepers sprinkled the floor three times a day but as soon as the water dried the dust rose into the air and settled on the children's clothes and skin. There were too many of them, scores of little boys and girls crowded into one wooden stable, and their faces were constantly covered by smears of dirt. The matrons washed their clothes under the taps but the water was dark with sediment and the wind so loaded with soot that the rags were not any cleaner after they had been washed. There was nowhere to hang the tattered shirts and the children held their clothes against the wind or spread them on the tepid chimney where they gathered more dust.

Yet even worse were the sleeping quarters, which the children shared with the grown-ups. The dampness and overcrowding bred lice and outlandish boils that spread from one child to another. The wounds festered under their scabs and when they healed they left behind blue scars. There was also the smell, the stench of rot and stale soup and excrement, the odour of too many unwashed bodies, and the decay of the dead at the back of the barracks. It was a smell that pervaded the whole camp, from the entrance gate to the Hospital Block at the far end of the road. The Children's Block was better because the instructors played the game of cleanliness and the children scrubbed their stalls to win the weekly prize. They washed each morning and as they spent most of the time under the roof, their clothes were less filthy than those of the people who worked outside.

Even Mietek the Pole, who from time to time stole books for the children, sniffed and shook his head. He was a perseverant suitor and though Magdalena laughed off his small gifts, she looked forward to his visits. He came and went freely because there was always a leaking roof to be mended and thus he was a link between the Block and other camps.

'How strange.' He looked at the wall with its meadows, trees and geranium flowers. 'They even smell like a garden.'

'Wrong,' said Fabian. 'It's the turpentine Lisa Pomnenka mixes with her paints.'

The children competed not only in cleanliness and mathematics and geography, but there was also a prize for the best drawing, for a short story or for a poem. Himmelblau perambulated among the groups and checked on the children's reading, their writing and their handicraft. He took down his findings into an old notebook, and towards Wednesday summed up the results. Alex Ehren's children were angry with Adam, who made them lose points because he played hooky and disturbed the lessons. However, he was an asset in soccer, which they played with a rag ball. He was ambitious and whenever Alex Ehren's Maccabees lost, he quit the field and sulked. He spent much of his time with Jagger, the hunchbacked Capo, whose runner he had become. Yet he needed children's company and occasionally came back – small, fierce and dressed in good clothes and real shoes. He sat among the children but he was restless and created a commotion during the reading sessions. He wouldn't read but jeered at other children's mistakes, pulling Majda's hair until there were tears in her eyes and picking a fight with Bubenik. He was worse than ever, tense and nervous, his eyes burning with anger. When Alex Ehren tried to separate the fighting boys Adam jumped back, and hunched like an animal, drew his sharpened spoon.

'Just keep away, you bastard. You come closer and I'll cut off your prick.'

There was a circle of fear around the child and even boys from older groups treated him with respect, not only because he was Jagger's runner, but also because of his sudden flare-ups and his scimitar-like spoon handle. The boy was at the same time a menace and a mockery, a small child dressed like an adult and wielding power through his master. He spoke in a high childish voice, but the words he used were those of a seasoned crook. Alex Ehren tried to see him as he was, a little boy with a sweet face and clear eyes, even though his mind was infected and his mouth corrupted by filthy words. Most of the time the boy was his enemy, a torturer who wouldn't let him teach and made him angry. He was like everything in the camp, Alex Ehren thought; good and evil, black and white, and nothing in between.

He sat with the boy after school and held out a card he used for reading drill.

'Read,' he said. 'We won't lose every week because of one lazy brat. Today you will learn to read.'

'Who needs reading?' Adam struggled to get his arm free. 'Reading won't get me a potato peel. I spit on your school. I get more bread for my errands than all of you together.'

'Read,' said Alex Ehren again and held the card close to his face. He was angry now and he tightened his grip on the child's arm.

'I won't.'

'Today you will.'

The little boy shook his head. 'I can't read,' he said in a huff. 'You never taught me.'

It was a lie and an unfair accusation and he held the boy's arm so tight that he winced. He had tried harder with Adam than with any other child, but even when the brat did attend a lesson his mind was on the wild things he saw at the Capo's cubicle.

He taught him the letters and the syllables and then some short words. It was like eating sand and pebbles but Alex Ehren was perseverant and unwilling to be defeated by a small boy, however fierce and corrupted he might be.

One day something happened that broke the ice between them and afterwards they were friends at least for some time. He discovered, quite accidentally, that the boy had an extraordinary gift for poetry. His words flowed like a natural stream, a brook that cascaded from a mountain, or rather like a subterranean river that suddenly burst above ground. He didn't have many words but what he said was bold and fresh and painted in sharp colours, sometimes terribly profane but still touched with a sensitivity of soul.

Adam Landau wasn't an innocent child; he had lived in captivity for three years and was infected with the rot that grew on people in the ghettos and concentration camps. For much of his time he was in the company of the Capo, who had been an executioner in the ghetto, who lured women into his cubicle with soup and a piece of bread and who was depraved and evil. The boy was a small, foul-mouthed brat, inconsiderate of others and cruel when it served his survival. But at the same time he was still a child and the few mornings he spent on the Children's Block were, like Lisa Pomnenka's wall, a window into a world of decency. He was, Alex Ehren thought, like an evil imp with the wings of an angel, a rotten apple with a sweet core.

The Maccabees never won a citation for orderliness because even if the girls – Majda and Ina, and the twins Eva and Hanka – shushed the boys to be silent and work at their assignments, there was always one with unwashed ears, or a messy bunk, or another one reported for foul language at which Himmelblau clicked his tongue and took off a point.

Yet far more important than points for cleanliness was the competition for creativity. The best drawings and the best poems and stories were hung on the wall, where they remained until the next Wednesday, when they were replaced by the new winners. The children drew, wrote little stories and prepared plays to be performed on the platform, which Shashek, the jack-of-all-trades and master of none, had hammered together over the middle section of the chimney stack. It wasn't the prize, a handful of crumbled cake, that mattered, but the respect a child harvested when his drawing was pinned on the honour wall. They didn't know it because it was never spelled out, but their stories and drawings and their puppet theatre were a revolt and a mutiny against the German attempt to rob them of their humanity and reduce them to an animal existence.

And as long as they wrote stories and painted and danced, even if their art was often trivial or mediocre, they were still victorious because their artefacts were a shield against exposure to death.

Adam had to memorise his words, because, unlike other competitors, he couldn't read from a piece of paper. At the beginning he stumbled and stuttered but towards Wednesday he recited the whole poem smoothly and almost without a mistake.

It was difficult to work with the boy, who lacked discipline and who, like a wild animal or a squirrel, was distracted by every sound and movement on the Block. Alex Ehren felt proud when the boy finally climbed on the platform and recited the poem in his high-pitched childish voice. He got stuck once or twice, and Alex Ehren had to help him with the next line, but even so the Block grew silent with the magic the poem had woven between the child and his audience. He was the smallest child who ever won the weekly poetry prize and he stepped down from the stage and walked through the Block with the bearing of a cockerel and a hero. In the following weeks he wrote more poems with Alex Ehren but he never won first prize again.

Himmelblau kept the winning poem together with other children's stories and drawings in a cardboard box on his shelf. The poem was called 'Green':

*A green world*
*With a green door*
*And a bird with green feathers*
*On a train*
*We ate darkness.*

*The smoke was my brother*
*Who ran backwards with the trees*
*A man in a shirt like blood*
*Cut a field*
*In half.*

*Today I am big*
*And have a knife*
*To cut my fear*
*In half*
*But also people.*

Of course it was a childish poem, which had no rhyme and whose rhythm was haphazard and loose, but it was genuine and it won the first prize in spite of its cruelty and shortness. When Alex Ehren wrote down the words, his heart went out to the little boy, who remembered the green world of his distant past. He was a pest and didn't let Alex Ehren teach arithmetic and bits of natural history, but still Alex Ehren understood why Himmelblau never raised his hand against a child, save against Foltyn, the youth assistant who hadn't warned the teachers of the approaching Block Senior. For he couldn't forget, not even for a moment, that the boy would never grow up, never fall in love, never sleep with a woman or look back at an accomplished life.

They would all die – the fair-haired Majda, Bubenik who drummed time on his bowl, the dark-skinned Hanka with her rag doll and the boys who fought among themselves and cheated at marbles – they all would die and not survive the end of June. It wasn't a good poem, but in the context of their short lives it sparkled and shone like a firefly in darkness, because in some strange and inexplicable way, it carried an intimation of immortality.

Some doubted that Adam had authored the poem himself and chided Alex Ehren for his assistance.

'Sticking your feathers into Adam's cap,' said Fabian when he read the poem on the wall. 'The brat cannot read and you exhibit him as a poet. Lucky for you that Himmelblau swallowed the hoax, hook, line and sinker.'

Alex Ehren felt hurt but in the evening admitted that he had helped the boy with the spelling of difficult words like 'feathers' and 'knife' and had corrected the sentence structure.

'You've always been a fool,' said Fabian. 'First you cheat and then you admit your sin. If you stick to a lie long enough it becomes the truth.'

He didn't believe in what he had said, since, in spite of their starvation, none of the instructors would steal bread from a child or fellow inmate.

April began with a string of warm days and Magdalena took the kindergarten children behind the Block. They stood in the sun and followed the light with their upturned faces like a field of flowers. The children arrived at the Block early because their mothers worked additional hours at the *Weberei und Flechterei*, the weaving sweatshop, where they produced ammunition belts for the German army.

On the first of April the children celebrated All Fools' Day, and there was much giggling and whispering among the pupils. They came out joking about increased bread portions, an exchange of the Czech prisoners for trucks and gold, or a sudden landing of the Americans in France, all of which, needless to say, was based on nothing but their imagination and wishful thinking.

The instructors went along with the jokes and pretended that they believed. Later in the day the grown-ups swapped roles with the children, who then conducted the lessons, organised games and even handed out the evening bread ration. One of the older children, a thin boy called Aryeh, impersonated Himmelblau and threatened everybody that he 'will two boxes on thine ear you give', which caused much mirth and laughter.

Yet the warm spell also liberated the germs that had lain frozen during the winter months and there was an outbreak of infectious diseases and festering wounds. Two of Beran's children contracted typhoid fever and lay in the infection ward of the Hospital Block opposite the Children's Block. Their friends crossed the road and tapped on the wooden wall but the male nurse chased them away,

'Sha,' he said and waved his hands in the air. 'Go away, you little fools. There is nothing the German doctor dislikes more than typhoid fever. He stopped visiting the hospital and wouldn't even see his precious twins. If there's an epidemic we'll all go up the chimney. Sha, go back to your Block and don't come here again.'

The awareness of the impending mutiny pervaded all their activity. Alex Ehren worked with the children, argued with his friends about politics and Palestine and in the afternoons ate his bread with Lisa Pomnenka. And yet the uprising was with him all the time, in his waking hours and in his sleep, when he visited an old relative and when he was alone or with Lisa, because the thought of the fire, the fighting and the possible escape were stronger than his love for the girl.

He was more fit now than he had been a month ago, but worried about his task. He joined the children's sport lesson behind the Block to strengthen his muscles. Sometimes he looked at the wires that ran high around the camp and wondered whether he would be strong enough to cast the heavy anchor and cause a short circuit. He found a blue-veined rock on the road and exercised with it, lifting it to his chest and lowering it to his knees. The strain left him pale and exhausted but he persevered, afraid that because of his weakness he would fail his comrades. In his mind he saw the welded hooks and pipes, but the more he thought about them the heavier the contraption grew. He would have liked to see the iron thing again, to touch it and become familiar with its weight and shape, but Felsen wouldn't let him visit the ward. Alex Ehren didn't speak about his task, not even with Beran or Hoch with whom he shared the bunk, but the children noticed his rock lifting and the girls whispered behind his back and giggled.

'I know what you are doing,' said Majda, touching the end of her ash-blonde braid. 'We all know.'

'Yes?' he asked, fearing that the children had found out about the uprising.

'You think Lisa Pomnenka will love you more if you are strong.'

There were no secrets on the Block, though certain things remained unsaid. He was relieved that they seemed unaware of the anchor and his assignment.

# 5.

THEY WOULD NEVER HAVE CELEBRATED PASSOVER WITHOUT Dezo Kovac. The music teacher was small and dark-skinned and his eyes were narrow and sparkling. He had been born in Slovakia, and his speech had a lilting Hungarian accent, which, together with his religion, made him different from the others. Sometimes Alex Ehren saw him pray opposite the wall, the rocking backwards and forwards, with his eyes closed and his lips forming Hebrew words.

'No Passover for me,' said Hynek Rind. 'Isn't it bad enough to be a Jew? Why rub it in?' He pointed his finger towards the roof. 'God?' he asked. 'If there was anybody up there I wouldn't be in here.' He looked around and laughed bitterly. 'Or if he is up there he sure doesn't give a damn.'

The Seder feast was a dangerous enterprise but all camp life was dangerous, thought Alex Ehren, because people died so easily. Each day there were trains with new arrivals, men and women and little children, who were beaten into rows of five and marched away. Alex Ehren watched them through the barbed-wire fence and sometimes caught wisps of their voices carried by the wind. They spoke many languages: Polish, Russian, Hungarian or even French. In his first camp days he wondered where the Germans would lodge them in the overcrowded barracks.

The transports were like rivers flowing into the sea, multitudes of human beings. Sometimes there was a train or two each day, boxcars that arrived full of people and left empty or loaded with loot. How did the Germans dispose of the excess deportees, the old, the sick who were not strong enough for labour, and the children? There were too many prisoners, endless crowds that seemed to well up from the depth of the earth, and as there were so many, he thought with horror, their life had no value. It was as if for each Jew that died there were ten others to take his place and so there was no end to the killing. And again, as always when Alex Ehren remembered his death, he gritted his teeth, and resolved that he wouldn't die meekly.

They argued about the Passover feast for several evenings because some of the instructors shied away from the unnecessary effort, others thought about the danger and still others, like Hynek Rind, denied their Jewishness. Yet the longer they spoke the more real the idea became and with all the argument and contestation the project grew flesh and bones until all of them, some grudgingly and others with resignation, accepted the idea of the Seder night.

Dezo Kovac taught the children Passover songs, and even Fabian, who usually mocked matters holy and profane, climbed on the chimney, and when the children demanded '*Alouette*', he shook his finger and made them sing one of the new tunes. The music teacher selected twelve children with the clearest voices and prepared with them Beethoven's 'Ode to Joy'. Sometimes Himmelblau attended a rehearsal but wouldn't join in, knowing how hopelessly out of tune he sang.

It was a feverish week, and though they went about their daily tasks – washing in the morning, the games behind the Block, their reading and Marta Felix's philosophy lessons – there was expectation in the air as if the Seder night were the most important event in their lives.

Some of the instructors bickered and others, like Felsen and his communist cabal, asked questions.

'Why barter bread for a bone and a horseradish? Why not call it a freedom day and leave out the religious nonsense? What matters is to avoid the Germans' attention.'

He met with men from other camps and they sat in the corner behind Shashek's workshop and spoke of the uprising, of arms and ways to escape. The Children's Block was the hub of the mutiny and Felsen was reluctant to arouse suspicion.

'The Seder night is a symbol,' said Beran slowly. 'The Germans have taken away our homes, our jobs and our families. We are for them like vermin, less than human beings. The only thing we have are symbols. The children will forget their bread rations in a day but they will remember the Pesach celebration as long as they live.'

'Until death do us part,' added Fabian. 'How long will they live?'

'Of course the Seder night matters,' Beran went on, disregarding Fabian's black remark, 'because it is—' he groped for a word '—it is a token.'

'What token?'

'That miracles do happen. From slavery to freedom,' and he circled his hand over the bondage of the wooden barracks with its leaking roof, the sooty chimney, the smell of decay, and the bunch of orphaned children who stayed on the Block because they had nobody to meet in their free hour.

'Nonsense,' Rind exclaimed testily. 'A token of a fairy tale. Who believes in miracles? There are no miracles in hell.' He laughed. 'Even on Doomsday the Old Man won't put us back together. Part of me blown away by the wind, another part in a cake of soap and the rest washed down the Vistula into the Baltic Sea. He won't know which part to send to heaven and which to hell. Who needs a myth?'

'We all do,' said Beran, 'because without a myth I am nothing. It's easier to die with a myth. Whatever it might be. Something greater than myself.' He stopped, embarrassed by his own words. 'One has to belong,' he said. 'It's not much to be a Jew, but it's all I have.' He grinned and touched his face with his sleeve. 'I am a part of the Jews who lived in slavery but I am also a part of those who left Egypt and became free.'

'I refuse,' said Hynek Rind, and his voice was loud and angry. 'There is no link between me and the Jews of your Bible. Three thousand years among the nations. A hundred generations of fornication and rape between their blood and mine. A dog is more wolf than I am a Jew. What about the Jews who lived among the Babylonians and the Persians? What about the Greeks, the Romans, the Crusaders, the Turks and the Arabs with whom we mingled? There were Petljura and Chmielnicki and the Khazars on their shaggy horses, and people and tribes whose names I don't remember. We slept with all of them, either by force or of our free will, and if you want proof, look around the Block. The Hungarian Jew has the slanted eyes and cheekbones of a Mongol, the Russian Jew the broad face of a Slav and the Sephardi looks like an Arab. Like his host nation,' said Hynek Rind, 'only more so.'

'It's not the blood,' said Himmelblau, who, at the sound of the argument, had come closer, 'it's the awareness.'

'Which leaves me out,' said Hynek Rind, 'for I have no awareness. The Germans branded me a Jew but who says I have to comply with it? I've given up Abraham and Isaac and Jacob. My forefathers climbed a different mountain and my promised land lies between the Elbe and the Moldau.'

For a while nobody spoke and Hynek Rind stood in their midst with his mouth defiant and his forehead low and aggressive.

It is strange, mused Alex Ehren, that with our death barely three months away, we argue about blood and myth and religion. We quarrel about politics and moral codes and how to celebrate the Seder as if our lives depended on our decisions.

Neither could Himmelblau have managed without the help of Julius Abeles. The Wednesday competition and Lisa Pomnenka's painted wall were of importance, but Julius Abeles supplied the goods they needed for survival. On first sight he was like everybody else, fortyish and insignificant. Once the Kitchen Capo had caught him smuggling potatoes and broke his teeth, which made him speak with a lisp. On his arrival he carried stones and as he laboured side by side with Alex Ehren, he told him about his shop in a narrow street of old Prague.

'Sold the business.' He snapped his fingers and grinned. 'Left it to an assistant for a trifle. Others waited for the

Germans to grab it for nothing. He'll keep the shop until I return. Reliable fellow. Leather is a safe investment because everybody wears shoes these days.' He looked at his muddy clogs and shook his head. 'Well, almost everybody. The rich do, the poor don't. The same thing there and here. It's the money that counts. The stupid starve but the smart survive.'

He secured a job on the *Rollwagen* Commando where he pulled a cart, harnessed to it like a horse. They transported the dead to the incinerator, garbage to the dump and rags to be deloused, and they returned with coal or beetroot and potatoes for the soup. The commando people stole provisions, bartered them for other goods, which they sold at a profit. They were the only inmates that left the compound and could trade with the Kanada prisoners, who sorted the looted luggage.

At the beginning Julius acquired a needle and a spool of thread, which he leased for a slice of bread. He was shrewd and perseverant like a peasant, and was ready to go hungry for days in order to buy more goods. At night he slid down from his bunk and cut off buttons from the dead, which he sold for a spoonful of soup. Some prisoners refused to pay the price and stuffed paper under their shirts against the wind, but by the evening they gave in and paid Julius for his wares.

He had a stock of white bread and a powder against diarrhoea, but above all he traded in tobacco, which he bought from Mietek the Pole. The tobacco was poor stuff, black and coarse, mixed with sawdust and crushed stubs thrown away by German soldiers. There were prisoners who, like Himmelblau, couldn't wean themselves from their habit and smoked away their bread rations. They rolled the tobacco in rough paper, which scarred their throats and burned fast and unevenly. The wood shavings flared up in fiery sparks and the cigarettes grew moist and went out. All that didn't put off Himmelblau, who relit the fags until he smoked them to the last. At the end when the cigarette was so short that it burned his fingers, he stuck the stub on a match and sucked the last bit of smoke.

Julius Abeles bribed the Block Warden with half a bowl of soup to keep an eye on his treasures because he still worked with the cart. By now he could have bought himself a job under a roof, in the kitchen, in the carpentry or even in the Registrar's office, but he preferred dragging potatoes and beets from the main storage where he met with the storeroom people.

'You buy cheap and sell for a better price,' he said to Alex Ehren. 'That's the trick.' He leaned closer to his ear. 'Look around and see for yourself. No funerals for the Block Seniors and the Capos. It's the poor and miserable that die.'

He struck a deal with Himmelblau and became the Block's go-between and supplier of goods. The Children's Block got the parcels that couldn't be delivered because their recipients were dead. The parcels were looted by the Capos and the SS, but they still contained a trove of food, bread and cake, dried apples, instant honey and sometimes even a glass jar of lard.

It was exciting to open the parcels, almost like looking into other people's bedrooms, thought Miriam the head matron, because she often found in the bread, at the bottom of a jar, or once even inside an onion a message on a piece of oil paper. The parcels came from different countries and were a link with the world, a token that the prisoner was not entirely forgotten. Yet they were also a symbol of lost hopes because they were intended for people who were no longer alive. She thought about her husband, who was imprisoned in the Main Camp and of whom she knew nothing.

The Block would never have celebrated the Seder night had Julius Abeles not provided the food.

'A shank bone, an egg and a piece of horseradish? And flour for the unleavened bread?' He shook his head and wondered at the strange request. 'The flour won't be a problem but the other things will be difficult,' he lisped with his eyes on the list. 'Difficult, but not impossible.' He always said that it was difficult but in the end he found – with a little profit for himself – what he was asked for: a Czech book; a piece of red cloth for the puppet theatre; and nails for Shashek, who was building decorations for the Wednesday show. He provided Himmelblau with his tobacco and the rags, which the girls sewed into mittens and mufflers.

The Auschwitz camps were a wilderness where nothing was impossible. The convicts' food rations were so poor that each day scores died of starvation. There were selections and the weak and the old were sent to the gas chambers and then incinerated in the electric ovens. Yet while the barracks people died of hunger, the Block Seniors and Capos of the Kanada Camp lived in obscene abundance on the goods stolen from the new arrivals. The better foodstuffs and the valuables were to be sent to Germany, but some of the loot found its way into the camps.

'One day,' said Julius Abeles, 'I'll have enough gold to bribe an SS officer.'

'An SS officer?'

'Everybody has a price. An SS officer isn't any different from my shop assistant. For the right price he'll let me run away.'

He dreamt about getting into the Kanada Commando, which packed the crates that went to Germany. It was a vain dream because the Family Camp inmates didn't work on labour commandos and Julius Abeles had to content himself with trading in Himmelblau's orphaned parcels.

They started their Seder feast in mid-morning because at dusk there was a curfew. They had only one Seder plate for all the children, which they passed from one group to another. It was a round piece of plywood with a bone, an egg, a sliver of horseradish and a tin cup of salt water, which were the tears of the slaves and the oppressed.

Aunt Miriam stirred beetroot jam into their morning tea to create a semblance of wine and she kneaded the dough and rolled it into small flat cakes. Shashek produced a baking grill from a piece of wire bent into a double loop, and Bass, the oven boy, held the dough over the fire until it was singed and browned on one side and then on the other. There was a bunch of children who watched the making of the bread, the mixing of flour and water, the kneading and rolling out and finally the mystery of baking the matzot. The smoke blackened the cakes and some of them were burned and crumbled, but at the end they had seven pieces of matza spread on Himmelblau's table. At that time there were three hundred and sixty-seven children on the Block and so each of them had a bite, a tiny portion not bigger than a berry.

'It is enough,' Dezo Kovac said, 'to have a taste of the matza. No need for more than a morsel as big as an olive. This is the unleavened bread our forefathers ate at their Exodus from slavery to freedom.'

Alex Ehren didn't know the Haggadah because in his religion lessons he had barely mastered the square Hebrew letters, and he couldn't understand the Aramaic sentences of the old text. However, as he told the story of the Exodus to the children, the boys and the girls, Hanka and Majda, and even Adam Landau the unruly brat, were silent, transfixed by the tale of the Jews for whom the sea had parted to let them cross from slavery to freedom. They drank the brew, which they called wine, and they chewed their one bite of sooty matza, and though Alex Ehren wasn't as good an actor as Fabian, they listened until he finished the story.

Alex Ehren had taught them to ask the traditional four riddles about the difference between that night and other nights, and they sang the answers in their high-pitched childish voices. They weren't strict about the ritual because they celebrated the Seder night at noon and the wine they drank was but the dregs of beetroot jam and their matza only a morsel of ordinary singed dough. They knew little about Jewish tradition and nothing of Jewish law and yet, as Alex Ehren looked at the burned bone, the egg, the bitter herbs and the salt water, something in him moved. He passed the one and only Seder plate to Beran in the next stall, who would pass it on over a beam to another group of children until it made a full circle of the barracks. They substituted day for night and tea for wine and they certainly wouldn't eat a Passover lamb, and yet, though they lived in a world of make-believe, the Seder night was genuine.

Never before, he thought, had there been a more real Passover. They were humiliated and debased and deprived of their humanity. Their lives were like the dust of the earth and worth nothing. Their torturers had starved them until some prisoners went mad and others turned into animals. Yet as long as they believed in miracles, they weren't entirely lost.

Alex Ehren looked into the dark abyss of the Block, at the beams, the stalls, the chimney and the walls. He saw his friends, the instructors and matrons, the Zionists, the communists, the Czech Jews and the German Jews, and beyond them the children who listened to the choir with their eyes bright and wide open.

Dezo Kovac gathered his group of sweet-voiced children and they sang Beethoven's 'Ode to Joy'. The melody was, Alex Ehren thought, like a bird that rose to the rafters, through the narrow windows, to the tar-paper-covered roof and then into the freedom of the sky. It overrode their hunger, their misery, the smell of decay and their fear.

'Joy, thou divine spark of Heaven, Daughter of Elysium … '

The tune spanned time and the barrier of space and carried them away from their death. They sang only eight lines, only sixteen bars of music, because that was all Dezo Kovac could teach them in such a short time. But they had rehearsed the melody so many times that all the Block children knew the eight lines by heart and as soon as the choir started, they joined the singers in an all-encompassing chorus. The three hundred and seventy voices grew into a chorale and reverberated from the roof and the wooden walls, where Lisa Pomnenka had painted her meadows and birds. They sang the melody again and again until, as if by magic, the song sprouted into a dream and all of them – the children, the youth assistants and the teachers – were, for a short moment, for a breath of time, unfettered and free from bondage. And in that one moment they defeated the Germans. They sang:

*'All men become brothers*
*'Where Joy's delicate wing rules'*

and their voices branched out and flooded the adjoining blocks, the Hospital Barracks, the Clothes Storeroom, and the washroom and latrines. They even reached the SS doctor who knew the words and the melody, but wasn't aware that the Jews were celebrating their freedom. He got up from his desk, crossed the camp road and listened. And when the children finished singing, SS doctor Josef Mengele nodded to Himmelblau.

'Well done, Children Senior, carry on.' He turned and left the Block.

At the time none of the Germans knew that on Passover day, which fell on Friday the 7th of April, they had been doubly defeated.

The children set themselves free by their voices, their wine and their unleavened bread. Their freedom, which they would remember until the end of their short existence, lasted but an hour, because shortly afterwards there was a roll call that lasted for the rest of the day deep into the night. They stood in the cold wind and the news travelled from one row to another.

'Did you hear?' the instructors whispered and repeated. 'This afternoon, while the children were having their Seder feast, a Block Senior, one Slavek Lederer, escaped from the camp. Despite the electrified wires, sentries, dogs and chain of mines.'

The sirens started in a low voice but then they grew into a frenzied pitch. They howled for a long time, rising and falling until they died with a growl. At first the children didn't pay them much attention since the sirens went off every time there was an escape. It was the Russian prisoners of war who broke out, but they were usually caught and brought back, bloody and exhausted, to be publicly hanged. Several days before, there were rumours of two prisoners, Rosenberg and Wetzler, who had reached the Slovakian border and who had promised to send a report of their plight to America, to England and to the Pope in Rome. There were similar reports almost every week but most of them were untrue and thus it was more important to survive the hour than to live on false hopes.

'Who cares about the Jews?' said Fabian. 'Even if they got a report they wouldn't lift a finger.'

They were in a place removed and forgotten, a planet so dark that it was invisible among the stars.

'Some did escape,' said Alex Ehren, 'and not all of them were caught.'

'Rumours, fairy tales and wishful thinking.'

There was, however, no mistake about Lederer's escape because the Block Senior was indeed gone. He had been in the camp the day before and now the Deputy Senior took over, at first sheepishly and reluctantly, but after a day or two he became accustomed to his new rank, to the cane and the whitewashed cubicle at the entrance to the Block. It was immensely exciting that one of them, a prisoner whom they knew, broke through the fence, the ditches and the chain of armed sentries and was on his way to freedom. They didn't know how he had managed to escape but in his feat there was hope for them all. Even the sick and the old, who dragged their feet and walked around wrapped in their blankets, awoke from their lethargy and spoke to one another.

'Did you hear? Ran away in spite of the fence.'

'Perhaps he rubbed himself with garlic to confuse the dogs.'

'Where does one find food? Or shelter? Suppose one has to sleep in the open?'

The old men knew they wouldn't escape. They were ill and weak and on the verge of death, but it was good to dream and have hope.

The Block Seniors made the prisoners stand on the camp road in the dark rain. The children, who were usually allowed to take the roll call inside the Block, had to remain together with the adults, hour after hour in the wind and drizzle. The smaller ones cried because they were hungry and cold and impatient. The older boys, Adam and Lazik and Neugeboren, pushed and pulled and tried to leave the row, but the sentries beat them back with a rubber hose.

Next evening all the male prisoners had to shave off their hair.

Alex Ehren didn't know how many prisoners were involved in the underground movement. They were organised in triads and he knew nobody except Felsen who gave him his orders and Beran to whom he passed the word.

'It's a precaution,' Felsen said, 'against informers because people crack and confess under torture and pain.'

Alex Ehren knew little of the overall plan, of the leadership or of the contacts with other camps and he sometimes looked at his fellow instructors, at Fabian, Shashek and even Hynek Rind, and asked himself whether they too, like himself, had been given a task, a mission which they would perform at a given moment.

He was glad that it was Beran with whom he shared the secret because there was tranquility and poise in the tall ugly man, whose hair grew low on his forehead. A month ago they had learned the date of their execution and he counted the days and the hours he had left. There was no subterfuge, no protection, no walls between him and the truth and thus he stood naked against time.

'Everybody is exposed to death,' said Beran, 'but some refuse to take notice. People hoard money, paint a picture, write a poem or compose music as a remedy against dying. They are fools because nothing protects you from death. Even the most miserable day is worth living.'

Sometimes Alex Ehren couldn't follow Beran's arguments and he shook his head.

'Look how we live. How do I make my days worth living?'

Beran grinned and opened his palm as if to receive a gift. 'Be like a fish. Don't swim against the current. There are things you can't change.'

'I won't die without a fight,' Alex Ehren exclaimed. 'Even an animal struggles when it is caught in a net.'

'Struggle is all right, I suppose,' said Beran, 'as long as you don't fight against time.'

Sometimes he wondered why Beran had joined the underground. If he was like a fish and didn't fight against time, would he be ready to fight against the Germans? He collected poems, which he recited and taught to the children. The poems spoke about love, nature and fine feelings and were but another shield against fear. He was in love with his wife whom he met for an hour each afternoon and they stood leaning against each other in a silent touch. Neither of them was handsome, and Sonia's bespattered coat and Beran's ridiculous hat didn't make them any more graceful. Yet there was tenderness and caring between them, and Alex Ehren wondered whether his gawky friend had indeed made peace with the current of time. In the uprising Beran was to set fire to the paliasses, and guide the children through a gap in the fence into the open.

The SS guards, who used to watch the puppet theatre or clap hands in time with Fabian's '*Alouette*', stayed away or walked through the Block with locked faces. An SS sentry had been involved in Lederer's escape and the camp commanders had forbidden any contact with the inmates. Many of the warders were not genuine Germans but Poles, Ukrainians and Magyars of German origin, who remembered their Teutonic grandfather only after the German conquest. They often spoke better Slovak, Romanian or Hungarian than the language of Goethe, and felt more at ease with the prisoners than among their comrades at the guardroom. They were a long way from home and sometimes slept with Jewish girls whom they paid with bread and potatoes for their favours. The women were young and attractive, and most of them better educated than the soldiers.

It so happened that one SS guard, a man called Pestek, a Romanian, fell in love with a prison girl. For some time they met at a Block Senior's cubicle, but then the young man decided to defect, to save the girl and wait for the end of the war in a safe place. It was a daring decision for which the SS soldier needed money to buy papers, pay for a hiding place and provide food for the period of hiding. At last he found Slavek Lederer, a Czech Block Senior, who had the necessary means and friends in a village where they could find shelter.

It was a good bargain for both sides and thus on the 7th of April, the very day Alex Ehren and his friends celebrated their Seder feast, Unterscharfuehrer Pestek and the Czech Block Senior, dressed in SS officers' uniforms and provided with stolen papers, walked out through the camp gate while the sentry stood at attention. They rode their bicycles to the nearest railway station, boarded an express train and by evening had arrived in Prague.

The story was leaked into the Family Camp by the man who swept the SS guardroom, the woman who worked at the post office in the Main Camp, and the artisans who came to the Block to have a look at the children. It was like a puzzle or a mosaic, which had to be collected piece by piece until they had a full picture. Alex Ehren waited a day and then another, but Lederer was never caught and never brought back to be hanged. After a week the Germans gave up their search, but the sentries remained cold and suspicious for a long time afterwards. They even stopped attending the children's charades and shows.

When, in the evening, the Block Wardens shaved the men's heads, their razorblades were blunt and the prisoners left the barber's chair with their scalps torn and bleeding. Some of the prisoners ducked and hid on the bunks because it wasn't only their hair of which they were being robbed, but a part of themselves, a part of their body and their personality. For a long time they possessed nothing. On their arrival they had lost their clothes, their luggage and the little store of food with which they came on the train. However, they differed from the other prisoners because they had been allowed to keep their hair.

'We are privileged,' Hynek Rind had said, 'and one day we will be rescued. There must be a reason why they haven't shaved off our hair.'

They didn't know the context of their lives and they divined and guessed their future from small, almost invisible signs and insignificant omens – their hair, a word from an SS sentry, a scrap of a newspaper and a rumour about the Russian Front.

Alex Ehren was among the last to sit down and let his head be shaved. None of the prisoners was given his midday soup unless he submitted to the procedure. Alex Ehren stood aside for a long time watching his bald-headed mates eat their grey mush. Finally he gave in to his hunger and to the inevitable and closed his eyes as the barber cut and tore at his scalp.

Pavel Hoch lent Alex Ehren a shard of a mirror, and he moved closer to the light to see his new self. At first he couldn't recognise his naked face, the unprotected mug, a face amazed and bare like the moon, with eyebrows raised, a visage gaping, stupid and round as if he had reverted to infancy. He was ridiculously different from his former self. Was he this ugly prisoner whose nose jutted out like a mast and ears protruded like the oars of a boat? He raised his hand to cover his scalp, but he knew there was no use hiding it because from now on his baldness would be a part of him as were his eyes, his chin or his hand. He felt humiliated as if he had been deprived of the last shred of his humanity, the only difference between him and other Birkenau inmates. It was a shock and a setback because, in spite of the departed September transport, they still fooled themselves that they were privileged, that they were pawns in a game and that, despite all odds, one day they might escape or be set free. All that was suddenly gone and without his hair he felt exposed and vulnerable.

He looked around and saw how ridiculous everybody looked. Fabian's head was flat and Beran was robbed of his brow and Felsen looked even more like a turtle than before. Shashek, however, remained unchanged as if his frozen smile were a mask and a protection against disfigurement.

They were grotesque and tried to hide their embarrassment with laughter, but even Fabian's ridicule was awkward and jarring.

Alex Ehren ran his hand over his bald head and thought about his escape.

'The shaven head will betray us when we meet a Pole or a Slovak.'

'Time enough to worry when you meet one on the other side of the fence,' said Beran in his unhurried voice.

Yet even more did he fret that Lisa Pomnenka would find him repulsive, a monster, and refuse to sit with him in the dark corner of the Block. He was too shy to mention his concern to anybody, not even to Beran his bunk-mate, who might have had similar misgivings about Sonia, his wife.

After the Block Senior's escape the SS sentries patrolled the camp road and the children couldn't wander too far away from their Block. They were unable to collect paper from behind the Registry Block and Alex Ehren soon ran out of the supply he kept on the shelf. The only one who was allowed to leave was Adam, who ran errands for the Capo, cleaned his cubicle and warmed his food on a little stove. The children asked about the Capo, his food, the gold he kept under his bed and the women he invited. But Adam kept his mouth shut and if they prodded him too long, he drew his scimitar and hunched his back in imitation of Jagger.

'Get off my back, bastards,' he'd exclaim, standing against the wall until they stopped pestering him and left him alone. Yet sometimes he'd slip behind the Registry and steal paper from the garbage bin. He'd bring it to Alex Ehren, stuffed under his seven shirts.

'Today you write a poem with me. Yes?' he would say, grinning. Yet, although they sat together many times, their writing fell flat and didn't sparkle any more, as if the child had lost his touch of innocence.

At first they couldn't get accustomed to their shaven heads. Fabian looked around and his mouth twitched but when he remembered his own bald pate he suppressed his laughter. On the camp road and during the roll call they wore their hats with the torn rims but it was inside the Block where Alex Ehren felt naked and ashamed of his appearance.

'What is hair?' said Lisa Pomnenka when she saw him. 'It grows and in a month or two you will have it back.'

He thought about the two months and his heart contracted and his mouth grew dry. Two months, he thought, will bring us to the verge of our lives.

On Monday two of his boys arrived with knitted caps that covered their shaven heads. The fashion caught on and the women, the matrons and even the youth girl assistants unravelled old sweaters and rolled the yarn into skeins. They knitted round caps on 'needles', which they peeled from their bunks and rubbed on a brick until they were smooth and pointed. Most of the children had mothers who produced their caps, but there were also orphans and for them the girls knitted caps during Lisa Pomnenka's handicraft lessons. The caps became a fashion and soon everyone had one – the teachers, the youth assistants and even the small boys in the kindergarten – so that the girls quickly ran out of knitting material. In the end they turned to Julius Abeles, who squinted at the crate with Himmelblau's parcels and clicked his tongue.

'Not easy,' he said. 'I'll have to get some from the main storeroom. It's still cold and they won't let them go cheap.'

Two days later he brought a bale of knitwear, multicoloured underwear and pullovers and single socks, which the girls unravelled and turned into caps. After a while the Children's Block was alight with colour because the knitters invented patterns and stripes, white and blue and red until the shaven heads disappeared under the make-believe gaiety of the caps.

One of the adolescents, Foltyn the guard, was among the last boys without a cap. He was awkward with girls and even in the history lessons, which he attended with the older children, he blushed and stammered whenever Marta Felix made him answer.

'I don't need one,' he said in a huff when she offered to knit for him. 'They are a children's game.'

'It would be a privilege,' she said.

She was alone in the camp and was often glad that she was free from worry about a husband, a lover, an old parent or a child. Yet at other times she felt abandoned and bitter that there was nobody for whom she could knit a cap. In the end he reluctantly accepted and Marta Felix produced for him a cap with a tassel which dangled at the back of his head.

Lisa Pomnenka gave Alex Ehren a brown cap and then knitted another for Shashek, her secret admirer. The handyman often stood and watched her work with the children or held the ladder, which she climbed up to paint the sky. He made her a toolbox with a shoulder strap and carved the heads for the puppet theatre.

A week later the German doctor came to inspect the two pairs of twins – the kindergarten girls and the two boys Zdenek and Jirka – on whom he proved the inferiority of the Jewish race. He looked around and noticed the coloured caps.

'You Jews are a dangerous lot,' said Dr Mengele with a frown. 'You turn even a punishment into an advantage.'

Alex Ehren's love for Lisa Pomnenka was a remedy against his anguish. He looked forward to their evening meetings, which were like a harbour to his days. After her father's death the girl was alone and he tried to be her guide and support. They kept sitting in a corner and holding hands and sometimes, when they thought that nobody was watching, they even kissed. They played lovers' games of hide and seek, and shared each other's dreams. They walked the camp road, and though the barracks, the fence and the railway ramp were a wretched, desolate landscape, they were happy to breathe the same air, to tread the same ground and touch each other's arm and elbow.

After a month on the Children's Block, Alex Ehren felt strong and healthy. Sometimes the instructors got a helping of the children's white soup, cooked from food left behind by the transports and he shared Pavel Hoch's love parcels. He also ate some of the bread Lisa Pomnenka earned by painting naked Gypsy girls for the German doctor. He was still hungry but the occasional extra soup and slice of bread liberated him from his frenzy of starvation. In his first months in the camp he was unable to think of anything else but his midday soup and the evening ration of bread. His whole life and even his dreams were permeated by one wish, a terrible craving for food and filling his aching stomach. Now with the little extra bread everything changed. He was a young man and the touch of the girl's skin turned his affection into desire. There was no place where they could be alone and their relation was full of tension.

'Yes,' she said and laid her palm on his, 'I want to make love to you. One day we might find a way.'

Alex Ehren's awareness of time made him impatient and he was not satisfied with a promise. How many days do we have, he thought, a month, two? Each day may be the last and we could die or be parted at any hour. He had no doubt about her affection; she was gentle and ready to listen to his stories, but she still remained herself, a different entity, as if encased in a shell he couldn't penetrate.

He wanted to know all about her, about her childhood, her family, school and friends, and, though she talked, he felt that she kept the kernel, the core of the story, for herself. He wanted to have her entirely, her body, her soul, her mind. He begrudged her the time she spent with Shashek, the jack-of-all-trades, with whom she worked on the puppet theatre or prepared decorations for a charade. He suffered when the German doctor summoned her to work in the Gypsy Camp and he imagined the disasters that might befall her in the wilderness of the camps. He would have liked the girl to stay on the Children's Block where the instructors had created an island of security and where he could protect her. He thought that she was vulnerable and fragile and could come to some terrible harm without his help. Yet that was only a small shadow on the happiness her proximity gave him. He was glad to see her in the morning, eat his soup in her company and in the evening share his bread with her.

After work the instructors, the matrons and the youth assistants played a guessing game and even then they sat close to each other. They weren't ashamed in front of Himmelblau, Fabian, Hynek Rind and the children. The Block people had accepted them as lovers and they didn't feel embarrassed any more.

Fabian invented a new version of an old game based on brains and honesty. They called the game 'The Ring' because the players stood in a circle and held hands, but when the question fell on the girl she shook her head and stood back.

'I am not clever enough for the game.'

She walked over to Shashek's workbench and helped him dress the puppets he had carved from a piece of cherry wood.

'Some people have brains and others have hands.'

'Why don't you try?' Alex Ehren asked, annoyed that she had left the circle.

'Why should I? Would you love me more if I were clever?'

'You can learn,' he said.

'Maybe one day I will,' she answered, working with her needle. She rarely opposed him but instead escaped to an unidentified vague answer, which he hated. She had lost her mother when she was still a child. There was no school and she looked after her father, cooked, did the laundry and shopped for meat and vegetables. With the German occupation her father lost his job and she decorated tiles to pay their rent.

'One day,' she said, 'I'll catch up with my learning.'

She had no doubt that the war would end and that she would resume her life where she had left it before the camps. It was as if she were blind to the transports, the chimney and the rumours about the date of their death. Sometimes Alex Ehren spoke about his apprehensions but she wouldn't listen.

'I don't want to know about bad things.' She laid her hands over her ears. 'Fear makes bad things even worse.'

She was like a bird that lives its summer and doesn't care about the snow. She took life and death as they came, without thought or regret or deliberation. Sometimes he was tempted to tell her about the mutiny and his plans for their escape. He always planned for both of them to cross the river, to live in the woods or to work as farmhands in a village. Yet on second thoughts, he kept silent because like so many times before, he felt that she was like a child, simple and unworried and therefore happier than he was.

The German doctor liked her work and she often spent whole days in the Hospital Compound drawing diagrams and painting pictures of Gypsy girls. She still worked on the wall with its meadow, flowers and birds, but because of Mengele's commissions, half of the wall was still bare and empty.

# 6.

BENEATH THE GAMES AND THE CLANDESTINE SCHOOL THERE was rot. The Block was like a ship on a sea of corruption, which seeped in through the cracks with each flurry of wind.

The inmates of the camp fought for their lives. The convicts in the red-brick barracks of the Men's Camp and the Women's Camp, and even those in the remote labour camps of the immense Auschwitz complex, lived on borrowed time. There were too many of them and as the trains brought new transports, the redundant had to die to make room for the new arrivals. There was a daily quota of ten thousand who passed through the chimney, and Dr Mengele spent his mornings choosing the travellers.

Sometimes he inspected new transports and at other times he weeded out the veteran inmates. They paraded in front of him, naked or draped in their thin prison drills, and he ushered them with a cane left to their deaths and right to more labour and death afterwards. Even the sick and the weakest were desperate to live, and in pathetic attempts to look strong they inflated their chests, held their heads high and opened their mouths in a twisted grin. Yet they were unable to hide their bloated faces and the doctor made them shuffle into the rows of the condemned.

And if some of them, one or two, succeeded in slipping through in the morning, they certainly died in the afternoon or by the next day, because the selections went relentlessly on and on, in an ever tightening circle of dying. Never before was there a man who, like the physician, had sent so many fellow human beings to their deaths and remained sane.

'How does he spend his nights?' asked Alex Ehren.

And Mietek the Pole, who had been in the camp for so long that he knew its inroads and secrets, pursed his lips and grinned. 'Listening to classical music,' he said, 'Vivaldi, Bach and Brahms.'

There were, however, the fat cats, the obstinate survivors who worked in the kitchen or in the food storage, or those with the armband of a Capo, a Block Senior or a Registrar, who were not subject to Mengele's selections. There was a fierce scramble for life, a war without bounds or mercy, because it was either your skin or mine. It was a one-time gamble and therefore absolute and cruel and final.

Himmelblau sat with Aunt Miriam, the head matron, and ruminated about morality.

'What is moral,' he said, 'to cry out and die like poor Antigone or to steal and tread on others and save one's neck?'

He spoke German with the matron and his words flowed easily. 'It's the children,' he went on, 'we have to teach. The truth or the lie? Don't cheat and don't steal and love thy neighbour? Shouldn't we instead show them how to survive in the jungle? But how can I teach something I've never learned?

'"Helpful be a man, noble and good",' he said, quoting a German poet and laughing angrily. 'Goethe doesn't make sense in a concentration camp. How long can we play the game of make-believe? We tell them not to lie and we lie to them every day, because the Block with its little songs and with helping the small and the weak is only an illusion and a lie. One day when the Germans close the Block the children will be like fish without water.'

Sometimes the teachers argued about the value of honesty. 'The Germans have robbed us of everything. Our homes, our work and even our lives,' said Marta Felix. 'Why shouldn't we take back at least a piece of bread or a potato?'

'From whom?' asked Beran. 'From the Germans or from our fellow prisoners? Where is the limit? How can I explain to the children that one piece of bread is different from another?'

'Don't explain,' said Fabian, 'because there is no difference. How long do we have? Two months, three? Each day you can fill your belly is a blessing. Why confuse them? The Ten Commandments were not meant for concentration camp convicts.'

Without rules the Block doesn't make sense, thought Alex Ehren, but he didn't say it aloud.

There was little opportunity to steal from the German garrison who lived in a separate compound. The prisoners who cleaned the guardroom were scared to pinch a piece of bread because the soldiers sometimes let them have scraps and leftovers from their meal.

'A wolf,' said Fabian, 'doesn't choose to be a wolf. It's his hunger that drives him out of the woods. If you give a wolf a bone he will become a dog and stop biting. What to tell the children? The truth, of course. Save your skin, my little brats; fight for your life as best you can. And if you have to steal, to lick a boot, to swindle … do it. What else?'

And yet the instructors still told the children stories where good was rewarded and evil punished. The children often misunderstood and when Alex Ehren spoke about a poor family who lived on dry bread and lentils, Majda took her thumb out of her mouth.

'They were not poor. They could have bartered their bread and lentils.'

They took wrong sides and opted for the dragon, the witch or the giant rather than for the good and the simple-minded. They loved adventure and were ready to hear the same story again and then painted pictures of Robin Hood, the Slovak highwayman Jánošík, of Eskimos and Gulliver on scraps of paper, which Alex Ehren hung on the wall. Yet they also painted their fears and there were drawings of the fence, the dogs, the chimney and of soldiers shooting a prisoner. By the end of the month the escaped sentry Unterscharfuehrer Pestek was caught and executed and although they hadn't seen him die, he too began to appear in the children's pictures.

Alex Ehren produced a board on which they played draughts and snakes and ladders. They loved games, but the boys cheated and whenever Adam Landau lost, he started a fight. By the end of April he still couldn't read because he spent most of his mornings with Jagger, and was cockier and wilder than ever before.

For a while he made peace with the teacher, but when he didn't win another prize, he lost interest and stopped attending school. When Alex Ehren caught him lying, the boy spat on the floor and disappeared for three days, but then came back like a bad penny, for a round of tug o' war and a game of marbles. The boys dug a hole in the dirt, shot their marbles and then crept on the floor to roll them into the kitty. The game became a craze and an obsession and the children could barely wait for a break to go back to their sport. The game had complex rules about which they quarrelled, disturbing the older children, who sat with Hynek Rind doing some geometry.

'There is time for school and there is time for marbles,' said Himmelblau in his funny Czech. 'The teacher will keep your marbles and give them back at the end of the lesson. We will not close the school because of your game.'

Alex Ehren collected the marbles and kept them on his shelf until the end of the lesson, but the children never handed over all of their marbles, or else they produced new ones and ran behind the Block to continue their game. They chewed bread and rolled it into pellets which when dried grew as hard as stone. Bubenik was a master of the craft and even older boys paid a spoonful of soup for three of his marbles.

One afternoon Alex Ehren broke up a skein of fighting boys. They were excited and angry and, as so often happened, Adam was at the centre of the row. He stood against the wall with his fist clenched at his chest.

'He cheats,' they shouted. 'Come on, Adam, show him the marble you've got.'

'It's mine,' said the boy, and his eyes were like tiny flames of blue fire. 'I worked for it and no bastard will take it away.'

'Why are you hiding it? What is it, a secret?'

'A winning marble,' they shouted. 'A golden marble that rolls into the kitty by itself.'

They had no pockets and they kept their possessions in a knotted rag inside their shirts. This 'satchel' might contain a piece of string, a bread crumb saved from last night's ration, a coloured button and, of course, their hoard of marbles.

'Show him, show him,' they clamoured, eager to expose the cheat. Some of the children lived with their mothers, but many were orphans and had to manage on their own. They were very young, some only seven years old, but they had learned to help one another with food and clothes and the small things needed for survival. At noon Alex Ehren collected a spoonful of soup from each child to let one of them have a second helping.

'To give up one spoonful is nothing,' Eva had said, holding her rag doll close, 'but another helping is a treat.'

They knew how many days there were to their second bowl of soup, three or four, and it brightened their mornings to know that at noon they would have a full stomach.

They could survive only as a group, and though nobody said it aloud, they depended on one another like the organs of one body. The Children's Block was run like a summer camp, a game, an illusion, an island. The children existed in a make-believe world, detached from the cruelty of the camp, but the group was real and solid and without pretence. The children had forgotten their past, their families were torn apart or dead, they had no home, no neighbourhood and no landscape to remember, save the ghetto walls or the barracks of their prison camp. They were uprooted, stripped of their names and starved until they were like animals. For many of them the group became a substitute family, the community to which they belonged and the only wholeness in a fragmented universe. The group was their identity and when somebody asked them who they were, they wouldn't mention their father or their country, but the name of their group, because they were the Swallows, the Bears and the Maccabees more than they were anything else. But they could also be cruel and deadly to a boy who stole a piece of bread from his friend, cheated at marbles or broke the code of the community.

'The marble,' they sang now, 'show him the marble.'

Adam opened his fist and there was a golden bead, smooth and glistening and as heavy as a pebble. It caught the light that fell from the narrow window and it shone in its perfect roundness.

Alex Ehren knew that there was gold in the camps, gold that had been sewn in the hem of a coat, hidden in a glove or in an aperture of the body. There was also the gold of the wedding rings, the filigree necklaces and the earrings stripped off the dead women before they were burned. The gold was melted down to ingots and sent to Germany, but some of the jewels were stolen and kept in a cache behind the bunks. Alex Ehren hadn't seen gold since his mother handed over their Maria Theresa *thaler* coin to the Germans.

'They can take the gold but they can't take away the name,' she'd said. But she was wrong because at his arrival in Birkenau Alex Ehren had lost his name and became the number that a Polish convict tattooed on his forearm. He didn't mind too much because all of them had become numbers – Himmelblau and Fabian and his friend Beran and Marta Felix who had a PhD in philosophy. Whenever he met an SS sentry he had to snap to attention and present himself not by name but by number. Even the children had to remember their ciphers and he taught Bubenik and Majda and all the rest of his group to stand to attention and sing out the answer.

'Here I am, prisoner number one-seven-zero-five-six-three, playing marbles or skipping rope or learning the names of German weekdays.'

Alex Ehren was startled by the gold on the urchin's palm. It was unexpected and full of dangers. The bead was smooth and opulent and carried the memory of lights, carpeted rooms, a potted linden tree. It also trailed the intimation of femininity and fragrance.

'How did you get it?'

'None of your business.'

'Did you steal it?'

'Worked for it,' said the boy with his face sullen and angry. 'Ask Jagger the Capo.'

'Who pays with golden beads? What kind of work is it?' asked Alex Ehren.

The boy resented his questions and turned to run. He would stay away for a number of days, even a week and then return with a bribe. He was generous with his riches and handed out gifts with ease: to Neugeboren old sneakers; to Bubenik a mouth organ; and to Majda a kerchief. Sometimes he brought bits of food, a slice of salami, salted fish and even a raw egg. He was a small child and the Camp Capo's visitors gave him things stolen from the new arrivals. The boy imitated the grand style of the Capo, his protector, who allowed him to wear the black armband of a runner.

'The marble,' said Alex Ehren and looked at the glistening bead. 'Who pays with a golden marble? What kind of work is it that pays with gold?'

Alex Ehren thought of the danger hidden in the precious metal, because if the boy was caught, the SS might beat him to death to learn where it came from. Children were not exempt from cruelty and torture, and possession of gold, which was a door to freedom, was a mortal transgression.

He looked around at the other children but they were silent as if sworn to secrecy. They know, thought Alex Ehren, though for some reason they refuse to tell. Adam was a nuisance and a pest, who fought with the boys and cheated at marbles, but he still was a member of the group and they protected him like a wall of stones. Or was it not only his secret? Were others involved? He had to know, he thought, for their sake and for his own.

He held the boy fast and shook him until his satchel opened and some of the marbles spilled on the ground.

They were all grey and inconspicuous, and, save the one in his hand, none of them shone like gold. It was only much later that Alex Ehren learned about the boy's work and the source of his prosperity.

At last Shashek finished carving the puppets. He had worked on them for three weeks, sculpting their heads with a broken blade. Lisa Pomnenka painted the faces, and, together with the older girls, sewed the clothes. They lifted the theatre onto the brick chimney. The chimney ran horizontally on the floor along the whole block, like a heated low wall with an oven at each end. From the ovens the chimneys rose up through the flat roof but it was only in the children's block that they were ever lit. From underneath the trestle Fabian and Marta Felix moved the figures. It took a long time to produce the frame, the curtain and the decorations from the materials found around the Block. Shashek needed wood, nails and hinges for the trap door, items which he acquired one by one, from Mietek, from the camp carpenter and through Julius Abeles, the Cart Commando man. The decorations were important but the main attraction was the puppets, which Himmelblau kept in a wooden box in his cubicle.

At the beginning there were only three characters: Princess Marmalade, King Dumpling and the jester called Send Helping. Later Shashek carved the Devil and Prince Sof-Tov, which was the Hebrew word for 'happy ending'. They didn't know much Hebrew, although Dezo Kovac conducted lessons for the Zionists. But they all – the Czechs, Dutch, Germans and even the communists – used the word *sof* to describe the end of the war. When the *sof* comes, they said, I'll do this and I'll do that. I won't touch beetroot soup again, or I'll put on my best clothes and parade along the river, or work for the world revolution, or go to Palestine, or write a book about the evil in man. The word *sof* was an incantation that brought alive their wishes and hopes, and although for each of them the word meant something different, for all of them it was a crown and a fulfilment. Sof-Tov was an appropriate name for the Prince, who at the end of each play saved Princess Marmalade from the clutches of the villain. Their first performance, for which Alex Ehren wrote the script, was on Monday. The play was written in Czech, but the Devil spoke German and clicked his heels like a soldier.

'The language is not guilty,' said Himmelblau. 'There were Kant and Heine and Thomas Mann and even Albert Einstein who wrote in German. Why must the Devil speak German?'

'The road to hell is paved with German words,' replied Fabian, grinning. He enjoyed his satanic part; he didn't know much German and so he invented new words, twisted and frightening and meaning nothing. He sat cross-legged under the table and improved on Alex Ehren's script with rolled r's and rattling g's, and diabolic snorting, which the children loved. He was a good actor and soon the Devil was the most popular puppet on the stage.

None of the instructors was a skilled puppeteer, but by and by they improved and on Monday the Block was always full of visiting craftsmen, registrars and even SS guards.

They had to be careful with the text because some of the Germans understood a Slavonic language, Polish, Ukrainian or Croatian, and before every performance Himmelblau cautioned Fabian to curb his tongue and make the Devil speak Czech.

'All right, all right. I admit that not everybody who speaks German is a devil—' he grinned at Himmelblau and polished his broken lens '—though all the devils I know speak German.'

Shashek the handyman had marvellous fingers. He turned a piece of wood in his hands and then started carving, splinter after splinter, until he had a rough outline of a face. He deepened the hollow and smoothed the brow and then suddenly, out of wooden nothingness, emerged a shape, an image, a being.

He had only a knife with a broken blade and the wood was unpolished and rough, but each puppet was alive with an inner craving and ambition. Each of the five manikins had a heart and a soul; it was unmistakably itself, and once finished couldn't have been mistaken for anybody else.

'Where did you learn it?' asked Lisa Pomnenka, who admired his gift and artistry.

'A bit here and a bit there. Made a toy horse for a nephew, nothing serious. I wanted to become a car mechanic, but Jews couldn't be apprenticed.'

She looked at his hands, which were big and cracked by the many tasks he was doing on the Block, and which moved as if they had a life of their own. He turned his palms upwards in a gesture of giving.

'They don't look like Jewish hands,' he said and his face folded into its involuntary grin. 'I suppose I inherited them from my mother's side. My mother wasn't Jewish. Her people were Protestants. Working class folks, one grandfather a smith and an uncle a coal miner. Big hands and small heads.'

He stopped and blew away the wood shavings and the dust.

'I didn't want to be a Jew and sell shoes like my father. I wanted to use my hands.' He paused and then went on. 'My mother pushed me through school. "Jews are fine people," she said. "They read books and live in good houses. They don't come home dirty and don't spend their evenings in a pub drinking beer. I want a better life for you and your children."'

He looked up and his voice was angry. 'I'll die because my mother wanted a better life for me and for my children. Why can't parents let their kids live their own lives?'

Lisa Pomnenka saw that he had carved her likeness into the face of Princess Marmalade and was flattered. What she wasn't aware of was that he was in love with her and suffered each time he saw her together with Alex Ehren.

According to medical science the prisoners should have been dead. Sometimes the Jewish doctor crossed the road from the Hospital Block to listen to the children's chests and to run his fingers over the boys' spines. He was one of the survivors of the September transport and it was he who had brought Himmelblau Fredy's whistle. The Youth Senior wore it on his neck as the gym teacher had done, but it took him a long time until he dared to use it. It was like wearing a dead man's clothes, he thought, and he blew the whistle only in times of alarm or emergency.

The physician conducted a study of sorts. He weighed the bread and calculated the nutritional value of their margarine and beet jam.

'We live on four hundred and fifty calories a day,' he said, and shook his head. 'How long can a man survive on so little? According to the book we are all dead.'

The hospital staff got more food because the Block Registrar wouldn't report the deceased immediately and for a day or two the doctors and the nurses shared the dead people's bread rations. The labourers, however, lived and pushed the iron wagons up the road, cleared the ditches and marched to work through the gates while the orchestra played 'Marinarella', 'The Blue Danube' and 'Roll Out the Barrel'. True, many inmates died of exhaustion and disease, and each morning Julius Abeles and his Transport Commando mates carried their bodies to the crematorium. They went through the deceased people's clothes and scavenged their last possessions, their buttons, the crumb of bread and sometimes even a coin or a banknote.

Most of the prisoners owned nothing, not even their time. Their days belonged to the Labour Capo, and their mornings and evenings to the SS, who counted them at the roll call with the movement of a gloved hand. Sometimes they even worked at night in the white light of the projectors or had to forgo the one free hour when they met their families.

Nothing was permanent in their lives. From time to time they were moved to another block or were shifted from one commando to another like pawns on a chessboard.

'I have nothing,' said Beran, 'and so I have nothing to lose. Think of the people who have a home, a garden and a bank account. They are afraid to fall asleep because of burglars, fire and earthquakes.' He spread his arms like a gawky bird. 'I am free, because nobody can rob me of anything.'

There was another freedom of which the SS couldn't deprive them – the freedom to dream. Most of the deportees dreamt of food and in their minds they cooked imaginary feasts and indulged in orgies of food and drink. They compared lists of restaurants and argued about recipes for meats, gravies and salads. They spoke of fish, of fowl, grilled or fried in oil, and fought about condiments, soups and confectionery. The children had no memories of fine foods or cakes with whipped cream. They had never seen a fruit – a lemon, a pear or a bunch of grapes – because after the German conquest the Jews were not allowed to buy fresh fruit. Some of them had lived in camps for four years and the only delicacy they remembered was the yeast dumpling, which were handed out in the ghetto.

Sometimes a visitor brought an apple to the Block and the fruit circulated among the children, who touched its skin, smelled it and fondled its roundness until it was cut up into tiny pieces and distributed among the smallest of them.

'Close your eyes,' said Alex Ehren, 'and dream that one day you'll have as many apples as you wish ... a basket, a barrel and a cart.'

The children chewed the bit of fruit and dreamt about the world.

The puppets made Fabian even more popular than his '*Alouette*'. They asked him to roll his r's and rattle his g's and speak like the Devil, which he did with relish and gusto. He sang '*Alouette*' with them and made them laugh with his fibs, but in the evening when the children left, he mocked himself and his friends who dreamt about Palestine, and memorised Hebrew words.

'Aren't we funny,' he sneered, 'with one foot in the grave and with the other in a kibbutz in Palestine.'

The Block instructors looked like scarecrows in their rags marked with red paint, their shaven heads covered with knitted caps, shuffling along in their wooden clogs. The men were unshaven, the women gaunt. Their coats were either too short or trailing on the ground. They knew that they would die on the 20th of June, but they remained committed, making the children wash in icy water and write words and sentences in straight lines.

Alex Ehren wrote little plays for the puppet theatre and Beran collected poems on scraps of paper. But their inspiration was often tinsel, and their convictions false.

Alex Ehren preached one thing but believed in another, and Fabian's mockery kept him down to earth. It helped him to see himself as he was – an ordinary man, a number, a scarecrow and not a very good teacher. They all – Beran and Himmelblau and even Marta Felix – needed Fabian, whose crooked mirror provided them with true proportion and kept them sane and sober.

Fabian was an artist at eating his soup. He started out holding his bowl in both hands. He closed his eyes, felt its warmth and inhaled the fragrance of the potatoes, the beet and bone, which the cooks sometimes threw into the cauldron. His spectacles had only one sound lens and he had to crane his head like a raptor to see his dish. In the process of cooking the soup had disintegrated into grey mush. Yet sometimes, on a lucky day, when the ladle came from the bottom of the barrel, he struck a piece of potato or a slice of beet, which he saved for the very end of his meal. He held his spoon as delicately as if it were a musical instrument, a flute, an oboe or a horn, on which he was about to produce a theme. He scooped the top crust and licked his spoon with his tongue as if it were the cheek of his beloved. He sank his lip into the liquid pool and sipped the soup but didn't swallow and held it against his palate, savouring its ingredients, and only then allowed the food to flow down his throat. Each time he swallowed he did so with remorse, knowing that what was gone could never be recovered. He worked slowly along the banks of the bowl, sometimes leaving a mound in the centre, yet at other times he ventured right into the deep and sailed stately towards the shores. His meal took him a long time, longer than anybody else, and often when the children returned from the washroom with their cleaned bowls, Fabian was still at the last remnants of his soup.

He sighed and tied the bowl to his trousers.

'Eating,' he said, 'is like making love: either you put your heart and your groin into it, or you don't do it at all.'

He was small and twisted like a mountain tree and hungrier than other instructors. Sometimes when Lisa Pomnenka got bread from the German doctor, she broke off a piece and gave it to Fabian. He was gruff in his thanks and hid the bread in his jacket.

'Much obliged, my princess,' he said satanically. 'Ask the doctor if he doesn't need an actor.' He was aware of her likeness to the puppet and sometimes, as if by mistake, he addressed her as Princess Marmalade.

And so each one had a dream. They lived terribly and without a shield against death. They were exposed to cold, starvation, to the ever-present stench of decay, the festering canker of their wounds and the bittersweet smoke of the burnt offerings, which rolled in wreaths over the landscape. It was a borderline existence, devoid of light and murky as if living under water. Their life had no value and even the trivial matters were like climbing a mountain.

Alex Ehren washed, waited in a queue for his pittance of bread and beetroot jam, and each day he felt lucky that he hadn't contracted diarrhoea, which caused dehydration and sudden soiled death. He lived with the children and taught them a bit of reading and writing and a little about the world they had never seen, but each task was like swimming against the stream. Yet he knew that as long as he fought he was alive and could indulge in his secret dreams.

He kept his world of dreams to himself and didn't share it even with Lisa Pomnenka, whom he loved. He had an ability, which he had developed at school, where during boring chemistry lessons he learned to conjure up white towns and landscapes with exotic trees. It was an exquisite gift, which he used sparingly on sleepless nights. He knew that the panacea of his dreams was only a temporary freedom, which would disperse like mist in the morning, but even that was a remedy and a relief.

One evening he had a vision that came to him uncalled for and of its own. He was in the hollow of a rock. It was a secret cave, a womb sealed off by layers of lava hardened into basalt. It was so deep within himself that there were no words, nor light, nor air and, as it was utterly self-contained, he was detached from his outer self. He was not alone but shared the cave with a pride of animals. They emerged from dark pools and sprouted like mushrooms, in the soil of his desires, some of them corporeal and others inchoate, shadowy and vague. They prowled the forests of his soul and tried to lead him astray.

Yet then the beasts were gone and he was alone. And from there, from the constriction of the chiselled cave, he cried out upwards, like a tree. At first he was shy because he had never been a religious person and didn't know the words of any prayer, but then he understood that reaching upwards didn't require words or religion, and he wasn't shy any more. He was scared that his voice wouldn't pierce the rock, the distance and the unknowing clouds, and he raised his voice to a shriek. He didn't mind whether there was anybody who listened or loved or cared, because what mattered was the striving, which was like water for his very self, parched with fears.

And then there was an answer. It didn't come in a flash of light or the raising of a curtain or from any direction, but grew like a flower or a crystal from within and spread outwards. He suddenly understood, unwillingly and reluctantly, and with a great deal of resentment, that the camps were not what they seemed to be, but a part of a whole. Life was an immense gift, a miracle of miracles, exquisite and unique and bestowed only once. His ordeal, his degradation, and even the children who were condemned to die before their time, weren't for nothing; the children hadn't been born in vain and did matter terribly, because by having existed they made an imprint in the dust of the universe. It was therefore of utmost importance how they used their gift of life, because each thought, each word, each deed and even the breath from their mouths would be indelibly imbedded in the abyss of time to come. He was an outcome of all that had ever been and the beginning of everything that would ever be, and thus he could never be abandoned or forgotten. His life, like that of any man, tree or rock, was a link in the chain and thus of instrumental, infinite and cosmic importance.

He became aware that there were other worlds beyond his world, worlds that moved in circles within circles, intertwining, separating, growing and dying into nothingness, out of which new stars were born. He knew, though not in his mind but from somewhere within, that there were other lives beyond his life, lives that occurred on planes of consciousness different from his. They were transient and subject to the chaos of dying, though all of them – the formed and the formless and those yet to be formed – were part of the whole.

The revelation was simple and self-evident and Alex Ehren wondered why he hadn't stumbled on the truth before. After some time the experience waned and lost its sharp outlines but it stayed with him like a flash of light in darkness, as long as he lived.

However, most of the time he dreamt about food. His life was stripped of pretence and he had little need for religion or the transcendental. There were some inmates, like Dezo Kovac, who occasionally joined a group of old men, who, in the darkness of early morning, swayed backwards and forwards and mumbled words of prayers which they barely understood. Their prayer was a longing for things past rather than piety, because it was difficult to praise God in a place devoid of human dignity.

There was a boy in Beran's group who had a Bible. It was a small volume in black covers, which Aryeh had rescued through the showers and the tattooing ordeal. The book was printed in Hebrew with a Czech translation on facing pages, and the teachers borrowed it from time to time and read a chapter about the kings and wars and the creation of the world to the older children.

Many of the instructors were members of the Zionist movement, who intended to emigrate to Palestine when the war ended. Sometimes they argued whether to travel directly from Birkenau to join a kibbutz or stop for some time in Prague. They had little knowledge of the climate, the work and the language, although some of them could form a number of twisted Hebrew sentences.

What they didn't know they substituted by imagination, and Alex Ehren played a game with the children called 'When I come to Palestine, I'll see a lemon tree'. It was a memory game where each child added an item until there was a string of objects they would see in Palestine. The one that couldn't remember the proper order of words had to quit. It was a good game but less useful than a drill called 'What I will do when an SS comes in'.

'We'll play a game, we'll play a game,' they shouted and the one who forgot to shout lost a point. Alex Ehren often sprang the question on the children but they knew the trick, and by the end only Majda, who was a dreamer and sucked her thumb, lost a point.

Aryeh was thin and serious and the only child that spoke Hebrew. He was the son of Miriam, the matron, and Edelstein, who had been the Ghetto Elder. When Eichmann visited the Children's Block, he took Aunt Miriam's letter, but was evasive about a possible visit.

'It's not in my hands,' he said, 'but I'll see what I can do.'

He was lying, of course, as all the Germans were when they spoke to the prisoners. The Jewish prisoners were kept in the dark to prevent them from planning an escape. The Germans always altered their regulations, and what was permitted one day was prohibited by the next morning. Since Pestek's escape they even rotated the SS sentries lest they became friendly with an inmate.

There were rumours about a Jewish uprising in Warsaw, and Mietek swore that he had spoken to a man who had escaped through the sewers of the burning ghetto. The man had lived for some time in a village but was caught and sent to Birkenau. There were other rumours about resistance in Treblinka and Sobibór and Majdanek, names Alex Ehren had never heard before, but the rumours came and went and nobody knew whether they were true or false. The Family Camp was like a house without windows and the prisoners were isolated, not only from the events in the world but also from other compounds in Auschwitz. Most of them worked inside the camp, and when a commando was marched to a working place beyond the gate, the sentries kept them apart from labourers from other places.

Some of the prisoners, like Hynek Rind, who called himself a Czech of Jewish descent, saw in it a good omen.

'Even the Germans know that we are different from the Polish Jews. One day they will set us free, exchange us for prisoners of war or for money. They don't want us to mix with the rabble and learn about the chimney.'

There was no logic in what he said because the truth filtered in with a craftsman, the Cart Commando and even with a German sentry. Everybody knew about the executions that went on daily in the gas chambers, about the occasional escapes, about the war that raged all over the world and even about the events in the German garrison.

On Mondays they played charades. They staged Julius Caesar, Napoleon at Waterloo and Diogenes in his barrel. There was Moses and Forefather Czech, and Fabian even impersonated Adolf Hitler, whose name they pronounced with fear and trepidation. It was a dangerous idea and Himmelblau stationed Bass, the oven boy, as an additional guard at the back door, to look out for the Priest.

Alex Ehren wondered how the children solved the riddles, because many of them had never attended school and their knowledge was shallow and full of holes. Yet they were keen on new things and intent on stories that substituted for their unlived experience. It was the Block, he thought, that replaced their twice-removed world. They were confined to the camp, but within the Children's Block they grew like plants in a glass house, on the words of the stories and on Lisa Pomnenka's meadow and birds on the painted wall.

In the last weeks the girl worked almost every day for Doctor Mengele. She charted family trees, drew diagrams and sketched the faces and limbs of his human specimens. Sometimes she was frightened by the cold fury with which he compiled statistics, as if a hundred examples were not enough to prove his point. He wasn't unkind to her and gave her bread but he flew into a rage at her smallest mistake, tore the sheets of paper to pieces and made her sit all night to repair the damage. There was something insane, she thought, in the doctor's obsession with bone structures, shapes of the heads and blemishes of the skin. Sometimes he didn't call her for a number of days as if he had forgotten her, but then she was summoned post-haste to draw a portrait or work with coloured inks on a diagram or sketch a family tree that spread over time and countries.

Alex Ehren suffered when Lisa Pomnenka was away and waited for her with longing and anxiety. He thought about the strange operations the doctor performed on women, the dangers of the Gypsy Camp and the SS sentries with their German shepherds. He had never been outside the Family Camp, which in spite of its stench and starvation became a familiar place, almost a home, compared to the wilderness beyond the gate. He was glad when he saw the girl return and he left the children and hurried to touch her hand.

Sometimes she crossed the camp road and visited the seamstress. It seemed to him a strange friendship because the seamstress was a middle-aged woman, a former Spanish war veteran, and he wondered what the two women might have in common.

'Is she more important than our love?' He was both angry and relieved that she had returned.

'Of course she isn't,' the girl said, 'but love has nothing to do with my visits to the Clothes Storeroom. I love you but you do not own me.'

He was cross but after a day he made up with Lisa Pomnenka because he couldn't bear being without her. In a peculiar way their relationship reversed and she became the stronger of the two.

He grew more involved each day but the more ardent he became the more distant the girl was, as if she were reluctant to give herself entirely. Alex Ehren felt that she was hiding something but he didn't know what it was. He grew jealous of Shashek, who assisted her with her painting, of the SS doctor who often kept her in his office overnight and of the seamstress, with whom she spent the hours, which he felt belonged to him.

The seamstress might have an ultimate intention with Lisa Pomnenka, he thought; a scheme possibly connected with her work for the German doctor.

'What does the woman want from you?' he asked, irritated, but she was evasive and laughed his question away.

'Women talk,' she said. 'She gives me material for my handicraft lessons.'

The ordinary prisoners were not allowed to enter the Clothes Storeroom. There were two sections in the block, one serving as storage for the prisoners' rags and the other, separated by a wooden partition, containing clothes looted from the newly arrived transports – articles that were sorted, packed and sent to Germany.

Clothes Capo Pavel Hock kept the rags on shelves, each kind in a separate heap – worn coats, trousers too long or too short to wear and tangled piles of shoes. Some of them were pathetic, decorated with mouldering fur and others still carrying a memory of elegance, though all of them were old and shabby from wear. They were marked with red paint, the trousers on the leg and the coats on the back.

Once a week they sent a bale of rags to be washed and when they came back, grey and crumpled and smelling of carbolic acid, they occasionally found a good shirt or a pair of leather shoes, which the Clothes Capo sold for bread or soup.

'It's not me who steals the bread,' he said, plagued by a bad conscience. 'If you live among wolves you cannot be a sheep.'

He was a political prisoner, a German Social Democrat, and not yet entirely depraved by camp life.

There was a cubicle to the left of the entrance and another to the right. One belonged to the Capo with the red triangle of a political convict on his tunic and in the other the seamstress mended prisoners' clothes, putting a patch over a patch on the torn elbows and knees. She worked on a sewing machine that Pavel Hoch repaired and oiled, but which was so ancient that a day or two later it would break down again. It still had the name and transport number of the original owner and he thought how difficult it must have been for him to carry the machine on the train. He remembered the crowded compartment, the overflowing bucket and the children who sat on the luggage in the corner. The owner of the sewing machine, he thought, might have been among the bodies he had seen along the bloodied path in the snow.

The children were always short of clothing. The boys tore their trousers, forgot their undershirts in the washroom and often sold an item for a piece of bread. There was hardly a week when Alex Ehren didn't have to take Bubenik or

Neugeboren, or one of the girls, to the Clothes Storeroom to beg for an article of clothing. He was not allowed to enter, but had to negotiate his deal like a beggar through the half-open door. Sometimes, however, when the Clothes Capo was away, Pavel Hoch let him in and they talked, perching on a pile of old blankets.

At one such visit Alex Ehren saw the girl. They were on the uppermost bunk in order to hide from the foreman and Lisa Pomnenka was unaware of their presence.

She came through the door, bent under the weight of her toolbox, looked around and disappeared into one of the white-washed cubicles. She didn't stay long and when she emerged, her box was light and empty. It was evening, almost the time of the roll call and there were no workers in the block. The girl opened the door a crack and hesitated before she slipped away and Alex Ehren wondered why she acted like a shadow and a thief.

What was the secret she shared with the seamstress? Lisa Pomnenka was open and outspoken, almost like a child, a maker of macramé patterns and a painter of flowers and birds. What was it that made her sneak in secretly and make sure to leave unnoticed? What did she carry in the toolbox that was heavy when she entered and empty when she left?

'Don't you know?' Pavel Hoch asked. 'Haven't you been friends for some time?'

'I don't know,' he replied. 'What is it?

'She carries bottles of kerosene and gasoline,' Pavel told him. 'We'll set the camp aflame before we go to the gas chambers.'

*

'Why didn't you tell me?' he reproached the girl in the evening.

He was irritated that she had a life of her own, matters of which he knew nothing, meetings with the underground people outside the camp and a mission as important as his own. He loved her but his love was possessive and he wanted her to belong to him only, boundlessly, unequivocally, and as a part of himself.

'It was my secret and not yours,' she said, and her eyes were like a mountain pool, blue and deep and cool.

# 7.

THERE WAS ALWAYS A CENTRAL PIECE AROUND WHICH THE ENTERTAIN-ment revolved. Once the pivot of the party was Aryeh's charade, another time it was a puppet show, a song or even a guessing game. The SS sentries stood at the far end of the Block and laughed and clapped their hands, although they only understood half the words. It was a strange relationship between the soldiers in their good green coats and sturdy boots, and the mangy children in their miserable rags. The German soldiers spoke to Himmelblau and even to the children, but they knew that when the time came, they would drive them into the trucks and impassively watch them die.

Many of the sentries were simple people – butchers, carpenters, farmers – but they knew that they belonged to the master race and the Jews were beings of a lower order, vermin, a cancer that had to be destroyed. Yet above all they obeyed their orders, and even when they laughed at the puppet theatre or the play, they wouldn't hesitate to inform on the children to the Secret Service. The instructors taught the children to be wary of the soldiers with the skull and crossed bones on their collars and hats. Whenever an SS man appeared on the Block, they changed the butt of a joke or improvised a new sentence. Even Fabian lowered his satanic German because one of the sentries might understand, grow angry and issue a punishment to the actors or the children – a curfew, withdrawal of food or even a beating. They learned to start a song or a dance or a German language drill in the middle of a forbidden school lesson. The boys had a rag ball and the girls a doll, which they had produced in one of Lisa Pomnenka's handicraft lessons, and at a moment's notice they switched to play. It was like a game, though it wasn't a game because the school, the newspaper and even the puppet theatre were like playing with fire.

The groups of children competed at their performances, which they planned and rehearsed on their bunks and in the corner of the Block.

When their turn came Alex Ehren held a consultation with his Maccabees and there was much shouting, excitement and disagreement. The girls wanted to perform a dance they had learned with Magdalena, and Bubenik and Lazik opted for cowboys and Indians, but in the end they compromised and agreed to stage Robinson Crusoe so the girls could dance and the boys disguise themselves as sailors and cannibals.

Alex Ehren hadn't seen much of Adam Landau since he had caught the boy with the golden marble, but now the brat was back – small, cocky and with the armband of a Capo's runner.

'We'll write a play together. Yes?' he said.

After the previous week's events Alex Ehren decided to punish him, to teach him a lesson, but when he looked at the child he was unable to refuse his eagerness. They sat together after school and Alex Ehren was again amazed by the child's gift for words and rhythm. He didn't know to read and yet he was like a fountain of imagery that spilled over in wasteful abundance and in two afternoons they produced a rhymed text.

It was a short play and when he read the draft to the children they wanted to change this and that and so they sat together and corrected and added until they were satisfied with the script.

Adam attended school without starting a fight or upsetting some girl's stool. He couldn't read with the others because he had forgotten the little he had learned, but he listened to the words and scribbled hooks and loops on a scrap of paper.

'The Capo will manage,' he said. 'I've told him I had to be an actor for a couple of days. Invited him to see the play. OK with you, Alex?'

There were two leading characters in the piece, Robinson Crusoe and Man Friday, but Adam wanted to be the ship's captain who defeated the pirates and sailed home with Robinson.

'A captain has a sword and a pistol, right?'

'A skipper should be armed.'

'To shoot bloody cannibals and pirates?'

'If necessary.'

'I'll sure make it necessary.'

They rehearsed on Alex Ehren's bunk because they didn't want anybody to know the tune, which Dezo Kovac had composed for the occasion. Lisa Pomnenka made Adam a captain's hat and used a tin of shoe polish to mask up Neugeboren as Man Friday, all naked except for a grass skirt around his waist. All the children had a part in the play. Three of the boys were sailors, two were cannibals, Eva was a parakeet, Majda Robinson's cat and the rest were animals in the forest.

There was not enough room for all of them on the small stage and they used the smokestack, which for a short while became a tropical island with Robinson Crusoe, Man Friday, the Captain, the cockatoo, the dog and the cat. Two children dressed up as baboons and sat in the tree Shashek had built from planks and a cardboard box. They were just eight years old and the play lasted only five or six minutes, but they transported their audience into another world and made them forget the camp.

Himmelblau had balked at the price Julius Abeles had demanded for a piece of foil, the red cloth and the feathers for the cockatoo. Yet when the play ended and the actors stood in a bunch on the platform, even he wasn't sorry any more. There were things, he thought, that were more important than a piece of bread from the orphaned parcels.

Everybody applauded and the actors repeated the refrain until the children knew the words and the tune. The hunchbacked Camp Capo pointed his cane at Adam, the captain with the cardboard sword and the tinsel hat on his shaven head.

'Damned brat,' he said in his booming voice. 'Who'd have believed the brat is an actor?'

The three SS soldiers rested their guns against their chests and clapped, and even the Priest, the shifty Block Senior, twisted his mouth and smiled. And then all the three hundred and seventy-two children with their instructors and matrons and youth assistants, the Camp Capo and even the locksmith, who came from the Main Camp to see the show, joined in and sang the words Alex Ehren and Adam had written for the play:

*Oh Robinson, oh Robinson*
*Leave your island*
*Leave your sorrow*
*There is for you*
*A happy morrow*
*When you board*
*The homebound ship*

Some of the sentries may have understood the words but only the inmates, the children and the youth assistants felt their inwardness. For they knew that Robinson's island was not a faraway wild place, but the island of Birkenau, and the ship that came to his rescue was the flicker of hope they carried within their despair. They knew that they were condemned to death and that the date of their execution had been written in their files. And yet, despite their utter exposure to death, they harboured a hope, a spark, an intimation of a miracle. For one it was an escape, for another an uprising and for yet another his belief that they would be exchanged for German prisoners of war. It was like walking in darkness and seeing the reflection of a star on the water. Or, as Dezo Kovac the believer, had put it during the evening:

'Evil is the space from which God withdrew. It is like a pocket empty of God's essence. But even in the void there remains the memory of his presence. If you believe you can survive. One has to learn from my loyal brother Job.'

'Your brother Job?' said Hynek Rind. 'Your brother Job wasn't in Birkenau. No selections, no starvation, no chimney and all that. Didn't he get everything back with interest? His home, his goats, his bank account and even his children? I would gladly switch places with him.'

However, the memory of the play remained and the girls asked Lisa Pomnenka to draw Robinson's island on the wall.

'I can't,' she said. 'There is no ocean in the middle of the meadow.'

She was behind with the wall because Dr Mengele kept her more and more occupied with his diagrams.

He wanted to move her into the Women's Camp but she begged him to let her finish the wall.

'The wall?' he asked and frowned behind his glasses. 'There will be other walls. One day you'll move anyway.'

He didn't know about her dealings with the seamstress and let her stay in the Family Camp.

The children under the age of ten lived with their mothers on the women's bunks. In the morning they came to the Block where they played, attended the clandestine lessons, had their meals and returned to their sleeping quarters late in the afternoon. There were boys who worked, like Adam Landau for the Camp Capo, as runners for a Block Senior, for the Registrar, or as apprentices with craftsmen where they got better food.

The kitchen helpers had a tame raven, which they taught to speak three words. The bird sat on their shoulder and picked their ear until they fed it a piece of potato or a crumb of stale bread. The orderlies had a privileged position; they were better dressed and supported their families with bits of food they stole from their masters. Yet even the runners and the apprentices came to the Children's Block for company and a game of marbles.

It was only by chance that Alex Ehren learned about the source of Adam's golden bead. One day a Polish Capo accosted him in front of the Children's Block. He had never seen the man before and was surprised when he poked his shoulder with his cane.

'Where is the runner?' He looked at the children and frowned. 'The Camp Capo's boy. Find the brat. Move, man, move.'

Adam hadn't been on the Block for several days and he wondered why the man needed the child.

'I've made a deal,' he said and winked. 'Agnes is the name.' He looked at Alex Ehren and narrowed his eyes. 'The little one is her go-between.'

It took Alex Ehren a while to grasp Adam Landau's part in the deal and he was horrified by its implication.

Half the inmates in the Czech Family Camp were women. They were starved, dressed in rags and often infested with vermin that bred in the dampness. Yet some of them, like flowers in a swamp, kept their beauty, poise and femininity even in the nether world of Birkenau. They were different from the Gypsies because they were considered well bred and their heads were not shaven. There were men in the Family Camp – their husbands, friends and former lovers – but they were not intent on their wives' bodies but rather on the midday soup, which was a watershed between life and death.

Yet the privileged – those who stole from the prisoners' food, those who dressed in warm jackets and boots and were not hungry for bread – lusted for women. The camp was a terrible place, a desert and a wilderness, lost and forsaken. It was life at its starkest and most basic, a world almost reptilian in its cruelty and struggle for survival. An intimate meeting with a woman was the memory of a lost home, of a wife and family.

For a woman to find a rich lover was a turn of good luck. Some of the concubines were made Block Seniors or Registrars and escaped the cold, the hunger and the slave labour outside the barracks. Adam Landau was an ideal go-between because as a child he could visit the Women's Block and arrange a meeting at the Camp Capo's cubicle. At first Alex Ehren was taken aback by the boy's corruption and he spoke about it with Marta Felix. She was the oldest among the women instructors, an intellectual and a confidante.

'We are hungry and have nothing to sell. The only thing a woman can offer is her body. If she finds anybody who wants to buy. Yes,' she said, 'some women use their children as go-betweens. You cannot cross a river and remain dry. Good and bad are relative matters. What is important is to stay alive, because once you are dead nothing matters any more.'

'It's immoral.'

'Is it? Should Agnes wait until her belly caves in and her legs turn into sticks and her breasts wither away like dry leaves? Moral? What is moral? To die and be thrown behind the block?'

'Majda will find out. Maybe she knows already. What will she think about her mother?'

'She will understand. Or she won't. What matters is life. Morality comes later.'

'And … you?' He was embarrassed to ask.

'No, I don't sleep with anybody,' she said. She held out her hand to touch his. 'Not because I am so chaste or moral but because nobody has asked me.' She paused and looked at the pained face of the young man. 'I know,' she said, 'you think of Lisa Pomnenka and about love. She may be as much in love with you as you are with her. But don't be a fool; if there is a choice between love and life, she'll choose life.'

He was angry, and he recoiled from Marta whom he now felt was coarse, cold and unfeeling.

Twice a week the children visited the old and the ill. The older children went one by one but Majda and Eva went together because it was easier to manage in pairs. They took the old woman's bowl and washed it under the tap, turned over her mattress and even dragged her for a walk around the block. And when they returned they spoke of their visit, because even those whose life seemed worthless had a story to tell. Some of the dying had been important, famous or rich, or had lived a thrilling life. Sometimes when Alex Ehren heard a name, he remembered that the person had written a book or had been an actor or musician, and he was surprised at his present wretchedness. It often happened that on their next visit the children found an empty bunk, because the old person had died during the night, but they had grown accustomed to death and weren't particularly alarmed. Alex Ehren made them draw pictures of the old people, because he felt that what was brought to the surface wouldn't turn into nightmares in their sleep. He kept the children busy with their small, daily matters – a game, a story and their weekly competition – to shield them from the dragons of fear. They were scared of separation, of pain and of transports to a new camp, but his wards who were still very young weren't afraid of death and spoke without terror about the old people who had died.

When Neugeboren turned eight each of the children gave up a slice of their evening bread ration, which the girls spread with beetroot jam and stacked like a cake. They lifted Neugeboren on a chair, once for each year and one more time for the next. Alex Ehren had a bit of foil from the captain's hat and they made the boy a tinsel crown and let him eat half of the cake. Aunt Miriam added a handful of sweets from the undelivered parcels and in the afternoon they sang birthday songs and played games. Himmelblau came around and shook hands with the boy and then his matron and the other teachers came over and all said something funny or encouraging to Neugeboren, the boy who had smuggled to Fredy his last bowl of pudding.

'Next year,' Beran promised, 'you'll do natural history.'

Neugeboren was too young to join Beran's group, where the children learned about animals and plants which they had never seen. He was curious and restless and always out for adventure. He had been Man Friday in the play and Fabian spoke to him in his best satanic voice rolling his r's and hissing his s's.

'Many happy returns, my little brother. We actors have to stick together.'

The games, competitions and birthday parties were modest and simple. They were like pebbles in a brook or grass along a path, scarce and unpretentious. In a different place or at another time they would have carried weight. Yet here their sing-alongs, their weekly performances and even the visits to the old people, made them look forward to the next day. Their reading and writing and the school routine were not only what they were on the surface, but a safeguard against perdition too.

The children spoke about the days and months to come as if the Family Camp and the Children's Block were to last forever … as if it was a solid base on which they could build their lives. Next year, thought Bubenik, I'll be in Fabian's class or take up carving lessons with Shashek, and Aryeh, who was in the senior group, hoped that Himmelblau would let him teach Hebrew when the school year was over. Even the instructors spoke about next year, not only for the children's sake but also for their own; without hope and pretence they wouldn't have been able to live.

The raven, which the cooks kept as a pet, was the only bird in the camp. The blackbirds, the starlings and even the common sparrows had died on the electrified fence and the skies above the blocks were empty and barren. It was queer and unnatural to live in a world without birds, and Lisa Pomnenka painted their winged shadows on her sky. She also painted them into the crowns of the birches and the birds perched there, blue, yellow and red-breasted, and the children pointed at them and learned their names. They were not real birds, just as the meadow was not real but only an imaginary stretch of grass, but the illusion and the make-believe kept them above water.

Some of the children became corrupted like Adam, who turned into a pimp, others, like Majda, wet their beds and sucked their thumbs, and others cheated at marbles and lied to get another shirt. They were imperfect like the lopsided trees and the fake flowers and the malformed blackbirds on the wall. The Block was only a substitute for life and Alex Ehren and Fabian were poor, mediocre teachers. Nor was Lisa Pomnenka an accomplished artist, but they did what had to be done because there was nobody else to do their task better. The Block was like a leaking boat, in constant danger of sinking. And yet it sailed on, limping and keeling to one side, but as long as it stayed afloat the children felt safe and at home.

Neither was there shame. Each morning Alex Ehren took his children to the washroom where they saw men and women in their nakedness. At first the boys were curious about the women's breasts, their bellies and their thighs. The little girls giggled and turned their heads at the sight of men's private parts, but by and by they got accustomed to the lack of privacy and weren't curious any more. There were young women in the washroom, and Alex Ehren ached for Lisa Pomnenka whom he loved. He wanted to feel her body against his, sweet and firm and yielding. The weather was better now and though the earth was still muddy there was no frost at night and at noon the sun was warm.

He learned to cope with the children, some of whom could read whole sentences from a book he borrowed from Dasha's library. Adam was away with Jagger most of the time and he conducted his lessons with relative success. The boy slept on the doorstep of the Capo's cubicle, but occasionally he did appear on the Block, well dressed and with the armband of a runner. Alex Ehren didn't know how to speak with the brat. Was he still one of the Block children or did he belong among the privileged, who were beyond Block regulations? Sometimes the boy stayed to play marbles or a game of tug o' war or to watch a performance, but he wouldn't attend any of the lessons. He was relieved when the boy left because he was like a rotten apple in a barrel, and he started a fight or broke up a lesson or teased the girls until they cried. He obeyed no one, came and went whenever he pleased and didn't let off until he had caused some mischief. When Alex Ehren cornered him for a talk, he laughed in his face.

'Who needs reading and writing?' he sneered. 'I work for the Capo. Why should I come back among the little children?'

He was a pimp, cocky and thoroughly depraved. The food and the fine clothes, which he showed off, made him a leader and he dragged Lazik into his evil adventures.

One day Alex Ehren caught him in the privy block.

The latrine was a terrible place; murky and ominous, it stank of excrement and the quicklime that the Cleaning Commando threw into the cesspool. The prison food caused diarrhoea and the inmates waited in long, painful queues for an empty place in the privy. There were six concrete rows in the barracks, each with sixty-six seats, but the holes were soiled and swarming with maggots and the ground was muddy with spilled urine. The SS sentries never stepped in and thus the latrines were a good place for barter in stolen goods and whispered talks about the mutiny. The block had male and female sections, which were separated by a strip of jute.

The screen was so narrow that it hid only the middle part of the body.

It was noon when most of the inmates were at work and the latrine was empty. The two boys crouched in ambush until Adam saw a victim for his prank. She was young, almost a girl, with a prominent nose and the dark face of a Sephardi.

Adam and Lazik followed her stealthily at their side of the screen like two thieves. When she lifted her skirt the two brats broke out into shrieks and threw stones into the cesspit. They used language so lewd and obscene that Alex Ehren barely understood. Yet he knew that the words dealt with excrement and human procreation. The young woman tried frantically to arrange her soiled clothes, her coat, skirt and her underwear, yet the two urchins followed her along the partition, hooting insults and obscenities.

'Go away,' exclaimed Alex Ehren. 'Go away this instant.'

He was angry and would have beaten them had they not escaped through the rear door and along the fence. He wanted to punish them, to mete out some kind of reprisal on the boys, but Adam worked for the Camp Capo and was beyond any rule or punishment.

By the end of April Lisa Pomnenka finished weaving the rope. It was rough and strong but at the same time flexible like a live snake.

'What kind of game will it be used for?'

He had never told her of his assignment but sometimes he wondered how much she knew from the seamstress or from the people who gave her the bottles of kerosene. She looked so innocent and fragile that she might have been mistaken for a child or for one of the youth assistants. Yet he knew that she had a will of her own and that under her smooth face she was strong and determined … probably stronger than himself.

'What if I fail?' he asked Felsen. 'What happens if I don't manage to cast the iron over the wires?'

'It doesn't matter,' he answered. 'Somebody else will take over.'

Alex realised that Felsen was talking about his death as if he were speaking about a stone thrown into water. He knew that in the context of the mutiny his life was unimportant and yet he was taken aback at Felsen's indifference. The communist saw only the goal and the end result; the fate of the individual was of no importance.

'It's the only life I have,' said Alex Ehren.

'Yes—' Felsen pulled his head into his collar '—we all have only one.' He shrugged and looked at Alex Ehren. 'If you are afraid I'll find a substitute. Better quit now than later.'

He was full of suspicion of the young people who spoke about Palestine but were blind to the needs of the present.

'We'll make our revolution when we come to Palestine,' they said. But what they really wanted was just to talk and postpone their decision. He thought about Fredy, who was supposed to blow the whistle but lost his nerve and died of too many sleeping pills.

'No,' said Alex Ehren hastily to Felsen. 'It's what I asked for. No need to look for somebody else.'

He gave the rope to Pavel Hoch, who hid it, together with the bottles of kerosene and petrol, among the ragged prisoners' clothes.

Sometimes the iron anchor emerged in his dreams. It was an inanimate thing and yet it moved and wriggled like an animal. The room was filled with Mengele's medical instruments, the spatulas, scalpels, gauges and probes. It was eminently urgent to extricate the anchor from under the bed and to start the mutiny, but the harder he tried the heavier and more unwieldy it became.

'Run,' he said to Lisa Pomnenka, 'run and save yourself.' But she wouldn't budge and waited for him to move the iron.

He knew of the SS doctor's operations. He would cut into a woman's belly and excise her organs, leaving her screaming in pain. The girl was on the bed now, white, exposed and lovely as a spring morning, but he was unable to lift the anchor and save her. He tugged and tore but his hands were helpless against the thing of iron. He cried out and Beran, his bunk-mate, shook him by the shoulder.

'I had a dream,' Alex Ehren murmured sitting up with a start.

'What dream?'

'It doesn't matter.' He fell angrily back on his mattress.

The dream haunted him for several days and he avoided the eyes of the girl, of Beran, Fabian and Felsen, as if he had indeed betrayed their trust and their chance to stay alive. There were still two months left and he was scared of the running time, though he also hoped for a miracle.

The Germans kept the inmates in darkness about their future. They promised one thing and did another in a cruel merry-go-round of hope and frustration. They played a game with the prisoners like little boys who trap a bird and enjoy its attempts to get free. They followed no rules, no laws and no commitments and that made the SS sentries, the carpenters, the butchers and the farm hands feel godlike and free from their own human bondage.

The Children's Block was the last in the row of sixteen barracks and there was a piece of grassy ground between the wooden wall and the fence. By the end of April the ground sprouted pale grass and some of the inmates, the most starved, who looked like cranes, collected dandelion leaves. Their stomachs could not hold the weed and they fell ill and died.

When there was no rain Magdalena conducted her gym lessons in the open and taught the girls a dance. She offered to take the boys also but they refused and sulked.

'Dancing is for girls,' said tiny Neugeboren. 'What good will it do if I dance?'

The boys were eager to show their pluck because they admired the brutal force and insensibility of the Capos and the Block Seniors.

The gym teacher beat the rhythm on a piece of corrugated iron and the girls moved their arms, walked on tiptoe and turned around with the tune they hummed.

'Now we are birds flying over a lake,' said Magdalena, and the little girls flapped their arms in pretended flight.

'And now we are bears and amble through the wood. And now we are bees who gather honey, and now flowers that bend their petals in the wind.'

The children had no recollection of birds flying over a lake and they had never seen a bear, though they had seen a flower or a stray bee in the ghetto. They danced not according to what they remembered but to what they imagined to be the flight of a bird, the ambling of a bear or the bending head of a flower, and yet their movements were true and graceful. It was strange, thought Alex Ehren, that their imagination was almost as good as reality but, then again, wasn't the entire Children's Block imagination and make-believe? It was a fiction, an absurdity and a denial of logic. The teachers, the matrons and the instructors together with the children lived in a small, closed world outside time, which, like a child in its mother's womb, fed not on what was now but on what had been in the past.

The boys wouldn't dance and Alex Ehren took them aside to do push-ups and calisthenics. At the end of the lesson they ran around the Block until they were tired and panting. He still exercised with his rock and he could lift the stone three times in a row. He practised every day until the gym teacher noticed.

'Want to win a prize in weightlifting?' Magdalena didn't know but she might have guessed his purpose, because in some way or another they were all involved.

There were other triads on the Block and Felsen talked to strange men in Himmelblau's cubicle. He wondered how many people in other barracks were involved – ten, fifty, a thousand?

The hospital orderly certainly knew about the anchor hidden in the spare room, Pavel Hoch kept the kerosene bottles among bales of old rags and the seamstress, who directed Lisa Pomnenka, must have been a pivot of the plot. Alex Ehren thought of the girl who could be caught every day and his heart skipped a beat.

In the last weeks he felt strong and alive. His running, the push-ups and the rock lifting made him aware of his body and when he held hands with the girl and touched her shoulder he was consumed by fire.

The thought of mutiny was constantly at the back of his mind. The idea of fighting the Germans was like a pendulum of a clock; it was at the same time a cause of fear and of exhilaration. For five years he had been conditioned to obey German regulations. The Germans were the conquerors of the world. First it was Austria then Czechoslovakia, then Poland and later Belgium, France and Holland and even Russia, until they ruled over all of Europe. There was no way but to bend and wait until the storm blew over.

At the very beginning, when the Germans had occupied his city, Alex Ehren had tried to retain his self-respect but the longer he lived under Nazi rule the lower he sank. First he was expelled from his school, then his family was robbed of their possessions and home. He was forbidden to use a train, attend a theatre or a concert, to own a carpet, a painting or a fur coat. The Germans closed streets and squares to him and the only green place he could visit was the Jewish cemetery with its stately tombs, overgrown with ivy. And then when he had nothing more left, he was shipped to the ghetto and from there to Birkenau to be put to death. Why was it that they accepted the Germans as masters of their lives, the lawful confiscators and executioners, as if they were a preordained cosmic phenomenon? Were the Germans perhaps the Satanic principle of the Book of Job against which there was no recourse? It was difficult to defy God but it took seven times more courage to stand up against Satan.

And there were questions.

'Why do they hate us?' asked the children. 'Why do they want us dead?'

They were more curious to know than scared.

It was a hydra of a question and each time he cut off one head there was another that grew in its stead.

'I used to live in Germany,' said Himmelblau. 'My uncle was a school teacher in a village on the Mosel. The farmers called him Herr Professor and at vintage time they presented him with a basket of grapes. I played hide-and-seek with the German boys and when the game was over we had coffee and cake in my aunt's garden. Yes, we had fights as boys do, but they never called me a Jew. On Sundays when the other boys went to church, we took a walk among the vineyards, and though I was tempted to steal a bunch of grapes, I never did. Solid German honesty. I never harmed anybody, paid my taxes and drank beer in moderation. And saved. Was like everybody in town. Strict rules and order. But so were they all, my schoolmates and their parents. Decent people. Why would they want me dead? Maybe it's a virus on their brain. An illness like mumps.'

'If it is,' said Marta Felix, who knew history, 'it has been endemic in Europe for a long time. During the Crusades the knights stormed the ghettoes of Frankfurt and Worms and Regensburg long before they laid siege to Acre and Jerusalem. Practice makes perfect, they said, and the Jews were an easy target because they were their neighbours and were forbidden to carry arms. The plague? Whenever the pestilence flared up they accused us of poisoning the wells and of practising black witchcraft. They didn't notice that the Jews in their overcrowded ghettoes died even faster than they themselves. Whenever there was drought or flood or an earthquake, disasters brought about by nature or by man, it was the Jews who were blamed and they paid for it with their lives. Nothing has changed even today. Doesn't Hitler blame the Jews for starting his wars?'

She laughed angrily and went on.

'Rape and pillage and burning of the Jews has always been a pastime because there isn't a better scapegoat for failure than a Jew. The Jews are different. They pray in a secret language, they eat different food and obey their own laws. And if, like in our times, the Jews look like everybody else, eat the same food and have forgotten the secret language of their prayers, the Germans make them wear the yellow star to separate them from others. With one difference. In the Middle Ages they burned us alive and today they choke us by gas first.'

Marta Felix's voice was bitter because there was no sense or reason in their suffering and death.

'There are good dead and there are bad dead,' she said after a while. 'There are dead who die for a reason. Trees die and out of their rotten wood grows a new forest. Animals die to feed other living things, vermin and bacteria. Old people die to make room for their children. But we—' she looked at her friends '—we are the bad dead because we die for nothing.'

She paused and scoffed.

'Not even for an illusion like God's greater glory. Not for king, fatherland or an idea.'

There was silence and Dezo Kovac moved his hand in a narrow gesture.

'Maybe it's their religion.' He hesitated. 'The Nazis brought back their pagan gods. Thor and Wotan and Freya.'

'Most of the Germans are Christians,' said Himmelblau.

'There is hardly a village without a church and the boys of my youth attended Mass every Sunday. Christianity teaches love. Religion has nothing to do with Birkenau and the killing of children.'

'Maybe it does,' said Dezo Kovac, rocking forwards and backwards as if in Jewish prayer. 'It is a matter of balance. There is the Holy Trinity – God the Father, God the Son and the Holy Spirit.'

'Yes,' said Hynek Rind, 'but what has all this to do with hating the Jews?'

'Isn't it obvious? The Holy Trinity is a triangle. But a triangle is incomplete and can be toppled and turned over. There has to be another angle to give it a firm basis and make it rooted in space. Another angle will change the triangle into a square and the Holy Trinity into a Holy Quadrinity and thus make it whole.'

'The Jews, you said. Aren't we talking about the Jews?'

'We are,' said Dezo Kovac, his mouth twisting into a sneer. 'What is the missing angle? The lower angle and the lower base? The Antichrist principle in the Christian universe, hell, darkness and the Devil. Don't the villagers believe that Jews have horns and a tail? Don't they speak of the Jewish smell, the *foetor Judaeorum*? And didn't the Jews deny and kill the Messiah, the living God?'

'If the Germans get rid of us, where is their whole? Don't they need to close the circle?'

'Not really,' said Dezo Kovac, touching his face with the back of his hand. 'We may die in the flesh and prevail as a principle. The dinosaurs died out a million years ago and survived in our fairy tales and nightmares as monsters and dragons. Destroy the Jews and the world will be paradise again.'

'Too simple,' said Hynek Rind. 'They can't believe such nonsense.'

'Can't they? It's so easy to see the world in black and white.' He looked around in silent despair.

'The Germans collect Jewish religious articles, to show their children the remnants of an extinct race. I know,' he said, 'because they made me work at the museum. Each day came a carload of Hebrew scrolls and candelabra from the communities that had been shipped to Birkenau. They looted the empty synagogues and I carried the books, the prayer shawls and the silver lamps into the vaults of an old house in Prague. They destroyed the Jews but kept the principle alive.'

He stopped and his voice trailed into a memory.

'When I was a child I saw the skeleton of a dinosaur. How glad I was that no monsters roamed the backyards of my childhood and survived only in my dreams.'

Even in the camp there was spring. In the morning, when they returned from the washroom, Majda pulled her thumb out of her mouth and pointed to the sky.

'Birds,' she said. They stopped in the middle of the road and lifted their heads to the seams of the clouds. There was a flock of birds, geese probably, flying in an arrow-shaped formation toward the north. And as they watched there was yet another arrow, larger and sharper and lower, so that the children could see their flapping wings and long necks.

They had never before seen migrating birds and later when the geese were gone and they sat in their stall, Alex Ehren played a spring game with them.

'In spring there are flowers,' said Eva. 'Little cats are born.'

'The ice on the rivers melts.'

'In spring it is warm,' said Lazik.

The boys took off their shirts and ran in the sunshine half-naked. After the long winter their bodies were thin and white, but otherwise, in that moment, they looked like ordinary children.

# 8.

PAVEL HOCH LENT ALEX EHREN A BROKEN MIRROR AND HE looked at his face. He had grown accustomed to the looks of others, but he was taken aback to see himself in the piece of glass. Was it indeed he, the haggard stranger that gazed at him from the mirror? His nose and ears protruded from his face and his eyebrows had risen almost to the top of his forehead. Lisa Pomnenka had knitted a cap for him but it was dirty and the tassel shabby from prolonged wear. He washed each morning but he had slept in his shirt since he had arrived in the camp and it stuck out from his jacket like a piece of refuse. The Block Warden shaved the inmates once a week, on Sundays, but his blade was blunt and Alex Ehren left the chair with his face bruised and bleeding. His stubble grew and by the end of the week he looked like a vagabond and a blackguard.

Sometimes he wondered how the girl felt about his face, his clothes, his grimy shirt. How could she love him with the countenance of a murderer, neglected and dressed like a scarecrow?

'Yes, your clothes are funny and if I was in a different place I would laugh. Your trousers are too short for your legs and your jacket smells. The canvas of your clogs is torn and you drag your feet so as not to lose them.'

He didn't know that she had noticed so much and he was ashamed of his appearance.

'And yet—' her eyes were blue and bright like fresh water '—I still love you.'

Next day Alex Ehren sold half of his bread ration for a razor blade and shaved even in the middle of the week. He was pleased when Lisa Pomnenka commented on his better looks.

Each day he was more attracted to the girl. She wasn't beautiful or soft and her movements were sudden and angular but she had the appeal of a squirrel or a mountain flower. Sometimes she was capricious and stubborn but on another day she agreed with whatever Alex Ehren said. He touched her fingers one by one and held her wrist to feel the beat of her heart. He ran his hand over her black hair and brushed the softness of her eyes. She had knitted herself a grey pullover in which she looked young and fragile like a child.

She was careless and he was concerned for her life. Day after day she left the camp and returned with a box full of inflammables but didn't seem to mind the risk. Once she forgot to deliver the bottles and he was shocked to find the contraband – ominous, dark and gathering dust – next to her toolbox and the rickety ladder. He touched the bottles with enmity and fear.

'How long will you carry them? Will it never stop?'

'Not until Felsen tells me. I can't refuse, can I?'

'No,' he said, and swallowed. 'I don't suppose you can.'

He didn't know how many prisoners were involved in the underground movement, yet once they set fire to the straw the whole camp would be caught in the uprising, those who knew and those who hadn't known. It was wrong, he thought, to take advantage of the girl who was credulous and didn't see the danger.

There was little time left and they would soon lose each other. Whatever happened in June – their death, a miracle or the uprising – it would possibly tear them apart forever. He put his arm around her shoulder. It was good to belong and to own and to meet in the touch of their bodies. He wanted to protect her and to save her from suffering and danger. He felt that he was the wiser and should be the stronger of the two and he was about to ask her to stop carrying the bottles. He was unhappy whenever she left to work for the SS physician, yet he didn't know what was better and what was worse, because the diagrams she drew for the German doctor might save her from death. Hadn't he reclaimed the Jewish physicians, the pharmacist and the nurses from the September transport? The awareness of loss and parting made him love the girl desperately, until his love turned into almost physical pain.

By the first days of May Lisa Pomnenka had completed about half of the wall. She had no overall concept, no grand scheme, and she worked from her whim and intuition.

'What will it be today?' He was curious in the morning but she laughed and shook her head.

'How should I know? I haven't yet climbed on the ladder.'

She went up the rickety ladder, which Shashek had hammered together from bits and pieces and which always needed another nail or rung, and she dipped her brush in the paint. She paused and let the idea float through her mind until it took root and she was ready to start. She drew the shape and then filled it with colour, light and shade. She painted a bunch of bluebells, a copse and the sky with a flock of birds. Another day she painted the wooden railing and the prominent red geraniums that spilled almost to the ground. She didn't know beforehand what she would produce, and in the evening she was often surprised at what she had created during the day. She moved with small, birdlike gestures, was happy one moment and sad in the next, and lived by the hour rather than by her head.

In the following weeks she had more time for the children because the SS doctor was busy with the Hungarian transports.

The Hungarians arrived, three trains a day, on the platform on the other side of the fence beyond the Children's Block. Sometimes the SS officers summoned the camp orchestra and the musicians played 'Marinarella' and 'Roll Out the Barrel' while the deportees were marched to their deaths. The children watched the locomotives, the wagons, the frightened people and the Capos that beat them into marching formations. Each day there were ten thousand fresh deportees, sometimes even twelve – men in large and stiff Sunday suits, women with kerchiefs printed with roses and children in oversize coats that were meant to last for another year.

There was an air of urgency on the platform and everything happened very fast – the disembarkation, the transition from darkness into light, the dogs, the Capos and the separation of the families. The dazed people rushed here and there looking for a husband, a child, an old relative or a basket with the last bit of food. There was no time and as soon as the prisoners were gone, their handbags and bundles were torn open and the contents built into mounds of bread, preserves, cheese and smoked meat. The commandos piled up the toys, the feather pillows and the clothes that the new arrivals had left scattered behind. All that was done in haste, at a trot – the descent, the looting of the luggage and even the sweeping of the platform. There was always a new train waiting on the rails and more villagers were processed and marched away. It was a colossal murder, a miracle of organisation, a crime brilliant and demented.

Alex Ehren tried to keep track of the numbers and counted a hundred thousand, two hundred thousand but then he stopped counting the dead because there seemed to be no end to the Hungarian Jews, who continued arriving in a perpetual sequence of trains.

Magdalena kept the children inside the Block. In the past there had been trains with new arrivals once a day, three in a week, and she tried not to take notice. She made the children look the other way and she beat the rhythm on her piece of tin and made the little girls move like birds and flowers and butterflies. She pretended that there were no transports and no marching convicts, but now with the avalanche of people, she was unable to pretend any more and she left the grassy stretch. It was wrong, she felt, a blasphemy, to let the girls lift their arms in gentle movements with so much horror on the other side of the fence. She conducted her gym lessons at the rear end of the Block where Shashek repaired chairs and produced toys for the kindergarten children. Yet her pupils wouldn't stay cooped up inside the Block, and when they heard the engine and the clang of metal, they ran to watch the trains, the people and the unloading of the luggage. They also came to listen to the music, because in the middle of the bedlam, the cries and the barking of dogs, the orchestra played its tunes until there were no more people and the platform was empty and ready for the new contingent. The children stood at the fence and the many transports made them indifferent to human misery. They asked no questions now.

There was nothing to ask, thought Alex Ehren, because they knew.

The Hungarian Jews were marched away and in the afternoon the chimney started belching smoke, black, dense and heavy and at night the sky was red with the glow of fire. The furnaces couldn't manage so many bodies and the Special Commando dug trenches, poured kerosene over the dead and burned them in smouldering heaps. The smoke wouldn't rise and the whole Birkenau complex, the Family Camp, the women's and men's compounds, the Gypsy Camp, the Kanada Blocks and even the SS garrison barracks were darkened by the cloud. It rolled over the landscape in wreaths and when the wind changed the smoke came back and the prisoners coughed with its charred sweetness in their mouths.

And with the smoke fell also the fine ash, which settled like snow on their hands and faces. Alex Ehren's eyes watered and when he ate he felt the gritty grains between his teeth. He knew what the dust was and his stomach turned and revolted, yet he couldn't stop eating because the soup was the only food he would get during the day and without it he would have starved to death. There was nothing to ask and nothing to answer, because even some of those who refused to believe in the gas chambers couldn't be blind to the killing of the Hungarians.

Yet even now – in the middle of the hecatomb, five hundred thousand, six hundred thousand dead, the smoke and the nightly fires in the sky – there were prisoners who wouldn't give up hope.

'It won't happen to us.' Hynek Rind shook his head. 'The Germans know that we Czechs are different. Assimilated and hardly religious. Why else the Family Camp? Why else keep the children alive?' He looked around for support. 'The Hungarians are practising Jews; they pray, study in Jewish schools, know the Talmud and whatnot. They speak the Yiddish lingo. We are modern, eat sausages with sauerkraut like the Germans. What is Jewish about us? Look at me. Even my birth certificate doesn't say I am a Jew. Without religion, that's what I am.'

'Yes,' said Beran, 'you don't speak Yiddish. And you are what you say. Modern, Czech, without religion. But the Germans have decided that you are a Jew. And that's what matters. There is a woman who was a nun. Had taken the vows and lived in a convent. One day she was called up like any other Jew. A nun, a bride of Jesus Christ. Because her father came from Jewish stock.'

Around this time Beran started to compile his volume of verses. He had always been fond of poetry and he knew many poems by heart – ballads, sonnets and lyrical poetry of love and nature. The instructors invited him to recite to the children and the older groups copied the verses and learned them by heart. He soon ran out of his repertoire and began collecting poems he and other instructors, matrons and even the children knew, and wrote them down in a booklet.

He got hold of used paper, which was still usable on the reverse side. He perambulated among the stalls, clumsy, awkward and slightly bent forward, and noted down each poem or a stanza or only several lines, according to the person's memory. It was remarkable, he thought, how much they remembered from their school days, because with one verse there came another – Czech, German, French or even Latin, a quotation or a part of a poem – which flowed back into the mind from the past.

'Why all the trouble?' asked Marta Felix. 'Is it not enough to remember?'

'It helps,' he said and smiled.

'With what?'

'You read a poem and you are transported to another place. You transcend yourself or you escape. I do what I can.' He shrugged. 'I can't stop the Hungarian transports but I can collect poems.'

In the evening Beran took the pages to Sonia and they held hands and read the poems together, leaning on the wall. The book of verses grew thicker and the teachers borrowed it and read it aloud to the children. They didn't understand French or Greek but listened to the fall, the rhythm and the music of the words.

Not all the Hungarians died. From each transport Dr Mengele selected the strongest, who were then sent to slave labour. Sometimes he pointed at one of the marching people and a scribe added the man's name to the list of labourers. He also saved identical twins, hunchbacks, cripples and a group of midgets he needed for his research.

One morning the adjoining camp was filled with naked women. There was no shame in the camp and yet the sight of so many female bodies was beautiful and disturbing. The girls stood in intense rows, young, nubile and with their heads and private parts shaven. There were ten thousand of them and they shuddered, pressing their bellies against other women's backs in an attempt to keep warm and hide their nakedness. They shivered in the morning chill, and though Alex Ehren was embarrassed, he couldn't stop looking at them because even in their wretchedness they were graceful and feminine. He saw the elegance of their necks, the proud curve of their breasts with the dark nipples stiffened by the cold, their strong thighs and their fertile groins.

They were like a herd of deer, shy and appealing and with their eyes large and dark under the domes of their shaved heads. They were kept in formation by female Capos, sturdy and brutal, and by a bunch of armed SS women warders in green uniforms. There was a bizarre difference between the two groups – the gross, peasant-like guards and the naked maidens, who in their helplessness looked exquisite and sensuous.

Two of the girls broke the row and when a Capo chased them back with a rubber hose, the rest fluttered in fear and called out in high confused voices, '*Lanok, lanok*, lasses, lasses,' to show them to which row they belonged. It was a spectacle bitter and sweet, cruel and delicate, a mixture of senseless hatred and squandered love.

The children had finished washing and put on their ragged shirts but Alex Ehren lingered, unable to turn away. Some of the naked girls noticed the children and stretched out their arms.

'Children, children,' they cried, appalled by the presence of children in the camp. Other groups took up the words and the whole compound, the multitude of naked girls, moved like seaweed in their direction.

'*Kis gyerekek*, little children,' they sang and their Hungarian voices were like the sounds of birds, falling, sad and reedy. Some of the girls cried and their tears fell on their bare breasts, necks and bellies.

Why did they cry? Alex Ehren had learned not to feel sorry for himself and for the children. Their misfortunes descended on them unrelentingly, like the oncoming winter, first one thing and then another until at the end they were robbed of everything and shipped to Birkenau to die. They were like a tree in autumn with one leaf falling and then the next and then many, until the whole tree was bare. Even here, in the hopeless reality of Birkenau, Alex Ehren needed Pavel Hoch's shard of mirror to see his face and the naked Hungarian girls to show him the misery of his existence.

The girls were cold and hungry. The SS sentries didn't allow them to enter their blocks and the girls stood in front of the barracks with their hands covering their breasts and groins.

The Family Camp inmates were utterly poor. They didn't own anything, for even the pockets of their tattered clothes were sewn fast to prevent them from hiding contraband. And yet, in the run of five months, each of them, even the lowest labourer on the ditch commando, had acquired a fistful of possessions – a piece of cloth to wipe his face, a foot rag, a shaving blade, a length of string or a speck of tobacco dust. During the day they kept their assets inside their shirts and at night under their heads to guard them against thieves.

They were also utterly hungry. They had starved for so long that their hunger couldn't be stilled by a piece of bread or a bowl of beet soup, because it was fathomless and all-encompassing. It wasn't only their stomachs and bowels that cried out for food but their hands and feet, their livers and hearts, their private parts and above all their brains. Food had become the hub of their existence and dominated their consciousness and dreams until they were unable to think of anything but their hunger. They gathered in groups to cook imaginary meals and when they fell asleep they dreamt of feasts and loaded tables.

They were starved, bereft of everything and beggarly and yet some of them gave up the pittance they had saved, and threw rags and bits of bread over the wires to the naked women. Neugeboren slid into the ditch and pushed a pot of soup under the fence and the girls knotted a stone to a muffler they had knitted in their handicraft lessons and cast it over the top wire. Some of the rags got caught on the barbs but nobody dared to take them off from the mortal wires. The women rushed forward to collect the gifts, but though they were starved, they were more intent on the clothes than on the bread. They tore the rags into strips, but as if they had forgotten all shame, didn't cover their breasts or crotches, but tied the kerchiefs around their shaven heads. The rags were white and black and yellow and after a while the host of girls looked like a field.

Next morning the women were issued striped prison uniforms, marched to the railway station and taken away.

There was hope in their departure because what happened to the Hungarian girls might also happen to the Family Camp inmates.

'Where did they go?' asked Majda.

'Probably to a labour camp. To Poland, to Germany. Who knows.'

'They won't die?'

'They won't die. They were shaved and given uniforms.'

He was surprised at the questions because the smaller children seldom asked about death. The older ones, the thirteen-year-old adolescents in Beran's group, spoke about being and non-being and even about God, but Alex Ehren's Maccabees lived in the present and cared more about a game of marbles, the puppet theatre, competitions and birthday celebrations than about God and their future.

'Does it hurt to die?' The girl held her rag doll close to her side.

'I don't think so,' Alex Ehren said. 'Like falling asleep, perhaps.'

'Falling asleep is all right,' Majda said and sucked her thumb. The Hungarian transports continued far into June, yet often when Alex Ehren watched a procession meander away to the sound of music, he thought of the ten thousand naked women. He remembered the curve of their necks, their breasts, their heads that looked like a field of flowers, and their birdlike voices.

The SS doctor billeted the dwarfs at the Hospital Block opposite the Children's Block. They were a family of seven but two of them were of normal growth and were their link with the outside world. The dwarfs were artistes of sorts and had toured Europe, sometimes as an independent group on their own and sometimes as members of a travelling vaudeville act. Some of them danced and others performed a wedding ceremony and they played an assortment of musical instruments – a fiddle, guitar, trumpet – but they also made music on wine glasses and on combs wrapped in paper.

They kept to themselves and wouldn't mix because they considered themselves superior to the Jewish deportees and exempt from their fate.

'When the doctor finishes his research he'll let us go,' said the one called Josef.

How peculiar, thought Alex Ehren, that so many consider themselves exempt from death – Hynek Rind, the Block Seniors and Capos, the craftsmen who came to repair the roof or build a wooden partition, and even the Jewish dwarfs who served Dr Mengele's research. They all clung to a reason, to an omen, which would save them: one because he was a plumber; the other because his father had served in the Great War; and the third because he was a freak of nature whose hands were malformed stumps. The dwarfs were better fed; they got a double bread ration and ate the thick children's soup cooked in the Gypsy Camp. One of them came to the Block each noon and was particular about the seven measures of soup, which he carried to the hospital in a bucket.

'We aren't Jews—' he spoke in a strange mixture of German and Hungarian '—and we were caught up in a transport by mistake. There is no reason why we should be here.'

Nobody knew who they really were. Lisa Pomnenka worked on their family tree but they changed their story each time the SS doctor asked them. One of them had one version and the other another, as if they had forgotten who they were or were lying on purpose. Once their grandfather was a Gypsy, another time they were the illegitimate descendants of a Hungarian nobleman and yet another time there was a Jewish connection of sorts. They crossed themselves and swore in Polish and in Hungarian that they were telling the truth. Their truth changed from one day to the next as if they were trying to confuse the physician until he let them go. The girl drew a chart of their grandparents, those who were dwarfs and those who weren't, but they constantly invented new ancestors until there were six or seven charts, though none of them might be the true one.

The doctor, who used to fly into a frenzy at the girl's smallest mistake, was patient with the dwarfs because he saw in the family of freaks a cornerstone for his racial theory. He kept taking measurements of their size, their body fluids, their skulls and he even cut off some of their hair and nails for some kind of test. He made the girl draw their faces and distorted hands in charcoal and pencil and sometimes they had to strip and he watched the girl as she traced their malformed backs.

However, he still spent most of his days on his official duties and needed less of Lisa Pomnenka's services. She worked on the wall, the meadow and the potted geraniums and the sky, until the painting covered three of the four Block walls.

'It will soon be finished, yes?' asked Himmelblau, who lived by the hour and the day.

'I don't know.' She looked at the dark planks. Himmelblau's question made her uncomfortable because she disliked commitments. It was not she who painted but rather something beyond her and she was only the tool and the instrument. Sometimes she spoke about it with Shashek, who understood.

There were days when she progressed quickly, but at other times she worked slowly, with relish, eager to taste every stroke of her brush. Sometimes she deliberately put off her painting and occupied herself with another task. There was always something else to be done – the handicraft lessons, the puppets' clothes and decorations for the performance. Some of the older children had good hands and helped with the work but she never let them paint the wall. She climbed the ladder up to the beams and Shashek held up her brushes and a pot of paint. He found a piece of cherry wood and carved a dog and a cat and a figurine of a woman.

'Don't hurry with the wall,' he said, grinning. 'As long as it's not done you can't lose it.'

'What can I lose?'

'The picture, of course. It's like an unfinished child. Once it's born it doesn't belong to the mother.' He had difficulty in conveying his thoughts and he motioned to the figure he was carving. 'When it's done it gets a life of its own. Like God—' he groped for words '—who made the world and lost it.'

He wanted to give her a present but he was shy and postponed the act of giving from one day to another.

Only Fabian became friendly with the dwarfs. 'We actors,' he said, 'are of the same kind.'

The vaudeville actors became bored in the Hospital Block and they came to see the children's performances. First came Josef and then another dwarf and then they brought with them the two women, one of whom was Josef's wife. They didn't understand Czech but they enjoyed the singing, the charades and Fabian's satanic voice, which he polished and improved from one performance to the next.

One of the dwarfs was a magician, a prestidigitator who swallowed fire and made things appear and disappear. He agreed to give a show, but as they had lost all their possessions on arrival, it took him three days to prepare his tricks. The dwarfs climbed on the stage, dressed in pied clothes and made music on improvised instruments. They used a comb, soup bowls, Himmelblau's whistle and even Shashek's pieces of wood. They performed a mock wedding with Josef and one of the small women. The bride and groom were malformed and their hands and feet looked like seals' fins. There was nothing beautiful about them. Their faces were prematurely wrinkled and when they walked over the stage they swayed and waddled like waterfowl. And yet they were human. They were small and misshapen, created by a freak of nature or a genetic error. They looked like living jokes, like caricatures of what had been the original purpose, but there was love and affection in the way they held hands and smiled at each other. They had acted out the wedding ceremony a hundred times; in fact, they had earned their daily sustenance by exposing their hunched backs and malformations, and yet even in their predicament they remained human.

The dwarf magician wasn't an accomplished conjurer, but the children were fascinated by the ball that came and went, by the pieces of cloth he pulled out of an empty hat and by the fire he swallowed. Himmelblau paid the troupe from the orphaned parcels that Mengele kept sending to the Children's Block. But when the physician learned about the performance, he moved the dwarfs to another compound and they were never heard of again.

As the days grew warmer, new grass sprouted along the blocks, but it soon withered, trodden by the crowded inmates. However, under the fence the grass survived and even small daisies bloomed in the lime soil. The children counted the flowers, twenty behind this block and fifteen behind that, but they didn't dare pick them because they grew under the electrified wires. The children were full of spring and when they washed and put on their shirts they teased the old man behind the washroom. He was always there, ancient, bent and poking the smouldering rags with a stick.

'Sha,' he said, 'don't come near, little children. The rags are full of vermin, which need burning.' He looked up with his watery eyes and made a quick movement with his hand. 'Sha, go away. I have the most responsible work in the camp, because if I don't burn the lice they will eat you all, flesh, bone and skin.'

It was a game between him and the children who came close to the fire and dispersed like drops of water when he chased them away, once and twice each morning.

One day he stood waiting for them some distance away from the fire.

'A surprise—' he turned toward the fence '—a surprise for the children.' He was excited and happy as if he had discovered a treasure or a source of food. 'There is a tree,' he said, 'a tree with leaves and branches.' He moved his arms to show the shape of the tree.

There were no trees and no vegetation in Birkenau. The barracks stood in long barren rows separated by ditches and electrified fences and no tree or bush was allowed to break their uniformity. It was a stretch of land, flat and immense, unbroken by any hill, valley or copse, where a prisoner might hide or idle away the time that belonged to the Germans. Sometimes when the wind lifted the bittersweet smoke, they did see the outline of trees on the horizon, but they were so distant that they couldn't tell whether it was a forest, an orchard or a row of poplars along a road. The tree lay to the west and the escaped prisoners Lederer and Rudi, the Quarantine Registrar, must have crossed them on their way to the mountains.

Alex Ehren looked at the distant trees and wondered whether he would ever touch the bark of their trunks and see the sun through their crowns.

The old man's tree was an apple that had taken root between the rows of barbed wire. It was a shy sapling born from a seed brought by water a long time before the Germans had conceived the idea of the camp. Its branches had never been pruned and sprang like unkempt hair, from the stem. It was small and fragile, but now in spring its twigs were full of delicate flowers. It was the only tree in the camp and possibly in the whole complex of Birkenau, but it lived and bloomed despite the smoke, the barbed wire and the electric current that had killed the birds, and the fine ashes that snowed on their branches. The tree was out of place, incongruous, absurd, and yet it was there like a reminder of a different world, a different planet that existed beyond the camps.

The children stood between the washroom and the latrine block and watched the buds, which towards noon opened into pink blossoms, and even the rowdy boys, Bubenik and Lazik, didn't clamour to go back to their game of marbles.

For several days the old man waited for the children.

'It is still there,' he said. He shushed them to silence as if the tree were a deer that might be startled by a sound. 'It is still there and blooming.'

After a week the flowers fell off and the tree sprouted pale leaves. The children painted the tree on scraps of paper and wrote a short story for the daily bulletin Felsen pinned on the wall.

One day the old man fell ill and died. Old men, those with wrinkled hands and white stubble on their faces, didn't last long once they fell ill. The children didn't know his name or the block on which he lived, whether he was alone or had a family, and they didn't visit him in his illness. Death was anonymous in the camp and when he passed away there were no mourners and no funeral. And yet, at least for a short time, whenever they came to the washroom, they remembered the old man, who had made them see the blossoming tree.

In the twisted world of the camps, strange, improbable friendships sprung up. Some prisoners banded together into communes to share the little they had, and children took to an old man who burned rags behind the washroom, and Mietek, the Polish roof repairman, fell in love with Magdalena, the gym teacher.

People who had nothing of their own clung to friends, to bunk-mates, who became a substitute for family or clan.

Foltyn, the gangling guard boy, became friends with Marta Felix who spoke to him about philosophy. He was fascinated by her wisdom and spent as much of his free time with the teacher as she would allow. He became her orderly, stood in line for her soup and roasted her bread in the oven. She was amused by his attachment and knitted him a sweater, which he wore under the heavy coat Himmelblau had brought him from the Clothes Storeroom.

For some reason Julius Abeles became Alex Ehren's friend. With the arrival of the Hungarian transports there was an abundance of wares, and he grew rich. There were rumours that he had sold an SS guard a watch and another a salami, which the soldier sent home to his wife. Sometimes he bribed the Labour Capo to leave him on the block. However, most of the days he still worked on the Transport Commando, where, hitched to the cart like a horse, he left the camp and met his contacts. He had an additional bunk where he kept his goods, loaves of white bread, sugar cubes, spools of thread, needles, razor blades, pencil stubs and a pouch of tobacco. He struck a deal with the Kanada convicts who provided him with goods to be sold in the camp.

'Difficult,' he would say. 'Come back tomorrow. I'll see what I can do for you.'

He opened his shop when the prisoners returned from work and he sat on his bunk, haggard and cross-legged, and traded in spoons and mittens and sometimes even pills against pneumonia, stolen from the SS infirmary. He drove a hard bargain and only inmates with parcels from the outside world, the Block Seniors or cooks, were rich enough to buy his wares.

'People need things and if you can supply them you reap a harvest,' he said to Alex Ehren. 'Here and everywhere. No difference.'

He was stingy and dressed in rags and ate little, but sometimes made Alex Ehren a gift of white bread.

'Don't worry. One day I'll take advantage of you. Your kind pays debts. But don't try to start a business because you'll lose your shirt.' And he grinned. 'You are worth as much as you have.' He fingered the knotted bundles under his straw mattress.

'I have nothing.'

'Wrong, my friend, wrong. You have the books you have read. Ah, here you are. You sell your knowledge in comfort while Julius Abeles drags the cart to make a profit. Don't pretend. There is no difference between you and me.'

He leaned closer and lisped over his broken tooth. 'What is life? It's buying and selling.'

He had some money and a handful of precious stones, which he believed would save his life.

'Everybody can be bought,' he said, 'the Capo, the Poles and even the Germans. Only the price is different. Have money, and you will live.'

He worried about tobacco in which he had invested most of his riches.

'The worst ones,' he said in a confiding tone, 'are those that die without paying. They buy on credit and then lie on their bunk cold and stiff. And I take the loss.'

He sounded angry as if the dead cheated him on purpose. Sometimes a prisoner was taken away by the Gestapo, the German secret police, and beaten to reveal what was going on in the barracks, who was a communist and who conspired to escape. There were whispers that Julius Abeles sold the SS not only watches but also information about the camp.

In mid-May there were several days of frost. The cold was caused by the melting icebergs in the North Sea. The Czech villagers used to count the days off on their fingers and called them after the three saints: Pankrác, Servác and Bonifác. Towards noon, however, the sun broke through the mist and the children could play behind the Block.

In the morning the washroom was empty. At dawn the prisoners came to rinse their bowls or sprinkle water on their faces, but after the roll call even the thin trickle of water dried up and there was no reason to linger around the smelly troughs. Alex Ehren promised Julius Abeles he would watch out for intruders, for Jagger or a German sentry.

'Half an hour,' said Julius Abeles. 'What is half an hour for a friend? Let the children run around for a while. Give the little ones a break. Himmelblau won't notice that you are missing.'

His wife came up the camp road and slipped into the washroom through the rear entrance, quietly and unobtrusively.

The man and wife didn't walk near the trough together, but each of them took a different aisle, Julius Abeles to the left and the woman to the right. She looked like an ungainly bird, a crow or a raven, with her prominent nose and her black coat tightly buttoned up to her neck. Once, a long time ago, the coat had been trimmed with fur, but it had fallen out and the bare patches were like islands of disease. She knew that Julius had hired Alex Ehren and when she passed him she hid her chin in her collar and turned her head. She was ashamed but walked on stolidly, perseveringly, until she met her husband at the oven.

The washroom, like all barracks, was equipped with an oven and a horizontal smokestack that ran through the block and up to the roof. The cast-iron door was open and Alex Ehren saw the sooty bricks, the grate and the cinders that were spilled on the floor. She reached the end of the chimney and took off her coat. She folded the garment inside out as if it were made of exquisite cloth and the bald collar were the fur of a beaver. She hung it on a dead tap and bent to enter the hole. The door was narrow and she had to crawl into the cave on all fours like an animal.

First she stuck in her head, then her shoulders and finally her thin legs with the mismatched stockings, one black and one grey. Alex Ehren stood at the far end and watched the road. The husband and wife were middle-aged and plain and they had been married for many years. There was terrible danger in their meeting; they possibly risked their lives, and yet they went through the ritual of lovemaking, despite the place and the time and the darkness around them.

Alex Ehren was suddenly startled by a noise and turned his head. He was relieved to see a bunch of his children, Majda and Eva and two other girls. How long had they been there, he wondered, and what had they seen?

He didn't speak about the event as if the girls had not seen Julius Abeles and his wife and him standing guard in front of the empty washroom. There were no secrets in the camp and the children must have known what people did in the oven. Majda couldn't be ignorant about Agnes, her mother, and about Magdalena, who met her Polish lover at the Clothes Storeroom, or the other women who sold their love for bread. What could he tell the children about Julius and his wife behind the cast-iron oven door? That they loved each other or that their lovemaking helped against fear? Were they hungry for the touch of their bodies as he was for Lisa Pomnenka, or was it an attempt to put a semblance of normality into their lopsided lives?

The day after, Julius Abeles gave Alex Ehren half a bread ration and a slice of hard cheese.

In the evening he shared his windfall with the girl. She cut the bread into thin slices to make it last longer and they cupped their hands so as not to waste the tiniest morsel of their bread. In the last two weeks the German doctor hadn't asked the girl to draw diagrams and they were often hungry. When they finished their meal they sat in silent contentment, and, as their arms touched, Alex Ehren felt the warmth of her flesh. He thought about the washroom, the sooty bricks and the lovemaking in the darkness. He loved Lisa Pomnenka and was consumed with desire, but he knew that he would never ask the girl to follow him to the washroom, to bend over on all fours like an animal and crawl through the iron door into the oven.

On the fifteenth of May a transport with 2,503 new deportees from Theresienstadt arrived in the Family Camp. Next day at noon there was another train with 2,500 more prisoners and two days later, on the eighteenth, there was yet another trainload of 2,500 people. There were all in all 7,503 new arrivals, but they were a mixed lot of 3,125 German Jews, 2,543 Czechs, 1,276 Austrians and 559 Dutch. Many of the newcomers were old or ill with tuberculosis and there was a disproportionately large number of orphans and small children.

The camp became choked with too many people. There was little space in the cavernous barracks and again Alex Ehren had to share his bunk with seven other sleepers. When one of them tried to ease his hip, they all had to turn as if they were an Indian deity, a centipede or a many-limbed animal.

He could bear the discomfort of his bunk, the painful latrine queues and his hunger, but he was unable to make peace with time. The camp was a terrible place, dark, squalid, enveloped in smoke and grey with the fine falling ash. He had learned to live on the crowded block, grown attached to the unruly children and formed friendships with Beran, Pavel Hoch and even Hynek Rind. He didn't want to part with his work, the white woollen blanket and the girl's proximity. He knew that the new prisoners arrived in order to replace them, just as they had come to take the place of the September transport.

# 9.

THE ARRIVAL OF SO MANY CHILDREN UPSET THE SCHEDULE of the Block. The three transports added more than three hundred new pupils, and Himmelblau had to set up German and Dutch groups with new instructors, more youth assistants and matrons. There were not enough food bowls, the children needed shoes, shirts, a foot rag and because there were not enough stools, again many children had to squat on the pressed earth of the floor.

Alex Ehren's group swelled to thirty and without Thomasina's help he couldn't have conducted his reading and writing lessons, let alone the bit of arithmetic he dared to teach. The Dutch girl had a small group of her own but she sometimes took half of Alex Ehren's pupils for a walk, sang a Dutch song with them or made them paint tulips and windmills. At first Neugeboren and Bubenik were confused by the Dutch and the German, but once they began to play marbles and sing '*Alouette*' with the new boys, they managed to communicate and some even became friends.

At the beginning it was exciting to have new people in the camp. The December transport had been cut off from the world for five months and they were full of questions about their friends and relatives in the ghetto, about the war and politics. The ghetto was only sixty kilometres northwest of Prague and sometimes the Czech gendarmes volunteered a bit of information and, for a bribe or out of compassion, smuggled a newspaper or a letter into the ghetto. Birkenau was cut off from the world by fences, watchtowers, a minefield and a chain of SS sentries with dogs. The news that filtered through was but rumours that spread by word of mouth. It was incredible that the ghetto people knew nothing of the gas chambers, the chimney and the death of the Hungarians. How was it possible that in the ghetto they saw transport after transport herded into trains and shipped east – their friends, children and relatives – and didn't ask themselves what was happening in the Polish camps? Was there no suspicion, no message and no warning? Some of the Birkenau inmates had written coded postcards to the ghetto with hints and hidden meanings. Hadn't they ever arrived? Were the Czech Jews indeed so simple-minded to believe that the tens of thousands of deportees – men and women, but also old people, invalids and children – were in labour camps and alive? It wasn't easy to escape from the walled ghetto or to start a revolt, but it was seven times more difficult to save one's life in Auschwitz.

'There were rumours,' said Martin, who was Beran's cousin, 'but people refused to believe.'

'More than rumours.' Olga was one of the new instructors. 'I saw a coded postcard. And there was Lederer.'

'The escaped Block Senior?'

'A Czech gendarme smuggled him into the ghetto,' Olga went on, 'and he told us. Urged us to run away or to fight, to refuse to go on the transport, but people said that he was mad.'

'Life in the ghetto is not easy,' they said, 'but we manage somehow. Gas chambers? Half a million dead Hungarians? Ridiculous. Technically impossible. Where would they bury so many bodies? Hitler wouldn't dare. Couldn't hide it from the world. Isn't Lederer himself living proof that his stories are madness?'

Olga was a communist and a friend of the seamstress. She was still amazed by the electrified fence, the smoke and the falling ashes.

'How could we have believed—' she moved her hand in a circular motion '—in insanity? There is no reason in the killings.'

'There is a reason.' Marta Felix had been married to a German, who had divorced her to keep his position at the university. They'd been students together and married for love. She was bitter about his betrayal and her love had turned into hatred.

'The Nazis must believe in something,' said Himmelblau.

'They do,' said Marta Felix. 'It's an insane reason but even insanity may have its logic.'

They were not alone by then because the Block people flocked together whenever there was a discussion. They were unshaven and ragged, hungry and frightened, but they argued about abstractions as if a thought or a theory could fill their stomachs, sweeten the stench of decay or cancel their death sentence.

'They have read Nietzsche and they believe in their birthright to rule.' She spoke German now to make the Dutch and the Austrian instructors understand. Some of the older children and the youth assistants, Dasha and Bass and even

Foltyn, who should have been at the barracks door, stood at the outer edge of the circle and listened.

'The Nazis don't act on a whim but rather on a theory. Logic may lead to insanity if the reasoning is based on a false premise. Haven't people in the past proved that the earth is flat and that three hundred angels can stand on the head of a pin? Insane asylums are full of patients whose delusions are based on faulty logic. The only difference between them and the Nazis is—' and she lifted her arms in desperation ' —that the Germans have guns and have conquered the world.'

She paused for breath and went on.

'Somewhere in the universe, they say, exists a spring, a source of energy that flows through all things – the sun, the stars, rocks and even people. It is the natural drive, the impulse, the gut feeling, the unfettered self. It is the soul which is in harmony with nature and therefore good. A spirit that permeates the world.'

'Even the concentration camps?' asked Fabian and smirked.

'Even the concentration camps, because they serve the purpose.'

Marta Felix looked at the faces of the adolescent assistants, the matrons and the teachers. She loved lecturing and went on with sharp eloquence.

'The enemy of the soul is the spirit. The do's and don'ts. The brain and the logic, which stems the flow of the soul. The Germans believe—' she smiled bitterly '—that by conquering the world they serve the course of nature. They impose the cosmic order of the higher and the lower, of lords and servants, man and beast, the human and the subhuman. They are born to rule as others are born to be slaves.'

'Where do we fit in?' asked Alex Ehren, though he knew the answer even before he asked. Yet he wanted Marta Felix to spell it out.

'Ah, the Jews,' she said in her accented German, 'where do they come in? The Jews are the *Geist als Widersacher der Seele*, the incarnation of the spirit that corrupts the soul. The cancer that spreads to kill the organism. The Jews are not a human species. And as such they have to be destroyed. Exterminated to the last specimen. Their blood and their seed wiped from the face of the earth.'

'Nonsense,' said Hynek Rind. 'The German carpenter, butcher and cobbler don't smash Jewish shop windows because they believe in soul and spirit. The SS man doesn't beat me up because of an abstract idea. And Eichmann didn't build gas chambers because the Jews corrupt the harmony of nature. With due respect for philosophy, I don't buy that.'

'Not the simple people,' she answered. 'They beat up the Jews because it makes them patriots and heroes. They burn a prayer house and save their country. Their cruelty is called a virtue and their aggression courage.'

She looked around at her friends and shook her head.

'No, I don't speak about the mob that follows and goose-steps. Their sin is simple because they merely obey. I speak about the educated people, the elite. Those who think and are able to discern between the truth and the lie. The university professors. Those who read Goethe and Kant and listen to Beethoven in the evening. I speak about those who give the Nazi movement its legitimacy. The scientists, the lawmakers and the preachers. Those who teach that torture and lies and killing are justified if they serve an idea. The worst crime,' she said, and her voice was shrill and angry, 'is not committed by the butcher and the beer drinker, but by the intellectual and the educated. The Germans are an orderly folk who listen to their teachers and obey their officers. Look around yourselves. Where are those that oppose the Nazis? How many German political prisoners have you met in the camps? Three, four, a dozen of the Protestants, the communists and the honest Social Democrats? The rest of the German convicts are murderers, thieves and homosexuals. I don't see many of the German philosophers, writers and physicians behind bars. Where are the German humanists and thinkers? They have put on the German uniform and joined the pack of wolves. They were reluctant to give up their piece of cake and chose to belong to the master race and be the conquerors of the world.'

It was getting dark on the Block and Marta Felix spoke faster and faster as if trying to conclude her lecture before the evening curfew.

'You want examples? I'll give you examples of how to poison human minds. Take the Ten Commandments, they say. Go over them one by one and you will find that they curb natural drives. For what is more natural than aggression, greed or lust? Why should a man not kill if he craves more territory, more money or power? Or if he lusts for another man's wife? Why should he give his slave a day of rest? The idea of equality between the strong and the weak is against nature and, to use the Nazi language, a Jewish ploy to corrupt the world. Don't stars swallow stars and galaxies cannibalise galaxies and suns rule the movement of their planets? The lion feeds on the gazelle and man takes advantage of his fellow men. If nature intended to make everybody equal, the tiger, the deer and the wolf would have the same hide and graze in the same field.'

She folded her palms in a roof against her chest and went on. 'They say it is the Jew who twists nature. Didn't the Jew Jesus preach to love thy enemy and isn't the Talmud the cradle of democracy? Wasn't it Marx who invented communism and the Jew Freud who took apart the human soul to analyse its hidden abysses? Jews have infected art and music by abstraction and Einstein corrupted science by his theory of relativity. The Jews have upset nature in order to suck the world dry.'

With malicious joy Marta watched the eyes that were locked on her.

'There is one hope for the world,' she said, and her voice was bitter with irony. 'Get rid of the Jews. Burn them along with their books. And when they are dead and their ashes scattered by the wind or washed away in the Vistula, the world will live happily under the rule of its natural master race, the Germans.'

It was a terrible sermon and they were silent for a long while. Marta's words were like stones, which hung ominously, arrested in their fall above their heads. There was no way out and no hope against the insane logic of the Nazi creed. There was only one way out, thought Alex Ehren, and that was with the iron anchor and the attempt to escape into the mountains.

Felsen wouldn't take part in the discussion and stood leaning on the smokestack, with his head low in his collar.

He had a cabal of communists who kept to themselves and knew better.

'Of course there is hope,' he said. 'In communist society there is no Jewish question. The Red Army has beaten the Germans at Stalingrad and the war will soon end with Soviet victory.' With the arrival of the Dutch and German instructors the Block split into even more opinions. There were the Zionists, the Czechs, the communists and those who believed that when the war was over they would take up their lives where they had been broken off.

There was Dezo Kovac, who hadn't lost God in spite of the smoke; there was Lisa Pomnenka, who painted her make-believe meadow; and Fabian with his cynical remarks, who dreamt of becoming an actor one day. They were as different as a group of people could be – they spoke Czech and German, Dutch and Hungarian; they were religious or atheists; young and middle-aged; simple and educated – and yet they had one essential thing in common without which they could not have worked with the children. Most of the Block people had a star, of whatever colour or shape, which gave their life meaning and direction.

The overcrowded bunks bred lice. The prisoners slept in their clothes and when they died their bunkmates inherited their vermin. Some of them fought against the infestation, but it was a vain effort because, for each insect killed, there were a hundred that crawled over from the next bunk.

The matrons checked the children for lice every morning. With so many new pupils they could not manage so the older children had to check one another. Before the lessons they squatted on the ground like monkeys and went over the folds of their clothes. Some of the girls, like Eva, were fastidious and came to Miriam twice a day.

'I have an itch here and here and here,' Eva said, and laid her head on the woman's lap. It was faster to check the boys, whose heads were shaven, but Bubenik and Lazik had four shirts, which they wore like an onion one on top of another, and which prolonged the procedure. At dawn, an hour before the morning roll call, Sonia brought a barrel with tepid tea in which the matrons washed the children's underwear. They believed that the bitter brew kept the vermin away and they made the children sprinkle the liquid on their collars. There was no place to dry the washed clothes and the children stood on the camp road waving their wet rags in the air. The boys had no patience and put on their damp shirts, letting them dry on their backs.

Fabian's actors produced a comedy about the vermin. There was a sick man with a puzzling disease. One physician claimed that he had eaten too much soup, another doctor said that it was a hernia and the third decided that the man was in love and suffered from a broken heart. They argued in Czech, in German and in Latin, quoted Hippocrates, the philosopher Maimonides and Doctor Mengele, came to blows and finally operated. They opened the patient's belly and found that he suffered from lice on the appendix.

The play was fun, though it was like everything Fabian touched, seasoned with cynicism and bitterness. He stopped teaching and took over the weekly entertainment, the games, the charades, the competitions and the theatre. He constantly invented new ideas and kept Shashek and Lisa Pomnenka busy with demands for more costumes and new decorations. He added two more characters to the puppet show – an animal, which was sometimes a dog and at other times a dragon, and Silly Billy, who in his innocence got the better of the Devil. He bought more tinsel and a pot of glue from Julius Abeles and coaxed Pavel Hoch into supplying him with outlandish rags for his theatre.

'You will be rewarded,' Fabian promised. 'When you come to hell I'll let you have the coolest place.'

He often spoke in his satanic voice and always cracked jokes about death and the chimney.

'Today it's warm and sunny,' Lisa Pomnenka said. 'Why worry about tomorrow?'

She was simple-minded and straightforward, and she refused to be drawn into the whirlpool of fear in which Fabian lived. She was one the few who met with long-term convicts, prisoners who knew the camps and the tricks of survival. She carried bottles of gasoline into the camp, but she had no faith in the uprising. She looked like a child with her box of paints, her long hair and her blue eyes, but she had spoken to Camp Seniors from the Main Camp and even to those from Buna and Monowitz, where the SS kept labourers for the rubber factory and the mines. She knew that only the very desperate, those who were on the verge of execution, would join a revolt. The camps were a cruel place where dog ate dog and nobody would risk his life for the doomed Czech Jews. She was a simple girl but she wasn't a fool and she knew that an uprising against the Germans had little hope of success.

'It's the only chance we have.' Alex Ehren was stubborn in his belief. 'Once we start, other camps will join in. We'll be thousands of prisoners against a handful of SS soldiers.'

She knew better but there was no point in an argument.

The strange friendship between Foltyn and Marta Felix grew. The boy took the night shift and during the day listened to Marta Felix's lessons. He didn't join the children but stood half hidden behind a wooden post and drank in the woman's words. He was fascinated by the kings and battles and fallen empires, and in the afternoon he came up to the teacher and asked questions. After some time they spoke about other things, about communism and democracy and the Platonic ideas of the state, of justice and friendship.

He was eager and Marta Felix enjoyed his young mind. He could have been her son, she thought, and was sorry that she'd not had any children. But then she looked around and wasn't sorry any more, because it must be a terrible thing to have a child and know that it would perish in the gas chambers.

The lice bred typhus. Three people fell ill at the beginning of the month and then there was a pause. Towards the second half of May, with the arrival of seven thousand five hundred new inmates, there was a renewed outbreak of the disease and the Hospital Senior had to add three more rooms to the infection ward. The typhus spread fast on the crowded bunks where the vermin proliferated in enormous numbers. There was no protection against the lice, which lived in the soiled clothes, in the mattresses and even in the cracked wood of the barrack walls. They sucked blood from the sick and deposited their poisonous faeces everywhere – on the people's skin, in the straw stuffing, the blankets and even in the air they breathed.

It took two weeks until the person knew that he was ill, and in the meantime, as he slept with six or seven other prisoners on a pallet, he infected his bunk-mates.

The prisoners were starved and exhausted and those who fell ill died. The process of dying was fast – first there was fever and nausea and in two or three days the patient lost consciousness and passed away in a coma. Three of Alex Ehren's children fell ill in spite of the washing and daily inspections, but Neugeboren, the smallest and thinnest among the boys, recovered and with additional soup and the crumbled cakes from the orphaned parcels, returned to the Block.

One evening Beran suffered from headache but the next morning he got up and worked with his group, taught chemistry to the older children and in the evening met with Sonia on the camp road.

She still scraped the dregs from the barrel bottom but she had grown haggard and tired. She worked with a new teammate because the Capo had found Agnes an easier job at the weaving workshop.

Beran pushed the bowl away.

'The mush makes me sick,' he said. 'There is something wrong with my stomach. Couldn't you barter the soup for a slice of white bread?'

He was impatient and his mouth was dry.

'I'll do it tomorrow,' she said, unaccustomed to his short temper.

The next day he was nauseous and couldn't eat the bread, which Sonia had bartered for her soup, and when she touched his hand it was clammy and very hot.

He stayed on his bunk for another day but he ran a high fever. Alex Ehren noticed the dark patches on his face and asked the Block Warden to send his friend to the hospital. There was no room in the Hospital Block and he had to stay on his bunk until some patient died and vacated a bed.

That night he was delirious and Alex Ehren wrapped a wet rag around his head.

'Take the book of verses.' Beran pressed on him the sheaf of paper. 'The orderlies steal everything. Even poems.'

He turned from one side to another in a restless sleep. In the middle of the night he awoke and sat up.

'It's not me who is sick.' He laughed at something he had dreamt. 'In the Carpathian Ukraine the Jews have a way with the Angel of Death.' His eyes were feverish and wide open. 'If a man is beyond hope they change his name. From Moshe to Abraham or from Mendel to Shlomo. The Angel of Death comes down with a list of names of those that will die that night. He takes one and then another and then starts looking for Menachem Mendel. But there is no Menachem Mendel in the village. He knocks on the door and looks into the window but there is no such man, only Slomo, Aharon and Moshe. And so he goes back with one name missing. How very clever to fool Death with a name.'

He rested for a while but then went on.

'The trouble is that it sometimes doesn't work, and when the Angel of Death doesn't find Menachem Mendel he may take somebody else, somebody whose name wasn't up yet, to complete the list.' He clung to Alex Ehren's arm and mumbled. 'It's not me who should die. I am the wrong man. It's a secret,' he whispered, 'but I am not who I am. Beran?' he asked, 'Beran is not sick because he is still in the ghetto.'

He shook his head.

'Another man was in the transport. A fellow member of my Zionist movement.' Beran held Alex Ehren's hand so tightly that it hurt. 'If you take his place he might stay. Volunteer for the transport because he is essential for our *hachshara* groups. He has a mission here and you'll look after the movement in the labour camp.'

He spoke fast and feverishly and Alex Ehren didn't know whether his words were true or the result of his illness.

'I volunteered,' said Beran. 'I volunteered and so did Sonia. Imagine, we volunteered for Auschwitz.' He laughed hoarsely. 'No, we didn't exchange names, only transport numbers. I won't tell you his name. It's between him and me. One day he will know how I died and he will have to live with it.'

Beran lay with his eyes open in the dark.

'He fooled the Angel of Death, but he won't be able to fool himself. Why should I tell you his name?'

He still clung to Alex Ehren's hand.

'The Zionist movement is important. Tell me I did the right thing to volunteer for Auschwitz. With Sonia, my wife. After the war we'll go to Palestine and live on a kibbutz. The more worthy will survive in the ghetto and start a new nation. The less worthy will die in Birkenau. Tell me it was right.'

'It was right,' Alex Ehren swallowed and said, though he didn't know whether any man or any movement had the right to judge.

The following day Sonia knocked on the planks of the hospital wall, but Beran didn't answer. They asked the orderly but he chased them away.

'He will die. So few recover from typhus,' she said, and her plain face was contorted with sadness. 'He could have refused. Isn't it stupid to die for an idea? Or for another person's rescue? How could they decide who is worthy to live and who isn't? What is an idea and what is a movement against Beran's life? Or mine?'

Next day, which was a Sunday, Beran died. His ashes, like those of all the other dead, were strewn into the River Sola. Alex Ehren left the book of poems with Dasha, who kept her library on the smokestack.

The Germans were scared of typhus. They had guns and ammunition and they kept the convicts behind electrically charged fences, and yet they were unable to contain the lice in one place. Twice a day, in the morning and at dusk, the SS guards counted the prisoners, but they entered the camp buttoned up and with their hands covered by gloves. They kept a distance from the inmates and when they came to see the children's performance they dared not enter and stood at the open door.

In the camp Dr Mengele continued to weed out the sick and the weak. The Special Commando sped up the executions and the bodies they couldn't process in the three incineration plants were doused with kerosene and burned in an open field.

At the end of May two events followed one another. After the evening roll call the prisoners were handed out postcards. They held the flimsy paper in their hands and stood in a queue for the pencil stubs, which Julius Abeles leased for a spoonful of soup or a bite of bread. They jostled and pushed and while they waited for the stub, they deliberated about the few words they were permitted to write in block letters on the card. It was tremendously important what they wrote because the postcards were their only link with the outside world. They couldn't write about their hunger, their diseases or the gas chambers. The inmates invented ploys to circumvent the regulation and to ask for food parcels without spelling out their misery.

Hynek Rind mentioned a relative who died of stomach cancer, another met Dalibor, a legendary Czech hero who starved in a dungeon, and Marta Felix wrote that she was reading Knut Hamsun, hinting at his book called *Hunger.* They were like drowning persons who cast about for a piece of flotsam, though the plank was often only an illusion or a handful of straw. Some of the postcards were never mailed, others got lost or were not delivered, yet after some time a number of prisoners did receive a parcel, which allowed them to survive another week. Others, mainly the members of the Zionist movements, banded into communes and shared their additional bread and margarine. Alex Ehren would have starved had the SS doctor not given Lisa Pomnenka bread and had Pavel Hoch not shared with him Aninka's parcels.

The cards were also a reason for panic. Alex Ehren turned the piece of paper in his fingers and remembered the cards they had written at the beginning of March. They'd had to date them 15th of April, to allow – so the SS sentries said – the censor in Berlin to read them. By mid-April the September transport had been dead six weeks. When their food parcels, robbed of the better items, began arriving in the Family Camp, they were sent to the Children's Block. They were of no use to their dead addressees, but the bread and crumbled cakes did help the children to keep above water.

When they were handed the new cards they were apprehensive. Would the Germans repeat the same ruse? Why should Alex Ehren write that he was well and working in Birkenau bei Neu-Berun, Deutschland, Schlesien? Why make his friends believe that he was still alive if he had been reduced to a wisp of smoke and a flake of ashes? Did they want to fool the people in the ghetto or the half-Jews who were still at large? Were they planning another transport to Heidebreck and wanted to assure the victims that there was nothing to fear?

'Take my card,' said Fabian to Alex Ehren. 'I have nobody who would send me a loaf of bread.'

'There must be somebody. A classmate. A girl you dated? A neighbour?'

'Small towns don't like poor Jews. My neighbours would read the card and say good riddance. Write the card and we'll share the bread. If there is any and if we are still about.' He also remembered the September transport.

In the evening they wrote their cards under the weak electric bulb in their section. They kneeled at the chimney or leaned the paper against the bunk, but above all they planned the words and the sentences. Each word was of supreme importance and they turned the version over in their minds several times before they wrote. To whom should they address it? To a distant cousin, a neighbour, a business partner or a former lover? In the afternoon Adam Landau came with his postcard in his hand.

'Will you write for me?' He hadn't been at school for many days and his eyes were hard like two small stones. He had an aunt married to a gentile to whom he wanted to write.

'Don't you play marbles any more?' asked Alex Ehren, remembering the golden bead.

'Marbles are for children,' said the brat. 'Write to my aunt that I've grown a lot. She might send me chocolates.'

He looked well and had good clothes, though he hadn't grown and his face was still that of a small child.

Two days later all the inmates of the Children's Block were sent to the showers.

Jagger, the Camp Capo, stood on the chimney, hunch-backed and leaning on Adam's shoulder.

'The Camp Commander,' he said, in his booming voice, 'has granted you a favour. You will have a shower and get a fresh shirt.' It can't be the time, thought Alex Ehren, with his heart pounding against his ribs. There were only two SS guards accompanying them, the one they called the Priest and another who spoke Romanian. Neither had they been forewarned by the underground movement. He looked at Fabian, at Hynek Rind and even at Felsen, who should have known, but they were as bewildered as he was.

Was it time for the uprising? He felt betrayed. He had prepared himself for the mutiny, he had dreamt and exercised with the rock, but when the time came he was locked up in the Children's Block and unable to defend himself.

They were marched down the camp road and when they passed the gate the musicians played 'Marinarella' and 'The Blue Danube'. He saw the men sitting on their platform, blowing their trumpets and fiddling away on their violins as if the procession of children was leaving for work and not passing the gate for the last time. What a pitiful crowd they were, the instructors, the matrons and the children, the youth assistants and Himmelblau with his glasses and Fredy's whistle around his neck. What fools they were, he thought. They had the kerosene bottles Lisa Pomnenka had smuggled into the camp, they had formed triads, with each member knowing his task, they had a pickaxe, a hatchet, five crowbars and an iron octopus hidden in the Hospital Block. And yet here they were, marching meekly through the gate. Why hadn't they seen the obvious – the May transports that came to take their place, the postcards, the overcrowded bunks and the outbreak of typhus? He was furious with himself, with Felsen and with the underground movement that had promised support, but when their time came, had abandoned them and let them die alone.

The two guards marched them between two rows of barbed wire, a way Alex Ehren had never walked before, and when he turned his head, he saw the older boys and the youth assistant Foltyn, Bass, the stoker and the new boy who was Shashek's apprentice. There were twenty adolescents on the Block, girls with small budding breasts who used to sit together and giggle, and the boys, some tall and lanky, with a shadow of moustache over their lips but others still round-faced.

He craned his head and looked for the girl and he saw Lisa Pomnenka at the far end with Aunt Miriam and the girl librarian who belonged to no group. Alex Ehren marched with his class, the Maccabees, the twins Hanka and Eva, and Majda with the blonde braid and the boys, who even now pushed one another out of the row and laughed at their own pranks. There was Bubenik and Lazik and Neugeboren, but Adam Landau was not among them and he thought how right the brat was when he wouldn't learn to read and write. Yet even now, in his time of fear, he was glad that the boy might be saved. He had the soul of a poet and the temper of a weasel. He pimped for the Capo, he probably stole and lied, but it was the camp that had taught him to be like that. He remembered Beran, who had died to let a better man survive and he wondered who was the better and who the worse, Adam or the other children, and had it not been for his desperation, he would have laughed at the absurdity of life and death.

The two SS guards made a detour. They led the column on a round trip, first to the Gypsy Camp, then to the Men's Infirmary, then turned a corner and stopped at the squat building with the brick chimney.

Alex Ehren had never seen the gas chambers before. He had looked at the tall chimney that spewed smoke and coloured the night sky, but the building was hidden in a copse and invisible from the camp. It looked innocent enough, like a small house, silent and shaded by a group of trees, and had he not known its secret, he could have mistaken it for a home, a laundry or even a well.

One of the SS guards, the Priest, took out a cigarette and smoked, watching the children with his pale eyes. There were three mounds, dishevelled like unkempt hair. One was a pile of shoes, which lay haphazardly, each unconnected to its mate, brogues and laced shoes, slippers and boots, all of them in poor repair, some wrinkled by age and others torn like gaping mouths. The other pile was of spectacles, entwined and tangled with one bent loop sticking out. There were thousands of them, thick and thin, gold-rimmed and tortoiseshell, worn and new, and their lenses blinked in the sun that broke through a cloud. The third stack was low, yet the most pathetic of all because it was built of baby carriages and toys that had belonged to children.

There were no additional guards and no Capos at the door and the house was silent and peaceful.

'Not our turn,' said Hynek Rind, encouraged by the quiet. 'They wouldn't dare touch the Czechs.'

The SS guard threw away the cigarette and marched them on to the shower rooms. There was an entrance for men and another for women.

Alex Ehren left his clothes at the concrete wall. They took off their shirts and the room was stuffy with the smell of unwashed bodies. He had worked on the road, carried boulders and slept in the same trousers for many months. When he undressed the rags were so stiff with filth they held the shape of his body and he could hardly fold them.

He heard the sound of running water but the shower might be a ploy to make them enter without resistance. For many weeks he had thought that he would fight for his life, but when their time came he was naked and unprepared. He looked around and clawed his fingers like a bird of prey.

'There are only three SS soldiers,' he said, 'and we could take away their guns.'

'There is no need,' said Felsen, who had spoken to a Polish prisoner. 'We'll shower and go back to the Family Camp.' He sounded as if he didn't believe his own words. 'When the time comes we will know.'

Alex Ehren kept the boys in a tight group. They were frightened and clung to one another, but only now, when he saw them without their clothes, did he notice how skinny they had grown. They were like a nest of baby birds and they entered the shower room in a skein of arms and legs and concave bellies.

The three Greeks were the last survivors of a Corfu transport. The Germans had taken their island in September and by the end of June there were no Jews left there, save a handful of fishermen that hid in the mountains.

The three were relatives – two cousins and an uncle – and they had been spared because they were barbers. One of them shaved the convicts' heads and the other their body hair, but their razors were blunt and their clients left the bench bleeding. The third man doused them with a disinfectant and the carbolic acid burned in their wounds and eyes.

There were many customers for the shave and they waited in a long queue. Alex Ehren didn't mind the time, the blunt razor or the carbolic acid because each shaven prisoner was a promise that they would live. The Germans wouldn't have shaved and showered people that were to be killed. He was exhilarated by the air he inhaled and by the beating of his heart and even the acid that burnt his cut flesh was a blessing. He felt as if he had been handed a gift, a prize, and he ran his hand over the stubble on the boys' heads.

'It's all right,' he said, and his voice was high with excitement like that of a woman. 'We'll have a shower and go home.'

They stood naked in the room, crowded and plagued by thirst, but it wasn't the day of their execution. The children would go back to their bunks, to their starvation rations and the smell of the latrines. Yet they would live and return to the Children's Block, which, with its lessons and games and Lisa Pomnenka's make-believe landscape, was their home. The windows at the top of the wall were almost blacked out with grime but he could see the sun and he felt light and happy. And had he not been scared of the SS guards, he would have thrown up his arms in joy and laughed.

Hynek Rind was among the last to be shaved. The Greek barber made him climb a bench and splashed water over his back and belly. He lowered his razor but stopped and gazed at his private parts.

He looked up.

'*Judio*?' he asked in a Jewish dialect with a surprised expression.

Hynek Rind stood naked on the bench, higher than the other prisoners, and Alex Ehren saw that he wasn't circumcised.

'Yes, a Jew. Not by choice but because of the Germans. Why else would I be locked up in this stinking place?'

'*Judio*,' the Greek asked again. 'What kind of a *Judio*?' He pointed his razor at Hynek Rind's penis.

'Go on,' said Hynek Rind, 'I am the last one and everybody wants to get it over with.' He felt that everybody was looking at his nudity and he raised his voice. 'Hurry up!' he exclaimed. 'I won't stand here forever!'

The SS sentry came closer. He was bored and the incident promised a break in the monotony of his job.

'A Jew and not a Jew,' said the Greek, and he shook his head. He spoke fast to his cousin and they both laughed at the idea.

'I could make you a Jew,' he said in broken German and poised his razor like a sword.

It was only then the SS soldier grasped his intention and nodded his head with a smirk.

'Make him a Jew,' he said to the barber. 'Do it quickly, man, and make him a Jew.'

There were other sentries in the room and they grew interested.

'You can't,' said Hynek Rind, holding his hands in front of his genitals.

The SS soldier stood very near and the Greek was scared. It was a joke at first but now he didn't dare disobey. And thus, Morpurgo, the Corfu barber, swung his razor and in one swift sweep cut into Hynek Rind's skin.

He gave one shrill cry, a shriek of pain and surprise and anguish and ran, with blood staining his thighs, towards the door. The German, still laughing, stepped in his way and with his rifle butt pushed him back into the row of prisoners.

Alex Ehren and Fabian helped him on his way back and he lay on his bunk, hurting, for three days.

# 10.

THE CLOTHES STOREROOM WAS AT THE FAR END OF THE CAMP. IT WAS so close to the Block that the children saw the commandoes unload the bales and then pull the cart, horse-like, down the road to return with a new heap of clothes. It was not only a storeroom for the prisoners' rags but also a sorting station for the new arrivals' baggage. With the incoming multitudes the Kanada people couldn't manage their task and some of the looted articles were sent to the Family Camp to be sorted and tied into bundles. The better coats and jackets were shipped to Germany where, through Hitler's 'munificence', they were distributed to German families, while the worst, the tattered rags, remained in the camp and were marked with red paint and worn by the Jewish inmates.

At the entrance to the Storeroom were two whitewashed cubicles, one of which belonged to the Clothes Capo, a German convict, a Social Democrat, and in the other sat the seamstress, who patched prisoners' rags on her ancient sewing machine. Like in other barracks the block was filled with three-tiered bunks, but instead of mattresses, they were full of shirts, underwear, shoes and jackets. On the surface it was a workplace similar to the weaving workshop, the mica block, the camp road and the ditch commando, but like so many other things in the camp, the Clothes Storeroom had two lives, one overt and the other secret, hidden from the Germans.

It was a privileged workshop because the coming and leaving of clothes enabled the prisoners to deal in tobacco and spirits for which the Block Seniors and the Camp Capo paid with bread and soup. Yet beyond the tobacco and vodka there was yet another secret, deep and dangerous, which the inmates hardly ever mentioned to anyone outside the barracks. The people who were arriving on the daily transports often hid a precious stone, a small jewel or even tightly rolled banknotes in their clothes. Pavel Hoch went over the seams, linings and cuffs and sometimes found a small trove of gold. The valuables, like the pillaged clothes, belonged to the Germans and had to be handed over to an SS supervisor, an officer, who collected them into a cardboard box. Each evening Pavel Hoch and his colleagues had to undress and an overseer checked their trousers, their mouths and even the orifices of their bodies for a possible theft. And yet, in spite of the officer and the search, he managed to conceal a stone, a coin or a small jewel, most of which he later handed over to the seamstress. Some of the prisoners grumbled but at the end they gave up their loot because they were afraid to be branded as traitors.

'We need arms,' she said. 'Crowbars and a pickaxe are children's toys. What we need are guns and hand grenades.'

The communists tried to come to an arrangement with Julius Abeles, to draw him into the conspiracy and make him buy a weapon for them. He refused point blank and pursed his mouth. 'It's a foolish idea and I don't want to get involved.

Dog eat dog, and every man for himself. One day you'll get caught and the Germans will hang you.'

After that day the seamstress despised him and spread rumours that he robbed the inmates of their daily rations. She never told them whether there were firearms on the block and where she had hidden the bottles of kerosene and gasoline, which Lisa Pomnenka had smuggled into the camp.

'The less you know, the less you'll tell.'

However, the contraband was somewhere, on one of the shelves, in her cubicle or in a dugout under the bunk. Each time an SS guard entered the Clothes Storage Pavel Hoch had palpitations, because had the soldier found a firearm or the bottles, they would have been tortured to tell where they came from and then put to death. There were seven prisoners in the storage and one of them might say a word to a friend or a lover.

'No, I am not afraid,' she said. 'There are ways to deal with informers.'

Sometimes Pavel Hoch mused about the seamstress. What kind of woman was she? Was she really as hard and unfeeling as she pretended to be? Did her faith in a communist revolution make her stronger and more determined? Didn't she have a lover, a husband, children perhaps? She never opened herself up to others and he felt uneasy in her company. It was difficult to be friends with a woman who had no doubts and who, like a devout Catholic, lived strictly according to the tenets of her faith.

'The world moves forward according to rules,' she said. 'Nothing is random. One stage leads to another and we can speed up the process or slow it down. But we can't reverse the flow of history.'

'Aren't there things beyond the material? Don't you believe in nature, in human goodness, in God?'

He thought about Aninka, his gentile girlfriend, and her loving parcels.

'I believe in a revolution. And the party that will bring it about,' she said. 'What happens to me is not important.'

There were communists among the older children. It was easy to be a communist in the camp because communism showed the world in black and white and explained the unexplainable. There were the communists who were good, and the fascists who were the reason of all evil. One day, when the good took over, all problems would be solved. They gathered around Felsen, who taught them Marx and Lenin and the boys felt that they had all the answers.

'For the communists there exist no Jews and Gentiles, only people,' said Bass, the oven boy.

'We cope with our Jewishness in three ways,' said Dezo Kovac. 'One is to deny your identity; to move to another town, to change your name and to marry a gentile wife. You'll live in hiding for the rest of your life but your children and your children's children might escape the curse.'

He looked around and was glad that Hynek Rind was at the far end of the Block.

'Some, like the Czech instructor, have tried but he was a generation too late. He concealed his Jewishness for thirty years but in the end it caught up with him. A Greek cut off his foreskin and an SS was his godfather.'

Alex Ehren thought about his name and his grandfather's house with its strip pasture.

'What is the other way?'

'If you can't change yourself change the world. Bring about a revolution. The communists don't have a Jewish problem, they say.'

He looked at the boy who was at the threshold of manhood and who believed that he could improve the world.

'Maybe they don't,' he said, imitating the singsong of a Jewish prayer. 'But maybe they do have a Jewish problem but don't speak about it. Can the party not decide one day that the Jews are counter-revolutionaries? That they are capitalists or cosmopolitans, or Trotskyists or enemies of the masses? Once a Jew always a Jew, and anti-Semitism is not a German invention. It is a poisonous plant that has flourished in Spain and France and Russia for a thousand years. Today it is in full bloom in Germany but who knows where it will crop up next?'

The oven boy wanted to answer but Alex Ehren held up his hand.

'Let him finish. Didn't you say three ways?'

'The third way is to be what you are. To make peace with it and draw the consequences. To go to Palestine.'

'And live with the curse?'

'Where everybody is Jewish the word Jew isn't a curse. It doesn't trail a bad taste, a smell. It is a word like any other. A Frenchman doesn't mind being called a Frenchman and an

Eskimo is not ashamed to live in an igloo. A shoemaker isn't insulted if you call him a cobbler and even a thief may not object to being called a thief. Once you accept your Jewishness you won't mind if they call you a Jew.'

The communists had an organisation that embraced all the camps and they all, even Dezo Kovac and Himmelblau and Hynek Rind, accepted their leadership. Most of the time Pavel Hoch handed over the money and jewels he had found. Yet some of the money and two small jewels he kept hidden behind a beam.

It was June and the silt had dried into hard cake, which cracked in spidery patterns. The prisoners had to work with a pickaxe to break the surface to lay the pavement. The stones didn't sink into the mud and the road had almost reached the Children's Block. Felsen's paper and the handwritten sheet were filled with hopes and promises. The children waited for the issue and when Bass pinned it on the Block wall, they read it and repeated the names of places and cities they had never heard before. But even the small ones, those who could hardly read, like Alex Ehren's Maccabees, picked up the names and asked: 'Where is El Alamein and what is Crimea? What kind of place is Tarnopol and how far is it for the Russians to come to Birkenau?'

Alex Ehren borrowed the torn atlas from the girl librarian and looked up the towns on crumpled maps with countries and frontiers that had long ago ceased to exist. At the beginning of the month the camp was awash with rumours and even the old and sick, who were swollen from hunger, lifted their heads and listened.

'The end may come sooner than we think,' said Felsen. 'Sebastapol has fallen and the Red Army is at the Carpathians.'

He had memorised a number of Russian sentences to greet the Soviet soldiers at the camp gate. There were other rumours, strange and exciting like exotic landscapes, about the German defeat in Tunis and Libya and about the British landing in Sicily and even about the fall of Rome. They were like ocean tides because they came and went – one day there was a rumour that the Americans had landed in France but the next morning a trainload of French Jews arrived at the platform. They heard that the Russians had conquered Hungary but the Hungarian transports kept rolling in, day after day, and their smoke eclipsed the stars and the sun.

The deportees had no way of knowing the truth and they lived on hearsay that spread like a grapevine on the barracks walls and on the electric fences.

On Mondays and Wednesdays, the children still had their afternoon parties and played Aryeh's charades. That week the actors showed the battle of Jericho and Fabian made Joshua's soldiers speak Russian. He sat with Marta Felix, who was good at languages, and she helped him write the dialogue.

Sometimes they were reckless and their little plays and songs were a revolt against the Germans. There had been three successful escapes from the camp: Rudi the Slovakian Registrar with his friend Wetzler; and Lederer the Block Senior, who had reported about the gas chambers in Birkenau. Their letters must have arrived in England and America, the Soviet Union and even Palestine, and by now the presidents, kings and governments of the world knew about the organised murder. They knew about the transports, the selections, the naked Hungarian maidens and even about the Children's Block in the Family Camp. Was it possible that they had heard and did nothing? That they slept at night, ate their meals, made love to their wives and forgot about Majda, Eva and Hanka, the twin girls, Adam Landau and Neugeboren? If only a part of the rumours of the German defeats in Africa, Russia and Sicily was true; if the American planes dropped bombs on German factories and towns, why couldn't they stop the trains with Jewish prisoners or destroy the Birkenau death factory? Or was the news about the inevitable fall of Germany only wishful thinking, an invention of the underground movement to keep up the spirit of the inmates? How was it possible that in the middle of a crumbling war the SS still had enough trains to carry Jews to their death?

They had only a very short time to live – two weeks, perhaps three, and each of them fought against time in a different way. Fabian defended himself with mockery and ridicule. He had a group of children actors with whom he prepared morbid sketches, one-act scenes, in which they poked fun at transports, lice, Germans and even the chimney.

He produced a play about a train to heaven. The passengers were met by St Peter, who conducted a selection of those who would go to Paradise, Purgatory or who would be sent to hell.

'Excuse me, is this Birkenau or heaven?' one of the arrivals asked.

'Of course it is heaven. *Protektorat* heaven, to be exact. Don't you know, you blockhead, that it has been taken over by the German Army? Operation Paradise. The SS have made it *Judenrein.* All Jews, including St Mary and Jesus Christ were sent on a transport to hell.'

It was a sad and cynical play but it made the children laugh, which was a remedy against their fear.

They had their sing-alongs with Fabian, who paced the horizontal smokestack and conducted '*Alouette*' or some other popular song. They sang loudly, with their mouths wide open, swaying left and right in rhythm with the tune, repeating the refrain again and again. The sing-alongs kept the children's community together because when they sang they forgot their hunger and misery and were like one body with a strong, healthy and even happy voice.

He was full of plans and ideas as if their time were not running out and he had years to carry them out. He basked in his popularity and enjoyed the children's applause.

'What is art—' he grinned and rubbed his cracked glasses '—if not a substitute for life? We have no life and so I make art.'

The Zionist instructors gathered the children in a corner, lit a stubby candle and sang Hebrew songs with words they only half understood. There was a mystique in their togetherness and when they sang they put their hands over their neighbour's shoulder and created a magic circle. Others sang Czech folk songs and German *Wanderlieder* with the children, but there was little rivalry and one group learned from another until there were no borders among the singers and their songs.

Since the Seder night Dezo Kovac had a group of children with the clearest voices. Sometimes, on Shabbat Eve, they sang the 'Ode to Joy', but he also taught them '*Dona Nobis Pacem*' from Verdi's *Requiem* and a march from a children's opera they had sung in the ghetto.

They had no instruments on the Block save a mouth organ and a cracked flute, but they produced music with their voices and there was hardly a day when the children did not sing.

'How can they sing in such a place?' asked Mietek.

'The birds are dead,' Magdalena said. 'Somebody has to take over.'

The children and the instructors grew accustomed to the music but the occasional visitors were struck by the tattered youngsters who squatted on the dirt floor and sang, '*Joy, thou divine spark of Heaven, Daughter of Elysium*'. Even the smaller children learned the melody and Bubenik, who was obsessed with drums, beat the rhythm on his soup bowl.

Alex Ehren knew that their make-believe Block saved not only the children but also themselves. They could have surrendered, like many others did, and sunk into despair, losing their humanity and rummaging in the garbage bins behind the kitchen for rotting rinds and spoiled potatoes. They could have become like wild animals and let the children fend for themselves. They knew that they would die; they even knew the date of their death, half a year after their arrival in Birkenau. They counted the days and were scared of time. They prepared to fight the SS guards with a sharpened spoon handle, an iron anchor, four crowbars and the handful of arms, which the seamstress hid under the bales of clothes. Yet as long as they stuck to

Fredy's rules, washed each morning and sang with the children about joy and peace and the brotherhood of men, they were not lost. They were like the pitiful toy soldiers, which Shashek produced from wood and rusty wire. The boys lined them up in rows and shot at them with their marbles made of hardened bread. The soldiers fell but the boys picked them up and made them stand again. What chance, Alex Ehren asked himself, had the conspirators against the dogs and the electrified wires, the watchtowers, the SS garrison and the German war machine?

'What matters is not what will happen,' said Lisa Pomnenka, 'but what is now.'

They used different weapons and fought on many fronts, against fear, dirt, hunger and vermin. They didn't fight because they were brave or well-trained or led by a military man. They fought because it was the only thing they could do. The Block and the painted wall were their El Alamein and Stalingrad and the plains of Crimea.

Alex Ehren made it a rule to save a slice of bread every day. He added the slice to the one he had already saved until he had a whole ration. He ate the old bread and kept the fresh for the next evening until he saved up two rations and at the end he had a whole loaf of bread. It was a treasure, a trove of food, which would sustain him for several days, even a week, if necessary.

The girl teased him about his miserliness and hoarding of bread.

'Why not have one royal meal,' she said, 'and go to bed with a full stomach? Tomorrow will take care of itself. I may get some food from the doctor.'

Alex Ehren could never free himself from the thought of tomorrow. He thought about the uprising, the breakthrough and walking in the darkness and about the deep woods of the Slovakian mountains. He knew that they wouldn't be able to buy food or to steal from a farmstead. He imagined how they would hide in a gully or in a cave, live on berries and mushrooms like hermits, until they made contact with other escaped prisoners or partisans. He also kept a finely sharpened knife hidden within his loaf.

'One day,' he said, 'the bread might keep us alive.'

There were two pairs of twins on the Block – two older boys and a pair of kindergarten girls. From time to time the twins were summoned to the Hospital Block where they stayed for half a day, a day sometimes, and then returned with a piece of bread or a slice of sausage. Dr Mengele sent an orderly to fetch them and soon the camp reverberated with the shouted summons.

'Twins on Block Thirty-two; twins on Thirty-two,' and all the inmates repeated the words. The labourers that worked in the ditches, those who knelt and broke rocks on the road, the men who stood guard in front of each barracks and even Sonia, who staggered under the burden of the soup barrel, all took up the call and shouted it in a frenzy of obedience. There was a punishment for those who wouldn't fall in with the shouting and the Capo beat the recalcitrant ones with a cane until they lifted their arms in defence and shouted with the others.

The SS doctor made Lisa Pomnenka the warden of the twins. She accompanied them to the Hospital Block, waited until he had completed his measurements and then took them back. The doctor's projects ran concurrently to one another. Sometimes he was more involved in his sterilisation scheme, another time in his research of inferior races and then again in his work with twins. They offered a rare opportunity because the identical twin would be an ideal control subject when he decided to infect his brother or cut out one of his glands. Birkenau, with its influx of death-bound prisoners, was a superb ground for research, as never before had a scientist had such an inexhaustible pool and supply of human specimens.

The Jews were abundant and dispensable, and when an experiment needed to be repeated, there were always thousands of others to replace the dead. Their lives were cheap, because, as they were to die anyway, it didn't matter whether they were suffocated by gas or died on the operating table. The people arrived in sealed boxcars – ten, sometimes twelve thousand each day ... men and women and children – and he had but to move his hand to have as many of them as he wanted. Sometimes, on his luckier days, he found three generations of the same family, which helped him trace a genetic flaw or malformation so frequent among the inferior races.

He had plans for Lisa Pomnenka, who, with her long skull and blue eyes might have some Germanic blood. He had taught her to draw family trees and diagrams in different colours and it would be a waste of time to train a new assistant. She spoke decent German and was good with the twins and there was no reason why she shouldn't serve him even when the rest were gone.

Once he showed her pictures to a friend, an SS officer who then commissioned the girl to paint a storybook for him. He brought her fairy tale texts and made her produce illustrations for *Hansel and Gretel, Little Red Riding Hood* and *Jack and the Beanstalk*. He was about to go on leave the next afternoon and he ordered her to stay in the Gypsy Camp overnight to finish the gift for his children.

'I thought you were never coming back.' Alex Ehren was bitter as if her absence had been her fault. He had waited for the girl on the road and was relieved when he saw her coming through the gate.

'One day I might not come back.' She laid her hand on his sleeve. 'The SS doctor wants to transfer me to another camp.'

Lisa Pomnenka felt sorry for the man in the tattered jacket. He tried to look neat, possibly for her sake, and his face was shaven.

He washed his shirt and wore the cap she had knitted for him at a rakish angle. He tried hard to keep his spirits up in spite of his fear and hunger, and he waited with his evening meal until she returned from the Gypsy Camp. He spun plans for an uprising, an escape and refuge in the woods. She looked at the one pitiful loaf of bread he kept wrapped in a piece of cloth and she knew how foolish, how impossible, his hopes were, but as she knew no other solution, she kept silent. She loved him, but what use was there in dying together when she might leave him and remain alive.

'I have a surprise for you,' she said, and kissed him on the mouth in front of the old men wrapped in their blankets and the old women that shuffled back and forth on their swollen feet. She stood very close and her black hair smelled young in the evening wind. 'Stay on the Block after the curfew.'

'How can I? The Block Senior counts us on our bunks.'

'He needn't know.' She held her hand over her mouth to hide a smile.

Alex Ehren had often dreamt about being with the girl, but it was always only a thought, far-fetched and imaginary. Sometimes, when they sat next to each other and he touched her hand or her shoulder, he was full of desire and pictured her naked skin and the shape of her body. But it had always been a dream, an idea, something that would never come true. Now, when she asked him to stay overnight in the Matron's cubicle, he was shy and self-conscious of his body.

He went to the washroom alone, long before the morning roll call, and he stripped and washed from head to toe in the sparse trickle of water. It was still dark and he saw the fading stars and a sliver of predawn moon. The stars were clear among the running clouds, though to the east they had grown pale with the promise of a new day. There was beauty in the June morning and yet he felt sad and abandoned. There was ambivalence in his existence, he thought, a double link of death and life, a taste of the end in each beginning. The breeze smelled of river but it was marred by the smoke that trailed, dark and bittersweet, over the landscape. There was an intimation of death in his daily routine of waking and falling asleep, his work with the children and even in the promise of lovemaking that night.

And yet the awareness of his imminent death sweetened the bread he ate and every breath of air became an experience because it was numbered and finite. He treasured even his squalor, the cold of his nights and the hunger of his days, because they were the only life he had. He shrunk away from the nothingness of non-being, but at the same time the finality of his time sharpened his sense of living. The insignificant trifles of his present – his towel, his mess-bowl, the broken comb – carried a luminescence, a beauty and meaning they would never have acquired in a different setting.

The Block was quiet without the children's voices and the bustle of the day. Alex Ehren had never seen the eighteen stands, the wooden stage and the chimney stack empty and silent. After the arrival of the May transports there were more than five hundred children on the Block and they took turns playing outside to let others squat on the floor and listen to the teacher.

The two bare bulbs over the chimney gave hardly any light and the corners were full of ghosts. Under Himmelblau's door was a bright chink and Alex Ehren stepped back.

Lisa Pomnenka motioned with her hand. 'He doesn't mind.'

He was embarrassed that Himmelblau knew but so did Fabian, who stuffed a blanket on his bunk and covered up for him.

The girl laid the table with a blue cloth. She put two enamel plates from the Gypsy Camp on it and stoked the cast-iron stove. They ate hot soup and a potato spread with cheese and then Lisa Pomnenka put a brown cake on the table. It was, like so many other things on the Block, a make-believe cake made of the bread the SS officer had paid for her storybook. She had cut the loaf into slices, spread them with jam and laid one on top of the other. She dressed the top with margarine sweetened with sugar. They drank tea she had saved from the morning and when they had eaten they sat at the wooden table, silent and at a loss at their sudden intimacy.

She had been formal and polite during their meal as if trying to keep up the illusion that they were in a different time and in a different place, and that the Block, the camp and even the next day didn't exist. It had been a long time, two years perhaps, since Alex Ehren was alone in a room and he stood up and paced the three steps from one wall of the tiny cubicle to the other and then stopped and held his palms above the stove. It was an exquisite experience to have a private place, a room all for himself. Yet he was still too shy to touch the girl.

Lisa Pomnenka took off her woollen jacket, which had been a gift from the seamstress. She stepped out of her skirt and unbuttoned her shirt and Alex Ehren watched in wonderment as she rolled back her dark stockings until the room grew fragrant with her nudity. She was, he thought, like a butterfly that had broken through its chrysalis. There were two separate worlds, he thought again, one dressed and the other naked, which were like two circles that did not touch during the day but intertwined at night.

She watched him with her open blue eyes as he undressed, clumsily and with his hand over his private parts, and then he turned towards her.

They touched and he felt the silk of her skin and his hand moved to the valley of her waist and he stroked her belly and navel. For a short while he drowned in the security of homecoming and was lost in time. They made love and Alex Ehren was surprised at the passion that flowed through the girl. It was as if they had exchanged roles and she was the stronger, the older and the more vital in the game of lovemaking. She gave herself generously, with total abandonment, though Alex Ehren was unable to shut off his awareness, to expose himself, to lower his defences and to speak about the pleasure they gave each other. It was as if the terrors of the last months had built a wall, which stood cold and forbidding, between his heart and the outside world. He knew that he wasn't her first lover but, afterwards, he was reluctant to ask about the men she had known before him.

She was lovely in her nakedness, delicate and with boyish hips and movements. The thought that he would lose her was like a wound and an affliction.

'I'll always remember,' he said, 'wherever we might be.'

'You won't—' she shook her head '—because we live what is and not what was or will be.'

She fell asleep with her dark head on his arm and he wondered whether their intimacy had brought them closer or had opened a wound and driven a wedge between them.

Next evening Lisa Pomnenka didn't return to the Camp. At first he thought she was working overnight for the SS doctor, but when another day passed and then another, he understood that she was gone, transferred to another compound or dead. He asked Mietek, Julius Abeles, who came and went with the Cart Commando, and even the Gypsy prisoner who brought the children soup, but they knew nothing of the girl.

The first days were the worst and he longed for her blue eyes, her smile, her hands and the touch of her body. One of the Clothes Storeroom prisoners might have informed the SS on her kerosene bottles, but when nobody came to search the Block, he dismissed the suspicion. The German physician conducted terrible experiments and he might have used her for one of his operations. She might also be saved, he thought, because the doctor wouldn't want her to perish with the condemned transport. It occurred to him that she had disappeared because their time was up and they were soon to die.

They had made love and her fragrance still lingered on his hands and he wouldn't forget her for as long as he was allowed to live. He loved her but he was unable to mourn for her deeply. He wondered how did she know? Were they all robbed of their ability to love, to mourn, to hate? Was it the utter exposure to death, the days and nights and weeks when he knew the date of his execution that made him lose his humanity? He didn't know. His time was like a spiral that spun around its axis, faster and faster in an ever-diminishing circle, and when the spiral and the pivot became one, he too would cease to exist.

He remembered the naked maidens in the adjoining camp, his friend Beran, who had died instead of another man, the September transport, the Hungarians and the frozen corpses that lined his road to Birkenau. They were all gone, like water in a sluice, in a sequence of arrivals and departures, and because there were so many dead in such a short time, he could feel little sadness or pity even for the girl he had loved.

# 11.

IN THE MIDDLE OF JUNE, THEIR LAST MONTH, AUNT MIRIAM fell ill. She ran a temperature, had a sore throat and in the morning couldn't swallow. She went to see the doctor, who diagnosed diphtheria and sent her to the infection ward. There were always outbreaks of contagious diseases in the Camp. Once it was encephalitis, an infection of the brain, another time typhus, which was transmitted by lice, or scarlet fever or an epidemic of festering sores. The vermin and bad food caused diarrhoea, which the paramedic treated with a white powder called *bolus* that stuck to the tongue and choked the throat. It was strange that the infections didn't spread faster, but possibly because the sick died so soon, they had no time to pass their illness on to others.

Aryeh bribed the hospital orderly to take his mother a bowl of pudding, the sweet mush they cooked from crumbled cakes. He spoke to Miriam through the wooden wall and she said that she felt better and would return to work in a week or two. She was a quiet, reliable woman, who didn't have an enemy in the world, and Himmelblau was relieved that she would be back on the Block in the critical time ahead.

The matron had a privileged position in the Camp because of Edelstein, her husband, who had been the

Ghetto Eldest. The Germans had arrested him for reasons she didn't know. Some said it was because a number of ghetto inmates had escaped; others believed he shouldn't have visited the Bialystok children, who passed through the ghetto on their way to Auschwitz and still others thought that he had learned about the gas chambers, which the SS wanted to keep secret.

At the beginning Miriam didn't know where he was. She thought that he was still in Theresienstadt, in another concentration camp or in a prison in Berlin. He had worked with Eichmann, and when the officer visited the Family Camp, he promised to take a letter to her husband.

'One day we may permit a visit,' said Eichmann and looked at her through his cold spectacles.

It was only later that she learned how close he was – half an hour's walk away – and she and the boy lived in the hope that they might see him again. They heard of Edelstein here and there, from a prisoner who had met him at the infirmary where he had come for treatment, on his walk around the prison yard and once when he carried out his bucket.

One day three SS officers visited the camp. They walked quickly up the camp road, inspected the workshops and even peered into the Children's Block. The next day the Block Seniors and the Registrars compiled lists of the prisoners, separate lists for women and men. They wrote down their tattooed numbers, age and profession and there was a rumour that the Family Camp would be dismantled and the inmates sent to labour camps in Germany.

There were other omens of an approaching change. The mica workshop and the weaving plant didn't get a new supply of material and when the women exhausted the stock, the shops were closed and the labourers sent to another commando. The same happened at the Clothes Storeroom, where all the workers were dismissed and the Clothes Capo was left only with the prisoners' rags, with the seamstress and Pavel Hoch as his only helpers. There were no new bales, no deliveries and no boxes packed for Germany. The seamstress had a hard time concealing the contraband on the half-empty shelves and Felsen warned the underground triads to be cautious and not to meet until the danger blew over.

On Monday two men from the Cart Commando were taken to the Main Camp for interrogation and in the evening the Priest discovered a cache of pickaxes and crowbars on one of the blocks. There was nothing unusual about prisoners being taken to the Camp Gestapo, the German secret service, and many Block Seniors had in their cubicles a stolen hammer, a pickaxe or a spade, which were needed to dig a ditch around the block. Nobody was publicly flogged or executed, and a day later the Cart Commando people were returned to the camp. Yet with the lists, the closed workshops and the visit of the three high-ranking officers, there sprouted a rumour about an informer in their midst.

At first it was just a whisper. Alex Ehren overheard it from the adjoining bunk but paid no attention. The bunks were full of tales; they bred and propagated like lice and most often proved to be fiction or a false alarm. There was no reason, he thought, why Julius Abeles should be an informer. Usually a rumour lived for a day and then died, supplanted by another story or other news, about the war, the Camp Capo or the distribution of the bread rations. Yet the word spread and grew wings and soon was all over the block until it burst open like a poisonous fruit. People spoke about 'Julius the Informer' and pointed him out to one another on the camp road. A man saw him stand with a guard and another watched him leave the block at night, another added some gossip and the next one took it for granted. The only person who seemed unaware of the suspicion was Julius Abeles, who left to work in the morning, hitched himself horse-like to the cart, and dragged a load of potatoes to the kitchen and then a burden of bodies to the incinerator. Like all the Cart Commando, he knew about the planned mutiny. In fact, the Commando people were an essential link with other compounds and with the underground leadership. They bartered bread for tobacco and stole from the prisoners' rations, but also smuggled news and contraband material into the camp.

It was true that Julius Abeles didn't believe in the uprising. He ridiculed the communist underground, Felsen and the seamstress, with whom he had a running feud because he refused to pay up into the weapon fund.

'The camp is more important than your profit. Only together have we got a chance.'

'It's dog eat dog here. Each for himself and no party or underground movement will help me if my number is up.'

He was ready to take his share of danger and carry forbidden stuff under a cargo of beetroot, but he was greedy and never parted with the small hoard of valuables he had stowed away.

'What nonsense,' he said to Alex Ehren, 'to fight the Germans with sticks and spoons. They will shoot us all.'

'What else can we do?'

'There are ways.' He looked around cautiously. 'The war can't last forever and there is a price for everything. Even from the September transport some survived. And who survived? Those who could pay. Do you think the SS physician saved the doctors and the apothecary for nothing?'

He was all set on buying and selling, and judged the world accordingly. Once or twice he had dealings with a German, an SS guard of Czech origin, for whom he procured a watch from a Kanada worker and another time a pair of leather boots. Yet he preferred to trade with prisoners, with the Block Seniors and cooks but also with ordinary inmates on his barracks. There was a great deal of envy among the people, who purchased from him a pinch of tobacco, a needle and thread, or leased a pencil stub for two spoons of soup; some prisoners hated the dealer who sold them tobacco on credit and for the next three days cashed the debt from their meagre bread ration.

One night there was a commotion among the bunks. During curfew hours the inmates relieved themselves into tin containers at the rear end of the barracks where the Block Services deposited the bodies of those who had died during the night. It was a murky place, smelling of death, spilled urine and excrement, forbidding and horrible.

'What is it?' exclaimed Julius Abeles, when the men closed in around him. 'No, I am not your man. I buy and sell but, no, I've sold no information.'

There were more men at the rear now. Alex Ehren saw the dark shapes of prisoners who climbed down from the bunks and joined the growing crowd. The ring swelled until there were a hundred men, some not knowing what the commotion was about, though others rushed forward with violent intent. He listened to the hum, angry and ominous like the roar of a waterfall, and Julius's pitched protestations.

'Why should I squeal?' he cried out. 'What good would it do me? Am I a Block Senior or a Capo? If there is a traitor among us, you will have to look for him somewhere else. Leave me alone; I am not the rat you want.'

There was no evidence against Julius Abeles. The prisoners who were taken for interrogation by the Gestapo, returned beaten and bruised, but none of them had been punished or put in solitary confinement. The Germans certainly didn't know about the mutiny because they hadn't touched Felsen or the seamstress, nor did they conduct a search at the place where the contraband material was concealed. It was a false accusation, either random or spread on purpose by his enemy.

Alex Ehren felt that he should climb down and defend the man, but he was scared of the angry multitude and didn't budge. He justified his cowardice by his responsibility for the children whom he couldn't leave. There were the adolescent boys who worked on the Children's Block but at night stayed with male inmates. The younger boys slept with their mothers on the Women's Block, but the orphans, even the very small ones, were on the Men's Block close to their teachers. The boys on the pallet opposite woke and lifted their heads.

'What is it?' Neugeboren was about to get down and see for himself, but Alex Ehren didn't let him because at the rear a terrible thing was happening.

'Death to informers. Go into the wires,' shouted a man and beat Julius Abeles about his head. 'Death to traitors. Into the wires.' The voices were like an echo that rose and grew and multiplied.

'I am no informer. You have no right!' lisped Julius Abeles over his broken tooth. 'I've done nothing. Check it out. I swear it's a mistake.'

He started out confidently, loudly, but his lisping voice weakened and fell until it became a shadow of a sound.

There was no reason and no pity in the crowd, and they beat the scrawny man with their fists and with their wooden clogs, which they took off their feet. They weren't men with names any more, but just an angry mass of bodies, hungry and scared and on the verge of death. They were frightened and desperate, and like dogs in a pack, ready to tear at anything. They didn't know what or whom he might have betrayed; they had no idea what the accusation was and yet they wanted him dead. Most of the men didn't know about Felsen and the triads or the kerosene bottles at the Clothes Storeroom. They hated him not for what he had done but because they ached to vent their own anger and frustration and fear. They fell on Julius Abeles with their clenched fists, their teeth bared, blindly, ferociously, they hit him on his head, on his back ... everywhere.

One of the men opened the back door and they pushed him towards the crack.

'I'll pay!' cried Julius Abeles in a desperate effort to save his life. 'There is enough for everybody. I'll get you two loaves of bread. What's the hurry? Wait for tomorrow. When there is light you will see I am the wrong man. It's somebody else, not me.'

He looked into the darkness of the block for support, to those for whom he had found medicine, white bread and a piece of rag. He needed a friend to come to his rescue. There was an immense mob by now, half of the block, two hundred men perhaps, and Alex Ehren knew that he should face the crowd, cry out, defend him, but he was helpless against their fury. He was ashamed of his cowardice, but he stayed on his berth and did nothing.

The noise at the rear abated but the fury didn't stop. The prisoners beat Julius Abeles until he bled from his nose and mouth but the slaughter went on. There was little sound save the dull blows and the man's stifled sobs, as if somebody had covered his mouth. The door opened wider and Alex Ehren saw Julius Abeles move into the light of the projector. He held his hands above his head and stumbled forwards, propelled by the hubbub of rage and hatred. He was outlined against the wires, small, miserable and bent with pain. The SS sentry shouted a warning. Alex Ehren heard two shots, and then like an afterthought, a third and final reverberation.

The dead man's bunk was empty. Then there were hands. They came from all sides, from the bunk above and from the berths underneath, greedy, grabbing, tearing and penetrating into Julius Abeles's blanket and mattress. The darkness grew alive with fingers, wild and uncouth, pillaging the bread, the jam and the crumbled cheese that Julius had hidden under his head. There was a squish and a rustle of spilled straw, but soon even that stopped and all was silent again.

'Go to sleep,' Alex Ehren said to the boys. 'There's no point in staying awake. He was mad to run out of the block during curfew.'

He knew that the boys didn't believe him but there was nothing else he could have said.

In the morning the Block Warden gathered the body from under the wires and laid it among the rest of the dead. He was very small and there was only a little blood on his chest and belly. Alex Ehren wondered whether anybody had found the satchel of gold and diamonds, with which Julius Abeles had hoped to bail himself out.

Life on the Children's Block didn't change. There were only a few days left, certainly less than a week, and Alex Ehren ticked off his hours, his mornings and his nights. They had arrived on two trains last December, one on the 16th and the other two days later. Would it be six months after the first or the second transport's arrival? It was immensely important to keep up the routine, the morning wash, the lessons and games and even the competitions, because each day the children were spared fear and chaos was a benefit, a victory over despair.

For their Wednesday party Fabian found a singer who gave a performance of popular songs and arias. The camp was full of artistes that had been on stage, actors, singers and musicians, who, for a piece of bread or an additional portion of soup, were ready to give a show. Yet even more important than the bit of food was the applause they reaped from the children.

The singer, La Baum, had been famous in the pre-war days and she came to the Block in her ill-fitting coat, wooden clogs and a kerchief over her hair. However, she had managed to find lipstick, and her face was made up and her hair combed into a crown. She wasn't young any more, and life in the camp had added a number of years to her age. Yet the moment La Baum climbed on the stage that Shashek had built on the chimney, she was transformed and young again. She wrapped a tattered shawl around her shoulders and she sang and moved in small mincing steps as if she weren't standing on an old table but performing in front of a full house with all the lights shining on her.

The last section of the meadow on the wall was unfinished and the bare planks stood out like an open wound. Lisa Pomnenka had painted half of a tree green and leafy but the other half was left only in a sketchy outline. There were still the ladder and her painting paraphernalia, a piece of rag, some turpentine and an apron, which she used to tie around her waist to keep her skirt clean. Shashek wouldn't move the ladder or the pot of paint, and kept it where the girl had stopped working.

'She may come back,' he repeated with his face folded into an involuntary grin. 'She wouldn't leave half a tree unfinished.'

Since she was gone the children had no handicraft lessons, but the Dutch girl was good with her hands and she could, at least for a day or two, keep the girls occupied with paper folding and with their little pictures of trees, houses and animals they had never seen.

Each time Alex Ehren looked at the make-believe landscape, the *trompe l'oeil* meadow, the copse, the birds and the wooden railing with the geranium pots, he remembered the girl. He ached for her proximity, for the touch of her skin, her fragrance and her sudden, birdlike turn of head, but he didn't grieve. She might be dead, or now live in another compound, but he had no power to change anything. He would probably never learn what happened to her and he had to make peace with his helplessness. It was as if his own fear had made him numb and impervious even to his feeling of loss. There was no sense in regret, he thought, because she might be better off where she was now than if she had stayed with the death-bound December contingent. His work carried him through the 16th, the 17th and the 18th of June. Even on the 20th, which would have been the day of their execution, nothing unusual happened – save for one thing, which, as they initially believed, might be a good omen.

In mid-morning a green military car drove up to the Registrar's office. Soon afterwards the three members of the Edelstein family, Miriam, her mother and the boy were summoned to the camp gate. The boy Aryeh heard the summons and he walked out on the camp road. There could be only one reason why the family was called to the Registrar's office.

He stood on the road where the labourers chipped stones and built them into a hard surface.

'I'm going to see Edelstein,' he said and his thin face was bright with a smile.

It is a good omen, thought Alex Ehren, who had feared the day for three months. We are alive and there is no sign of danger, no preparations, no curfew and no SS sentries with dogs. The boy is going to meet his father and things might look up. Edelstein's name carried a certain magic because back in the ghetto the Eldest had a way with the Germans. He used to haggle with the SS commanders about the number of transports and to intercede for the life of prisoners who were caught with contraband cigarettes or with a letter smuggled by a friend through the ghetto catacombs.

It was he who coaxed the authorities to establish children's homes, to allow them a playground on the bastion and increase their food rations. The visit might be a good turn because if they were to be put to death why should Edelstein be allowed to see his family?

The boy waited in front of the Hospital Block and then they went, the boy, his grandmother and his mother on a stretcher, down the camp road. And as they passed the dark barracks, the deportees looked up from their stones and there was a glint of hope in their eyes.

'There might be a change of plans,' said Felsen, who was in touch with the underground organisation.

Even Fabian woke up from his gloominess and watched the procession.

'Who knows, the Germans might grant us another six months.'

In the meantime, the group reached the green car at the end of the road.

'One sick prisoner,' announced the Hospital Senior with his arms at his sides. The officer nodded and looked at Aunt Miriam.

'Get up and walk. Two steps won't kill you.' He lit another cigarette and sat next to the driver.

A day later they learned of Edelstein's death. A Polish convict came to the Children's Block and told them. The SS officer had brought Aryeh, Aunt Miriam and her mother to the penal block in the Main Camp.

'You asked to see your family,' said Hessler, the SS officer. 'Here they are.'

He drew his revolver and shot the boy in the head, then his mother and then the old woman. At the end he shot Edelstein. None of them cried.

In the evening they gathered at the rear of the Block – the instructors and matrons, the adolescent youth assistants and the school children – and said *Kaddish* for Edelstein. For most of them it was the first time they said *Kaddish* because although there were many deaths, there were no funerals. Most of the children came from non-observant assimilated families and had little knowledge of religious matters. They were like Hynek Rind, who believed he was Czech, or Felsen the communist or Marta Felix, who didn't believe in God.

'How can you believe—' she shook her head '—even those who had faith must have lost it.'

'It is a matter of acceptance,' Dezo Kovac said, as if he were speaking to himself. 'God has little to do with religion. He doesn't need us. We need him.'

The children didn't understand the Aramaic in which Dezo Kovac recited the prayer. He translated the words and wrote them on scraps of paper and the children could read them in their language, in Czech, German or Dutch.

'*Yisgadal ve yiskadash,*' recited Dezo Kovac, facing Lisa Pomnenka's painted wall, which was the direction of Jerusalem. 'Blessed and praised, glorified and exalted, extolled and honoured, adorned and lauded be the Name of the Holy One, blessed be He, beyond all blessings and hymns, praises and consolations that are ever spoken in the world, and say *Amen*.'

Alex Ehren didn't want to praise God for death or for the misery and squalor and fear they had to suffer. He was reluctant to trust in a God that was indifferent to their death and who had no pity on Neugeboren and Majda and Bubenik and the rest of the children, who by now had learned to read whole words.

Edelstein, Aunt Miriam, her mother, and the boy Aryeh were irrevocably dead, and he was unable to acquiesce to the void of non-being, theirs, his or anybody's. Did they die in vain like the many thousands that arrived in Birkenau every day? Or were they perhaps executed as a symbol and sacrifice, which would allow the rest of the inmates in the Family Camp to live? Were they all – he and the ten thousand other prisoners – a burnt offering that would perhaps, somewhere in the future, serve a purpose? Or was the universe nothing but a matter of random, an absurdity, a maelstrom of accidental particles? He didn't know. He rebelled against a God whom he was unable to understand and whose justice was different from human experience. He didn't want to become resigned, to accept and make peace with his mortality and yet he said with all the others, '*Va yomar Amen*', and say Amen.

They stood with their faces towards the make-believe meadow, the flowers and the flying birds, which was also the direction of Jerusalem. They repeated the Aramaic invocation composed at the time of the destruction of the Temple. It was a prayer that made peace with death and which had been recited for every dead Jew for two thousand years. It was terrible, thought Alex Ehren, that the first Jewish prayer his children ever heard was a prayer for the dead. Yet at the same time it was as if they had returned home to what they had always been, without the lie and pretence that they were what they were not.

'Sometimes,' said Himmelblau, 'it is permitted to say *Kaddish de Rosh Galut*, a *Kaddish* for a teacher or the Head of the Exiled. I don't know,' he went on in his poor Czech, 'whether Edelstein was a great teacher but he certainly was the Ghetto Eldest for almost three years. I think—' he looked at the teachers, the matrons and the children '—we may consider him a Head of the Exiled.'

'We pray for the Ghetto Eldest Jakob Edelstein and for all the House of Israel,' chanted Dezo Kovac, and the children repeated the words in Czech and some in German. 'We pray for our teachers and their disciples and the disciples of their disciples, and for all that study the law here and elsewhere. May heaven send abundant peace and life to us and to all Israel, and I say Amen.'

And he tore away a shred of his tattered shirt and scattered a pinch of ashes on his head.

*

The day after, they mourned. They mourned as they had not mourned before, although there had been other dead – Lisa Pomnenka's father, the children who succumbed to encephalitis, the old man with the smouldering fire and Alex Ehren's friend Beran. There had been the frozen corpses that lined the road to Birkenau, the Hungarians and even Julius Abeles, who died of human envy and greed. It wasn't Edelstein and his family for whom they mourned but for themselves, and the *Kaddish* they recited was not only for the dead but also for the living.

Weren't they the Exiled and the House of Israel, thought Alex Ehren, and weren't they all as if dead already? Edelstein was, for them, more than a person. He was a symbol and a name, a kind of incantation against the unknown. Back in the ghetto they had grown to believe that his name created a protective wall between them and the Germans and now, when the wall was gone, they felt naked and exposed to evil. They also mourned Aunt Miriam, Edelstein's wife. The children had become accustomed to her quiet ministrations; it was she who handed out the morsels of sweets after their competitions and without her the Block was cold and orphaned. They mourned the boy Aryeh, their mate and brother, not only because he was dead, but because they saw how fragile their own existence was. There had been the children of the September transport, who were sent to Heydebreck and there were others who fell ill and passed away, but Aryeh was the first child that was taken away and executed. Why was he shot? For what crime? For what reason?

The instructors tried to assuage the children's apprehension.

'Aryeh may be well and alive in some other camp,' said Alex Ehren, but the children were no fools and were afraid and mourned.

The Block still functioned. There were no charades but the Satan in the puppet theatre grew even more daring than before and the children produced so many poems, little drawings and stories that there was no place to pin them all on the wall. The teachers perambulated among the groups and continued narrating the next chapter of their book, and in the evening they kept playing the game called 'the circle'. Marta Felix taught the older groups a bit of Plato and the boy Foltyn never missed a lesson and sat in the corner of the stall, fascinated by her explanations. Beran's book of verses was much in demand, and whenever Fabian read from it aloud, they remembered the tall, clumsy man, who had died to save the life of another.

They thought about the mutiny. One morning Alex Ehren brought the iron anchor from the Hospital Block to the Clothes Block where, so Felsen believed, it would be more accessible in time of need. He went to the Infirmary in broad daylight and extricated the object from under the bed. He wrapped the welded hooks into a blanket and then he and Foltyn carried the thing across the camp road as if they were disposing of a dead body. Alex Ehren tied a rope to the iron and hid it under a heap of wooden clogs.

The days were bright with sunshine and the children played games until the green stretch between the Block and the fence turned yellow and hard. The outlines of the prisoners' lives, like a landscape before a storm, grew more intense, clearer and more pronounced. Most of their future was not in their hands, but some of them had to make decisions.

Towards evening Alex Ehren met Agnes. She was looking good, and well groomed, though her eyes were tired. He noticed her smart jacket and boots and the woollen kerchief she wore over her fair hair.

Agnes had done well in the last weeks. She was a forewoman in the workshop, and the Capo had promised her that when they were transferred to a new camp, she would become a Block Senior or a Capo. There was a strange arrangement in the prison universe that convicts of rank carried their privilege into another camp.

'I am leaving Majda behind.' She averted her eyes. 'Who will look after the children when we are gone?'

'I don't know, some of the older women perhaps. They will not be alone.'

It was a lie, he thought, because once the Block was dismantled, the children couldn't survive.

She knew too but tried to pretend.

What did she want from him? To tell her to abandon the child and remain alive? Or die with Majda when their time came? Who was he to tell her, a stranger, a young man who could have been her son? Or did she think that the teachers, matrons and instructors should stay behind and look after their wards?

Children under sixteen were not in the transport lists. Most of the mothers wouldn't abandon their babies and asked the Registrar to strike out their names from the roster. However, some women like Agnes, who believed that there was no sense in dying with their children, opted for life. Nobody knew what would happen in the next days, though there were rumours that the strong and young would be spared and sent to a labour camp in Germany.

'I don't know,' he repeated and felt guilty together with the woman.

'I may have other children one day,' said Agnes.

She didn't look into his face and stood, young, feminine and desirable even in the squalor of the camp road.

After the Plato lesson Foltyn stayed in the stall. He lingered, leaning his back on the beam and waited for the teacher to fold the scraps of paper on which she had written her notes. They had grown friendly in the fashion teachers and pupils do and she enjoyed the boy's eager mind, his questions and his interest in philosophy. He reminded her of her own adolescence, she thought wistfully, the quest for answers, for direction, the confusion of a world too rich to be grasped. Yes, she thought, the boy had the mind and the curiosity of a student and she was glad to teach him. Yet how long did they have: a day, two, a week?

'More questions?' She was ready to sit with the boy and speak about Plato.

'I have never been with a woman,' said the youth, and his face was flushed with embarrassment.

'What is it?' Marta Felix was startled.

'I have never been with a woman.' He looked at her neck, her breasts and her hands that lay folded in her lap.

At first she didn't understand but when she did she was amused. She would have laughed but she didn't want to hurt the boy, and stopped herself. It was absurd, she thought, like incest almost. She was forty, an old woman by camp standards, and Foltyn was a child of sixteen, seventeen perhaps. What would people say if they heard about the proposal: Fabian; Himmelblau; or her lost friend Miriam? Yet then she looked at the boy again, young and inexperienced but eager to grow up before he died.

'Will you sleep with me?' he mustered all his courage and spoke fast and loud. 'For I have never.'

'I will,' she said, glad that she was still alive and able to do something for the living. Like most of the women in the camp, she had lost her cycle and hunger caused her to forget her femininity. Yet all that didn't matter in the last days of the camp, for the important thing was life at the time of its living.

'Yes,' she replied with abandon, 'I will sleep with you.'

She knew that it wasn't love but rather necessity that made Foltyn ask her, but she was flattered and almost happy. She felt more alive than she had for a long time, but at the core of her heart she was sad, and had she not been shy in front of the boy, she would have cried.

There were almost twelve thousand inmates in the Family Camp and the selections took Dr Mengele several days. He used the Children's Block for the task because all the other barracks were crowded with sleeping bunks and smelly with unwashed prisoners.

Alex Ehren undressed and folded his rags behind the Block where the children had played tug o' war, danced as flowers and bees and bears with Magdalena, the gym teacher, and where he had lifted the blue-veined rock. The stone was still there, close to the wall, large and unwieldy, and he wondered whether it would remain there after he was gone, forever. The Camp Capo, bent forward, limping and leaning on Adam's shoulder, marched the procession up the road. They were a strange pair, the hunchback and the little boy, dressed in identical clothes, a tailored jacket, a striped beret and polished boots. They were like grotesque twins, a caricature and a counter image of each other, reflected in a distorting mirror.

'Step sharply,' the Capo shouted, 'and look alive. You are going to work and not to a pub to drink beer.'

They took with them the youth assistants and the boys from Aryeh's group who could pretend that they were sixteen.

The younger boys remained on the bunks where they tumbled and caused mischief. They climbed like little monkeys with haggard faces, up and down the empty pallets, wreaking havoc on the folded blankets, and stealing bread from under the mattresses.

Alex Ehren waited in the naked queue outside the Block gate. The prisoners were let in one by one in fast succession and as he moved closer to the door, Alex Ehren's mouth grew dry with fear. For three years his life had been ruled by queues – the registration in Prague, the transport to the ghetto, the daily line-ups for food, for medical examination, for the train to Auschwitz, and the final queue for his life or death.

The SS doctor had a table placed in front of the door. He stood there, clean and elegant and well educated. He was the scion of a wealthy family and had never been hungry, degraded or abused. He felt nothing for the naked prisoners whom he condemned with his gloved hand, right to slave labour and left to their deaths. They came in, pale and cringing, stopped for a moment and then disappeared forever. They were like water that flowed in a stream, a job to be done, an order to be carried out.

'Your age and profession,' he said. It was a tedious and unclean task and he drank of the brandy that he put on the table. The table-top was scarred by Shashek's seven trades and an orderly had covered it with a baize cloth. Sometimes the SS physician looked up and saw the painted wall, the stalls and the scraps of paper the children had pinned on the dark planks.

The children, he thought, will have to go. Things had changed and Berlin had no use of them any more. He felt sorry for the Children's Block, which had been a responsibility for many months, and he was lenient with the adolescents. When Bass, the oven boy, lied that he was sixteen, he overlooked the obvious and sent him among the living.

He kept a vestige of decency and men and women undressed in separate contingents. When it was the day of the female barracks, the SS officers who were not on duty came in, stood at the wall and watched the selection, as they had done during the Wednesday children's performances.

They ogled the naked bodies, smoked cigarettes and exchanged smutty remarks about this and that, and sometimes regretted that such an exquisite nudity should go to waste. Some of them were aroused by the young girls, the virgins and nymphets with their budding breasts and only an intimation of hair on their crotch. The doctor was liberal with them too and let the girls pass because it didn't really matter whether they lived or died. They might grow up in a camp, or if they were not up to the slave labour, they would perish there. He was, he thought, not a cruel man and he didn't want to rob them of their chance.

Sometimes the German doctor played a joke on a prisoner. When Magdalena walked in, naked and barefoot, the doctor remembered her from the Children's Block.

'Profession,' he asked.

'A dancer.' The young woman blushed and looked away.

'Then dance.' He pointed with his cane at the horizontal chimney stack.

She was uncomfortable under the greedy eyes of the SS officers, but she climbed on the chimney, naked and unprotected by her rags. There was still the old table, the wooden stage where the children had performed their shows, their Robinson Crusoe and Beethoven's 'Ode to Joy' and where, once a week, Fabian and Marta Felix had put up the puppet theatre. She was ashamed of her nakedness and conscious of her pubic hair and bare breasts, but she stepped on the stage and danced. It was a dance, she understood, of life and death and she tiptoed lightly on her feet and turned and pirouetted. She moved gracefully and lifted her arms and held her head high like a swan and kept dancing with her eyes closed with fear and her cheeks hot with embarrassment.

Some of the officers clapped hands and laughed as they used to do during the children's parties. The gym teacher didn't know whether to go on or stop dancing and she stood irresolutely in the middle of the stage.

'Enough,' motioned Dr Mengele, grinning. And then, after a moment of pretend deliberation, he sent the dancer among the living.

Alex Ehren was exhilarated by his chance to live. There would be no need to fight, to torch the Children's Block and to gamble with his life. He forgot the mutiny, the triads, the underground movement and the iron contraption under a pile of wooden clogs. All of a sudden he was utterly selfish and refused to think about those who had been rejected and would stay in the camp to die. What mattered was that he was among the lucky ones who would be shipped to a labour camp, and the ten thousand others – the children, their mothers, the elderly, the weak – were for him of no consequence.

In the past he had steeled himself for a curfew, for Capos, SS sentries and trucks in the night. He thought that the horror of the September transport would be repeated, and he lived and clung to the idea of a mutiny, of setting the camp on fire, of desperate fighting and of many dead. He also thought about a breakout and a possible escape to the Slovakian mountains. In his mind he had rehearsed a hundred times the casting of the iron hook, the attack on the watchtower and the desperate dash towards the faraway trees. He had sharpened his spoon to a fine point and hidden it in a loaf of bread, and he kept a jacket without the red paint mark under his mattress.

All that was changed now. However, he still had doubts. Would they really be sent to work or were the lists, the selections and the preparations for a transport just a German ploy to deplete the camp of the young and strong? Hadn't Julius Abeles been a spy after all and weren't the Germans just getting rid of potential fighters?

During the days of the selections there was no school, and the children roamed the camp in packs and begged for food at the kitchen. There was chaos everywhere and yet the instructors still looked after their groups. They sat with the children on their bunks or walked outside or played games in an attempt to maintain a semblance of normalcy. In the late afternoon, a short time before the evening roll call, Adam Landau pulled Alex Ehren by the sleeve.

'Brought you something,' said the brat, and he handed Alex Ehren the golden bead.

'I can't. You'll need it perhaps.'

'I'm all right,' said the boy, who looked like a mannequin in his fine jacket and the armband of a Capo runner. His face was smooth and he smelled of soap. 'I'll be a runner in the Men's Camp. Plenty of food there.'

'I may lose it where I go.'

'There is a train to Germany,' said the child. 'I've got it from a German guard. You are going away all right.'

Alex Ehren had an urge to touch the boy and held out his hand. Yet Adam stepped back as if scared that he would be hit and played with his spoon honed into a scimitar.

'I won first prize for writing a poem.'

He lingered as if he wanted to say more, but then he turned and ran down the camp road, small, touched by evil and sharp like a weasel.

They slept on their crowded bunk for the last time. Fabian ran his hand under Alex Ehren's mattress and held up the loaf of bread. He broke off a piece and stuffed it into his mouth.

'Let's celebrate,' he said. 'Let's be merry because tomorrow we are going away.'

He took the bread without asking, the loaf which Alex Ehren had saved for his escape by scrimping and scraping and going to sleep hungry. He ate with his mouth half open, greedily and lavishly until the crumbs fell all over the blanket.

'Eat,' he said and held out a chunk of bread to Pavel Hoch and Rind and even Alex Ehren. 'It isn't my bread but Alex Ehren won't mind. I've let him have my postcard and he pays me with his bread.'

There was ecstasy and abandonment in his voice as if he had suddenly lost his mind.

'For once in my life I have taken what isn't mine and that makes me free.' For a while he played Satan again and rolled his words.

'Mutiny!' he exclaimed and tore off another piece of the black bread. 'What fools we were to prepare a mutiny.' He stabbed his finger at Felsen and laughed. 'The communists and the underground movement? Who would have joined us – the Men's Camp, the Kanada, the Buna people? They would have let us go down the drain. Many dogs bark but only the one in the corner will bite.'

It was true, thought Alex Ehren, and he wondered at how blind he had been. The uprising was like a house of cards, which collapsed with the first gust of wind. And yet he felt that he was betraying the children.

'Not true,' said Fabian. 'We've had our battle and we won.'

'I see no victory,' said Felsen, offended by his words.

'Aren't we alive? Look at the children, at the painted wall. Don't you see the poems, the pictures and the little stories still fluttering on the beams of the Children's Block? Uprising? We rose up all right and what's more we got the better of the Germans.'

'Yes,' said Dezo Kovac. 'We are alive. We could have lost and been dead inside. We and the children.'

For the last time perhaps, they slept on their overcrowded pallet like a many limbed animal, a centipede or an ancient Indian god.

That night Alex Ehren showed Pavel Hoch and Fabian the last two pages he had written. They wrapped the diary in an oilskin and a piece of tar paper and buried it in the hole they had dug under their bunk. They masked the hole with a plank and covered it with silt which, when dried, hardened into a stone.